LIFE AND MUSIC

MONTY RAYMOND

CORGIPAW
FILMS AND BOOKS

The content of this book is subject to copyright law. It may not be reproduced by any medium, electronic or mechanical, without the author's prior written consent.

The moral rights of the author have been asserted.

This book is a work of fiction inspired by true events. Any resemblance to actual persons (except the protagonist), living or dead, is purely coincidental.

Disclaimer: Statements about medical procedures made in this book are not intended as a substitute for consultation with a licensed healthcare practitioner, such as your physician, nor are they intended to diagnose, treat, cure, or prevent any condition or disease. Please consult with your own physician or healthcare specialist before you begin any healthcare program.

Cover designs by Emilija Prodic.

This book is printed in EB Garamond 12-point font for easy reading.

First published 2022

 A catalogue record for this book is available from the National Library of Australia

For my wife and forever

With all my love,

Monty

Dystonia is the third most common movement disorder after Parkinson's disease and essential tremor.
Many sufferers are ostracised and spend years suffering before being diagnosed.
There is no cure.

It was another world and another place, and as I look back, it was another person.

CECELIA

1. UNWELCOME

The traffic was dense due to a bottleneck outside the theatre, yet I managed to escape the concert hall car park in good time. I was hoping to see Sebastian before he fell asleep, so I rushed home as fast as I could. My adrenaline was high; I was eager to tell him about the concert and my success as I waited behind a queue of cars at a red traffic light.

I sat back to get comfortable in my seat, pushing my thick curls off my cheeks, and the world felt more tranquil than it had for a long time. The concert music still played in my mind, and I tapped my fingers on the steering wheel joyously to the melody. Life felt pretty good then and there.

Just at that moment, loud voices from the car next to me distracted my attention. 'It's you! It's Cecelia Cavendish!' they shouted. 'We loved your bassoon playing!'

I nodded and smiled. 'Thank you,' I mouthed.

Suddenly, a car horn tooted, making me jump in fright. The traffic light had turned green without me noticing. As a result, I instinctively put my foot on the accelerator before my head and neck faced the right way. The sudden jerk backwards as my car moved forward made the top of my body jolt sharply. It hurt, and I yelped in pain. I rubbed around my neck, chin and jaw, but that didn't help. The pain above my shoulders increased with every passing second, and I felt the need to get home quickly.

As my car increased speed, terrifyingly, my neck started pulling my head severely sideways until I couldn't see where I was going.

Without warning, a truck smashed into my driver's side door, sending my car spinning into a nearby tree.

CECELIA – EARLY YEARS
2. SEEDS

In her final year of primary school, a tall girl with bouncy, curly hair gazed lovingly at light reflecting off chrome. Her eyes followed the light towards long connecting tubes of polished wood and a bamboo mouthpiece, and she found herself falling in love at first sight.

She had just enjoyed a chamber group playing classical music in front of her class. She danced to 'The Teddy Bear's Picnic' and the *Lone Ranger* theme, two pieces of music she had heard before but never with such expertise and enthusiasm.

A captivating young musician played the chromed instrument. Afterwards, he went around the class, talking to each student one by one, ending with the young girl. She seemed the most interested, so he spent more time with her than anyone.

'What is it?' she asked.

'It's a baboon.'

'I like baboons and balloons.'

The young man laughed. 'Well, you'll like this. It's a bassoon.'

The young girl smiled, and the man let her play a note on it, or more precisely, a whooshing noise into the mouthpiece. For her, it was a note, nonetheless, and a wonder to behold.

Little did the girl realise that she would have played precisely one million notes on her bassoon while playing in a concert hall twenty years later.

CECELIA – EARLY YEARS

3. HALCYON

Two graduates joyfully accepted their Bachelor of Music degrees in Performance as they stood on stage in front of a noisy crowd clapping enthusiastically.

The graduates jiggled up and down next to each other, giggling at their excited parents.

'Let's go to Germany!' whispered Cecelia to Annie.

'Freiburg Music School is nice this time of year,' responded Annie, as she waved her degree in the air.

'Okay!' mouthed Cecelia. 'Woohoo!'

That's all it took—no weighing up the pros or consequences, just youthful impetuousness in all its glory. No extensive discussion needed.

But, as often happens, their youth got in the way and they barely made it to the airport. The night before their flight, they had a going-away party, one of many, many student parties, and they became separated.

'Annie, perhaps you shouldn't drink so much,' Cecelia had scolded, her curly hair bouncing with fury.

'But I don't know what German men are like. Stop being an A-flat, Cecelia.'

So, that was it. Annie left the party at midnight with a handsome man, and Cecelia was left alone, calling Annie's mobile phone for hours without an answer.

That night, Cecelia only had four hours of sleep. Annie had none. The following day at the airport, at 9:00 am sharp, Annie appeared, looking as fresh as a summer breeze, albeit panicky.

'I can't find my bassoon!' she exclaimed to Cecelia.

Cecelia smirked and then moved her suitcases to reveal Annie's bassoon, as well as another bag packed with clothes.

'Oh my God, you're my hero, Cecelia!'

'I'm not even going to ask what you got up to.'

'I love you too, Cecelia.'

Luckily, they still had the good sense to know what was important and what they wanted. From that day onwards, their parties quickly diminished, and they buckled down and studied.

Being fish out of water in a strange country, they stuck together like glue. They practised every day and night together, critiquing each other without fear. This honed their music skills even more sharply than students who practised alone. The two also played in student orchestras together. Sometimes Annie played first bassoon. More often than not, however, Cecelia was the lucky student to play first bassoon.

It didn't take long for their teachers to recognise their blossoming talent and urge them to play in professional orchestras. Their first paid gig was in the Black Forest Philharmonic Orchestra, playing the opera *Madame Butterfly*, filling in for regular players who had taken ill. The girls became known as the 'Koala Duo', undoubtedly due to their countless hours of practice and playing together. Not long after, they got sick of that name and decided on another.

'Let's call ourselves the Dynamic Duo instead,' suggested Cecelia one night after reading about themselves in a concert review.

'That sounds like a laundry detergent, but okay,' replied Annie.

So, that was it. Cecelia and Annie were the 'Dynamic Duo' from then on, especially when they high-fived each other before every concert.

Late in the second year of their post graduate course, and near the end of their time in Germany, the 'Dynamic Duo' were forced to become 'Separate Singles'.

They were both madly applying for permanent paid positions with any and every orchestra that would take them. They applied for jobs in orchestras around Europe, America, Asia, and even South Africa. The competition for permanent positions was tough. Annie remained in Germany playing casual gigs, but Cecelia overcame the competition to win a job in an orchestra in the Netherlands.

'Keep in touch,' they said in unison, as they hugged one another at the train station, Annie dripping tears on Cecelia's bassoon case.

CECELIA – EARLY YEARS
4. DIVERGENCE

Cecelia arrived at her workplace in Rotterdam, thrilled to have her first permanent job as a bassoonist in a professional orchestra. She relished the chance to try out her skills in this new environment and live a life full of music. However, only a short time had passed before she realised that she had entered a toxic workplace where everyone was divided over one issue: the proficiency of the principal trumpet player.

The trumpet player was kind and gentle with Cecelia, as he had always been with newcomers to the orchestra. In his thirty-five years as a professional musician, he had seen a lot of early-career players join. When he was a fledgling himself, the orchestra was a small, male-dominated affair. For most of the musicians, music training came about via music teachers paid for by their wealthy parents. But as the orchestra developed, new musicians came in who were better trained with higher levels of expertise, having learnt their musicianship skills from universities, prestigious music schools, and international orchestras. The trumpet player had seen many an elderly musician retire, superseded by young upstarts whose high confidence matched their considerable skills and dreams.

He was still a good player, and Cecelia enjoyed working with him.

However, according to many people in the orchestra, his time was up. Views were split. Generally, younger musicians thought he should go; older musicians wanted him to stay. Going against that rule, Cecelia felt the trumpet player should persist, as long as his playing problems were overcome with intense practice and a few lessons.

It was hard for her to come to that conclusion. On the one hand, Cecelia liked the trumpet player as he helped her to settle into orchestra life. On the other hand, she had to think of what was best for the orchestra as a whole and put aside her personal feelings.

Cecelia faced a lot of pressure from other players to change her mind, even though her opinion didn't mean much in the grander sense. When it became apparent she wouldn't change, she became somewhat ostracised herself, facing undue criticism of her playing as a result.

'You're playing too sharp,' or 'You're playing too flat,' they would say about the same passage of music in the same concert.

The whole thing came to a head when management tried to force the trumpet player to leave. He fought hard, maintaining that his playing was up to scratch the whole time and that the orchestra discriminated against him due to his age.

Management set up a task force and panel, where six of his peers would assess his playing and vote on his future. It was a challenging and draining time. They argued for hours about the future of their colleague, during which Cecelia heard many irrational and victimising comments that had no place in a diverse workplace. The panellists couldn't agree on the trumpet player's fate: three decided he should retire, three decided he should stay.

Eventually, management busted the stalemate. They stepped in and put him on probation for three months before declaring unceremoniously that his playing wasn't good enough and then giving him his marching orders.

The ordeal left a lot of bad blood that affected the orchestra's form as a whole for many months. In that time, Cecelia had to work extra hard to prove herself as a worthy member. Eventually, many accepted her. Some didn't forgive her, though, rationalising that she could not play well herself if she could not see bad playing in others. As a result, management didn't continue her employment after her six-month probation period. It became a permanent reminder of how fickle an orchestra can be and how little dedication and skill can mean when someone is out of favour.

It was a lesson that if you're not good enough, you're as good as gone in a coffin.

CECELIA – EARLY YEARS
5. FIZZWIDGENS

As she waited in the rehearsal room, Cecelia took deep breaths to calm her nerves. It was her turn to play the final piece after being successful in the first two rounds of an audition process. She was one of only two auditionees left. She and a young man were competing for a coveted principal bassoon position in her home country. It seemed an unmissable opportunity to move on from the shattered dream of her first job overseas.

A vibrant woman with neat blonde hair, wearing bright clothes, walked up to Cecelia.

'Hi. I'm Fleur. You're Cecelia, right?'

'Yep, that's me.'

'What are you playing for your next audition piece?' Fleur asked.

Cecelia smiled wryly. 'Something from Mozart. But I can't get 'The Teddy Bear's Picnic' tune out of my mind.'

Fleur laughed heartily. 'Yeah, me too. I played it last week at a children's concert.'

'Pity I'm not auditioning for a pantomime then.'

They chatted some more and, after the final audition round, went out to dinner at a cheap Italian restaurant. By the time they had finished their dessert of tiramisu, they had become best friends.

Fleur, as concertmaster of the orchestra, chaired a panel of musicians after dinner, deciding via a voting system which auditionee would get the principal bassoonist's job. Fleur recommended Cecelia for the role, but that got her into trouble. Some of the other panellists saw it as favouritism due to their apparent new friendship over dinner. In the end, it didn't matter. Other musicians on the panel voted for Cecelia, so the job was hers anyway.

Fleur's conflict of interest in that instance was the just the start of her troublesome behaviour, and Cecelia did not always approve. Still, Fleur made Cecelia laugh in a career where everyone needed laughter for pressure relief. More often than not, Cecelia forgave Fleur's foibles.

———

A few days after Cecelia heard the exciting news she was part of the orchestra, but before she had played a concert with them, Fleur organised a welcoming party for her. It felt way too soon, but as Cecelia was keen to meet her new colleagues, she agreed to be the guest of honour.

It wasn't the usual twenty-something party either. Booze and music were in full supply, and one or two people were stumbling around a little too drunk, but the difference was that this party didn't only have loud rock and roll music, it had other genres of music too. When Cecelia stepped through the door, booming Spanish guitar songs belted out through some speakers. Cecelia looked around shyly. Everyone seemed to be enjoying themselves, especially two trumpeters who were talking loudly outside.

Fleur ran bouncily to her once she was inside. 'Cecelia! Welcome!'

'Hi, Fleur!' Cecelia breathed a sigh of relief. She had been feeling a little awkward. A lot was riding on first impressions and last impressions, especially as she would be spending a lot of time with these people in the orchestra.

Cecelia reached inside her purse and took out a compact disc. 'I brought some of my favourite music from the Fizzwidgens.'

Fleur smiled excitedly. 'Ooh yeah! Good choice. I love their song 'Dance 'til it drops!'

Another girl walked up to Cecelia and gave her an unexpected hug. 'Did I hear someone say, Fizzwidgens?' she asked. 'They're awesome!'

Fleur turned to Cecelia and back to the other girl. 'Cecelia, meet Jayne, she plays second oboe in the orchestra.'

'Hi.'

Cecelia looked downwards, only greeting her with a simple, 'Hello.'

Jayne put her arm around Cecelia again, and it instantly relaxed both of them. 'Good choice in music, Cecelia. Come on, let's put this baby on.'

The two of them ran to the CD player.

Jayne smiled towards Cecelia. 'You saved the day. Thanks, Cecelia! This party was beginning to fall flat.'

Cecelia smiled back. 'You're welcome. It's what I do.'

'What? Fall flat?'

'No! Save the day!'

Jayne giggled. 'I know how good you are, Cecelia. We're good, and welcome!'

And before long, with the help of Fleur and a few more musicians, they sang, '*Dance 'til your toes curl up, dance 'til your arms pop out, dance 'til your head drops off, oh yeah ... !*'

As Cecelia sang, she gained confidence with each note. She felt more and more a part of the orchestra, and she was beginning to make new friends. She couldn't help looking around, though. People were looking, but not everyone was smiling at her.

Was it the music, her singing, or was it something else, she thought?

It made her think of her difficult times in the Netherlands and how she wished she had Annie with her.

———

Cecelia couldn't believe her luck getting a job back in Australia after she passed her probation period. It enabled her to see her family again after so long and enjoy the nice weather and relaxed atmosphere, amongst many other things on offer in the beautiful city where she now resided.

But Cecelia missed Annie and after a year in the orchestra her good luck changed for the better. She contacted Annie as soon as she found out the good news.

'Annie, the second bassoon position has just become available in my orchestra! You *have* to apply!' Cecelia pleaded.

'When's the next plane?' asked Annie.

Cecelia put in a good word about Annie with her orchestra management while wondering about her conflict of interest. In any case, after practising her heart out for the audition, Annie was the clear and just winner of the position.

The Dynamic Duo was reunited once more.

CECELIA

6. RUMBLES

In the Weistar Festival Theatre that night (we called it the 'Festival Theatre' or 'Weistar's answer to Sydney's Opera House'), all available seats had bums on them, as the marketing department would say. The patrons who were lucky or rich enough to get in were lost in the performance, while some of my fans were eagerly waiting for me to play my notes.

I had been at the Festival Theatre lots of times. Yes, I was nervous. All performers are. It would have made my nervousness more bearable if I had friends to discuss my anxiety with but, of course, they were too busy playing their parts.

My time to play approached. The eyes of the audience, and some orchestra members, were nearly on me. Usually, when I was on stage, that would lift and inspire me to play better, but on that night and at that moment, it felt like I had all the symptoms of wanting to be somewhere else. A dreadful feeling washed over me, and my heartbeat raced. My muscles tensed and my body started to tremble. I had a dry mouth and shortness of breath. I tried to inhale, unsuccessfully, which increased my sense of panic. Breath is one of the most important things for a wind player, and without it, I was history. As the seconds passed with my mind in that merry-go-round, my body responded. Sweat started to build on my brow and my palms. I quickly wiped my hands on my trousers to dry them, but they remained clammy.

What if I played the first note and it wasn't perfect? Some in the audience wouldn't notice, but some would. The musicians definitely would. We were playing a piece that the audience already knew, which meant they knew the notes and instruments, and they would know if I hit a wrong note or played out of time.

One note. One bad note. One note played at the wrong time. That's all it took to destroy years of work, years of dedication, years of toil. That one note, in one fell swoop, can ruin reputations faster than anything else. And I had a *considerable* reputation for nurturing.

All those thoughts entered my mind without invitation. Every musician grapples with them at times during their career, but they keep them at bay. As a seasoned musician, I hadn't thought of them for years. Why did they invade my mind during *that* concert?

When playing any musical instrument, there's always uncertainty between playing a note and hearing a note. In the next tiny fragment of time, I somehow managed to loosen my fingers and lean forward slightly. Then I started to blow. At first, I thought nothing came out. Then I thought if something did come out, it would sound like cater-wauling. At that moment, the smallest of moments, I felt my heart leave my body.

'Relax, Cecelia, relax,' I said in my head. 'Breathe in, breathe out —Dalai Lama in, Tibetan Monk out. I can do this. I can do this.' Suddenly I was aware that a beautiful singing tone was coming from my bassoon, reaching outwards. My whole body let go and felt joyfully heavy again, like the moment just before sleep. I smiled inside. I was going to be okay.

As I looked up to the conductor, my focus travelled to the audience before I played again. There was a collective sigh throughout the whole theatre when my bassoon sang for a second time. I sighed with them as my body became increasingly relaxed.

From the corner of my eye, I saw my friend Annie next to me. Her little face lit up in response as she lifted her bassoon and joined in. A moment later, we were playing an exquisite duo within the orchestra of ninety. We were singing together through our instruments, and for a few seconds, the world felt not just okay, it felt utterly right.

CECELIA

7. TERRIFIC THREE

The following night should have been just another concert, but for me, it was memorable for one reason and one reason only. I had to try even harder than the night before. Sure, concerts are challenging but this particular concert seemed more similar to a life or death situation requiring a fight or flight response. I couldn't flee because there was too much riding on me being there. The whole show, or movement at least, would collapse if I picked up my bassoon and ran off the stage during the middle of a piece. I had to stay and fight, and it felt like twelve rounds with a world champion boxer. The only thing that gave me the strength to finish was knowing I had to be there.

When the last note ended, I was shaking. It was a huge relief when the conductor signalled for us to rise and even more of a relief during the standing ovation from the audience. My playing didn't pass without notice, however. Many of the other musicians seemed to glare at me, except for Christopher on third bassoon who was studiously removing the reed from his bassoon's crook.

Christopher had previously played principal bassoon in another orchestra in Europe, but when his orchestra had unexpectedly folded due to a funding debacle, he had found himself languishing in the

Weistar Symphony on third bassoon and contrabassoon. He had subsequently thrown himself into looking after an alpaca farm as a distraction. However, when Annie and I were invited to his farm one day, once we had met his best and cutest alpacas, Charles and Winston, we realised his main ambitions lay with breeding, bloodlines and medals he could put around his beloved pets' long necks.

I did, though, occasionally catch him secretly practising my solo bassoon parts, and he also had a habit of telling me, 'You're playing too slow, too loud, too sharp, too flat,' whenever his passions were ignited.

'Maybe you need your hearing checked, Christopher?' I would reply with disdain. It was all I could do to put on a happy face and laugh about it.

Which is why Annie and I waltzed backstage together, giggling to ourselves after seeing his poker face. As we left the stage, Fleur joined us too.

Annie turned to me with the usual adrenaline-filled jittery smile she had after concerts. 'Cecelia, you're the cat's miaow,' she said admiringly. 'And I'm lapping up your milk.'

Fleur joined in, miming a healthy technicolour yawn.

I looked at both of them with a smirk as I let out a sigh of relief, trying to hide my shakes. I mean, it's nice to get a compliment, if you're at the top of your game. 'But my milk's curdling,' I murmured hoarsely.

Annie dealt with the situation, as only she did after a big concert. Well, as far as I knew. She popped a red pill in her mouth. When it came to drugs, I wasn't in the loop, or shall I say fruity loop.

Fleur looked at us both with an expression of understanding. I could see where Fleur was coming from. There were moments in the concert where I didn't have to play any notes, and in that time, I had tried to empty my mind with silly things such as how well the conductor had tied his bow tie or an itch in my big toe. I had looked around too and Fleur, being the concertmaster with several solo pieces, was the main distraction. She had played a couple of notes a little uncharacteristically sharp, as Fleur was always a perfectionist, putting more into her music than anyone else. She had worked towards perfection for a long time, enjoying it and taking it in her stride, especially in such a prominent position in the orchestra. I admired her for it.

She momentarily put her hand on my shoulder. 'Show me a musician who's never out of form, and you'll show me *nobody*,' she said.

I looked at her, feeling vulnerable. She stepped back slightly in defence, but my expression didn't deter her. 'Maybe you're not as good as you were in Europe,' she said cheekily.

Fleur's confidence and playful fighting spirit always rubbed off on me, even in the face of being wrong, so I proceeded to tip the spit from my bassoon towards her. She was nimble on her toes, and it landed about two millimetres next to her shoe.

She shrugged her shoulders to make light of her offence as she frowned at the spit on the floor. 'But you're still great. Must have been my self-help books,' she laughed.

My eyebrows furrowed at her. 'You can take them and that comment back, Fleur.'

Her mood lightened in the face of mock defeat. 'Sure, when we all retire to the funny farm.'

Annie's face, laughing at us in playful excitement, lit up. She loved being in the Terrific Three that we had become. 'We'll share a cottage at the funny farm!' she exclaimed happily.

Just at that moment, a cellist walked by. With a royal wave and a twinkle in her eye, Fleur made a bee line towards him, looking back at us with a cheeky smile as she left. 'I've got someone else in mind to take with us to that cottage,' she winked.

Annie shook her head. Her voice raised towards her departing friend, and she shouted, 'Really, I've always thought you only had yourself in mind.'

Yep, we were indeed the Terrific Three.

CECELIA

8. DISCO BAROQUE

We said our temporary goodbyes in the car park, and I headed towards my trusty old car, a pale yellow 1960's Renault. I smiled in relief at its familiarity. It had been in my loving ownership since I was sixteen when my dad bought it as a congratulatory present after getting my driver's licence. He loved old cars, and driving my Renault I affectionately called 'Ronnie', I soon came to love old cars too. Like my bassoon, having something old in my life felt comforting. Not that 1960's stuff was old.

The heavy traffic on the drive home required more attention than I wanted, and it distracted me enough not to pay much mind to the concert. While waiting for traffic lights to turn green during the car trip, I thought about Annie and Fleur's brief tiff a little, but the playful banter made me laugh more than anything else. I looked at the passenger seat and my bassoon case resting next to me, plastered with stickers gathered from orchestras I had played in over the years, from Europe, America, Asia and more. Its worldliness settled any doubts I had about my playing talent. When that calmed my mind a little, I tried to dissect what was driving my anxiety over the last two concerts.

I thought about my fingers and how they turned the steering wheel. It felt comfortable, just like controlling my fingers on my bassoon, and I certainly didn't have any trouble with corners or indicators.

The craziness on the roads felt somewhat comforting too. I was able to weave between cars and lanes with ease, skill and reassurance. After a while, I concluded that my fingers were okay driving, so they must be okay when they pressed and manipulated my bassoon's keys and finger holes. When I paid attention to it, I decided the concert was nothing more than an evening when I didn't play at my best. It wasn't my worst, either. After all, I did get applause.

With both of my hands full of musical paraphernalia, I found it challenging to fit the key into the keyhole of my front door. Still, once I heard the familiar click, I let out a deep breath, and my heartbeat slowed. It always took several hours to come down from a big concert, none more so than this night, so I decided to shake off the tension with some dancing. I walked down the long hallway to the lounge room, plonked my bassoon on a chair, and proceeded to put on some Baroque music.

Hearing beautiful music always made me feel free, so I spun my body around and slung my arms in the air like a seagull floating above a cliff with the help of a sea breeze. The music radiated through my body, and with it, my cares soon whisked away. With every shimmy, I thought about my luck. I had a great job, a gorgeous home, good health, contentment and love (although not necessarily in that order), to name a few. So, I did what any happy, modern girl would do. I brought out my inner John Travolta and, with the Baroque music providing a beat in the background, I disco danced to the bathroom to brush my teeth. Eat your heart out, Olivia Newton-John. After turning off the music, I found myself still hustling to the bedroom door, opening it quietly.

I blew a kiss towards Luciano Pavarotti, not the real one, but a poster of him above my bed, and jumped in under the covers. It made a book I had been reading, *The Forest of Being*, fall to the floor, but I didn't care.

I snuggled up against Sebastian. Beautiful, lovely, slim, dorky, safe, warm Sebastian. The man I loved.

CECELIA – EARLY YEARS

9. SEEKING

Fleur and Cecelia settled comfortably into two bright orange armchairs, as they enjoyed listening to Eric Satie's *Gymnopedies*. While they sat, they performed routine maintenance on their musical instruments, one swaying to the music gently, the other smiling cheekily.

Fleur turned to Cecelia, saying, 'This has to be one of the most romantic pieces of music ever.'

'But what about Rachmaninoff?' implored Cecelia.

'You've only just passed your audition and you're already in the groove!' Fleur laughed.

Fleur became lost in the music a little more, then, with her mind ticking over, stopped to stare at her friend. But Cecelia was too busy polishing the chrome on her bassoon to notice.

'Did you ever notice that the sides of a violin look like a man's pecs?' giggled Fleur.

'No, so don't tell me what part of a male's anatomy my bassoon reminds you of.'

Fleur flashed a smile while gazing at Cecelia. 'When was the last time you've been with a man?' she asked.

'It's been a while.'

'You need a man, Cecelia.'

'Maybe one day, Fleur, but you know what it's like with all the practice and concerts. I'm now married to the orchestra.'

'What about the horn player? He's, umm, recently single.'

'Dating inside the orchestra. Urrgh! It's too incestuous.'

'I know!' Fleur stopped, and her face lit up with an idea. She immediately ran to the phone.

And before Cecelia could stop her, Fleur had placed an advert in the newspaper that read: *Woman twenty-nine, quiet achiever, seeks the meaning of life.*

CECELIA – EARLY YEARS

10. UN HOMME ET UNE FEMME

A tall, slim man with thick black hair sank deeper into his chair as he read the personal ads in the newspaper. Reading these sorts of ads wasn't something he usually did, but one attracted his attention. It read: *Woman twenty-nine, quiet achiever, seeks the meaning of life.* He thought the person in the advert sounded like him and someone he wanted to meet. So, he phoned the number and mentioned a little about himself, including that he was a university student. A few minutes after he left his message, the woman called him. She introduced herself as Cecelia and said how much she liked his name, Sebastian.

They chatted for about an hour and instantly built a rapport. Both had a similar quiet tone and volume in their voices, and they bounced off each other amazingly. It wasn't long into their conversation when they agreed to meet for the first time at a local café.

When Sebastian first saw Cecelia, he thought she was sexy as hell. She wore a miniskirt and a shimmery white top, set off with white high heels. He could see Cecelia dressed to impress, and his body reacted appropriately. She walked towards him and stopped about a metre away. They didn't say anything as their eyes met. All they could do was exchange huge grins.

After a few seconds, Cecelia said politely, 'Hello.'

'Hello and well, hello!' Sebastian replied cheekily.

Cecelia smirked. 'Hmm, now where have I heard that line before? Perhaps another date?'

'*Johnah Wishes*, starring Tom Cardinalese and Rebecca Zane.'

Cecelia shouted a little too loudly, 'Money! Now!'

'Oh. You've seen it?'

Without warning, Cecelia's face turned a little serious, to Sebastian's surprise. 'No, really, money now! Come on hand it over, or else!' she ordered.

'Or else what?' Sebastian asked nervously.

'Or else, who's going to pay for lunch?'

Sebastian laughed. He finally realised Cecelia was joking, and his body relaxed. Sebastian stretched out his hand, which met with Cecelia's. As their fingers touched, they jumped slightly.

'Electricity,' said Sebastian.

Cecelia smiled again, and lost for words, blurted, 'Must be the humidity.'

'Yes, the ... umm ... weather seems to lend itself to it.'

Cecelia giggled at Sebastian's nervousness.

'Are we going to talk about the weather?' she teased.

Sebastian straightened himself.

'I'm sorry. I'll probably say a few inappropriate things, but I mean well.'

Cecelia nodded sympathetically. 'I know. It's okay. But enough of the movie quotes. Okay, buster?'

'Keaton.'

'What?'

'Yes, within Keaton, I mean, Buster Keaton, er, reason.'

'I'm watching you!' Cecelia winked.

'Okay. Umm. Perfection is when two people who are perfect for one another are there for one another.'

'Ooh, that's clever. Let me guess, from another movie?'

'*The Journey to Hunt*. 1979. Mike Dreamers ... oh ... sorry.'

Cecelia playfully tutted. 'You're a Holden driver,' she replied.

'No, I drive a Jaguar.'

Cecelia laughed. 'Very funny, but no. Holden Driver was Mike Dreamers' henchman in the film,' she said.

Sebastian looked at his feet apologetically before looking up. 'Oh, right. Of course.'

They walked inside, still gazing at each other, and sat down at a table situated next to a wishing well full of fish and turtles.

Sebastian looked around.

'Funky place,' he said.

'Groovy.'

And from then on, their awkward first meeting morphed into two people wholly focussed on one another (after Sebastian said a few more film quotes that Cecelia rolled her eyes at but secretly found cute). Cecelia listened to Sebastian talk about his difficult childhood, what his university film studies meant to him and how important they were, and a million different thoughts about the environment, the world, and just about anything.

Cecelia smiled. 'It's great that you're not content in a dead-end job and looking to fulfil your passions.'

'I guess so. Life is much more than what you do for a living. How about you, Cecelia? What are you passionate about?'

'Music.'

'Listening or playing?'

'Both. I play principal bassoon in the Weistar Symphony.'

Sebastian's eyebrows raised. 'Wow!' he exclaimed excitedly.

'Uh-huh ... wow.'

Cecelia continued to chat about her love of music and her career. She mentioned the word 'bassoon' several times but Sebastian looked puzzled and glazed. Still, he tried to listen intently, his thoughts interrupted by Cecelia's green eyes and long flowing hair.

Cecelia stopped talking.

'Are you all right, Sebastian?'

'Umm, yeah … it's just …'

'Oh! You don't know what a bassoon is?'

'Umm … no!'

Cecelia giggled.

'It's a woodwind instrument. It's a bit like a digeridoo.'

'Oh!' nodded Sebastian. 'I guess not everyone would know.'

'You're right,' chuckled Cecelia again. 'I've got mine in my car. I can play it for you later if you like.'

Cecelia talked more about her career, her travels around the world, her atheist views, her upbringing, and how much fun it was to eat gnocchi in Lido and pizza in Naples. Before long, and before they realised it, the waiters were packing up chairs and getting ready to close the café.

As Sebastian and Cecelia got up, they looked at the turtles in the well and gazed into each other's eyes. Sebastian could tell that something special was starting. Cecelia's soft and understanding face gave every indication she felt the same way.

'I guess we'd better go,' said Sebastian.

'Yes. I've got a concert to go to.'

'What … now?'

'Yes a concert for you, remember? To show you my bassoon.'

'Ahh, a concert for one. My favourite type of concert!'

As they walked out, Cecelia turned to Sebastian.

'You know Sebastian, you were the first person ever who, when we first met, didn't ask me about my job.'

Sebastian gently squeezed her hand. 'Well, I guess I'm not the sort of guy who asks what you do for a living to people they've just met as if someone's career defines them.' He shrugged his shoulders and laughed. 'It's funny. Why don't people ask, 'Nice to meet you, tell me about your beliefs!?''

Cecelia smiled, and for a few seconds, there was silence between them. Outside, she looked up and gazed into the setting sun.

'Such a big and lovely sunset,' she mused.

'Aye. It's very grand.'

Sebastian seemed to sense Cecelia was searching for something, so he went deeper.

'Sometimes, I do think about the beauty of the world and the true meaning of creation. But of course, I could be talking crap, and we can find the meaning of life in the chicken dance. Brrk brrk!'

They laughed again, more freely compared to a few hours before when they first met.

Cecelia turned to Sebastian and focussed her eyes on his. 'I like how we just changed quickly from deep metaphysical things to something silly.'

Sebastian continued his chicken dance.

'Brrk brrk! Do you believe there is something more to this universe?' he asked.

Cecelia reflected on her bassoon and how it made her feel when she played it. 'Yes, I think there is. It's hard to explain, but I think there is. Maybe something magical about it. I know I get that from music.'

Sebastian looked to the sunset for a few seconds, then back to Cecelia. She could almost see the cogs turning in his brain.

'Yet, you don't believe in God?' he asked.

'Full of contradictions, aren't I?'

'Humans are contradictions.'

They smiled in comfortable silence while they admired the sun again setting over the horizon.

After a few minutes, Sebastian broke the stillness. His words warmed Cecelia like the sun. 'A person can find mystique and magic, even if they clean horse poo,' he said. He smiled contentedly. 'As long as we can write stories in our head.'

'Or play music.'

Sebastian nodded in agreement. 'Cecelia, when loving someone, it wouldn't matter what job they had, and it wouldn't matter if they lived in a tent.'

Cecelia felt a thrill run through her body.

'Come on,' she declared. 'I've got a concert to play for you.'

As they got to Cecelia's car, a large group of people was partying loudly in an adjacent carpark.

'Looks like we're going to have a chorus,' joked Cecelia.

'Chorus interruptus.'

Cecelia proceeded to play her bassoon above the chorus in the car park for the pleasure of her newfound listener, laughing inside at the absurdity and perfection all at once.

Then, over the next few weeks and months as they grew to know each other more intimately, Sebastian found Cecelia very easy to love. He admired her long list of admirable qualities. They even wrote a book about every attribute they admired in one another. Sebastian wrote three volumes about her. That's how much he loved her.

In short, Sebastian saw Cecelia as vibrant, fun, talented, kind, considerate and super sexy. According to Sebastian, many people had those qualities, but he often said, 'Cecelia *overflowed* with them.'

Sometimes when Sebastian was alone, he pondered how his life could have taken a different path if he had not talked to Cecelia on the phone that fateful first day. It was a *Sliding Doors* moment when his life train could have taken him on a different track if he had been doing something else. But he felt so glad he made that infamous phone call and it took him where it did.

Cecelia continued playing in her orchestra, and Sebastian enjoyed studying film. Sebastian's family didn't understand his yearning to do something bigger in life. They wanted him to work in a steady nine-to-five job instead. Still, Cecelia understood Sebastian's grander plans, and that helped bring them together. Their eyes would light up as they discussed art, literature, writing, films, philosophy and whatever made life more than what it was. They couldn't wait to share their latest experience or epiphany in learning. She expanded Sebastian's world to opera, too. He saw her play in *Turandot, The Kingfishers*, and concerts with the Australian Ballet.

Sebastian loved seeing Cecelia walk on stage to applause and hearing her play, knowing that he would take her home afterwards.

She looked very sexy in her orchestra outfits, as well. He didn't want to be a groupie, though, like some other partners of players, partly because he didn't want to bask in her celebrity. He felt that her fame was hers and hers alone. However, some of it did rub off on him. Her friends and other musicians grew to know Sebastian. In turn, he became recognised by many in the artistic sphere.

There was even a fan club for Cecelia, and its members would crowd around her after each concert. Cecelia and Sebastian loved them as well and had a good laugh about it all. They both felt high, not only for being in love but for living in a shared state of being that seemed to be floating above everything and above the world.

Exactly two years to the day after Sebastian had met Cecelia, they proposed to one another, emphasis on, *they*. The proposal was more diplomatic than traditional. While laying on a bed, Sebastian said, 'On the count of three, if you would like to get married, rotate your legs in the air like you're riding a bicycle ... one ... two ... three, go!' Immediately, they lifted their legs and did their best *Tour de France* peloton impersonation. For the rest of the day, they were sore from grinning so much. And that was it. They were engaged, and three months later, they got hitched.

And Sebastian never did get around to thanking Fleur for putting the advert in the newspaper.

CECELIA

11. OSPREY

Sebastian woke slightly and snuggled into me with my arms around him. He stirred and mumbled, 'Finding the meaning of life again?'

'Mmhmm.'

'Mozart will do that to you.'

My adrenaline levels, already high from the concert, were getting higher, and I wasn't tired yet. I slid my hand under the covers and ran my fingers lightly along Sebastian's legs, hips, tummy and chest. He responded by turning around towards me. His eyes were sleepy, but he still turned up the left side of his lips in a cheeky smile.

'That's naughty,' he murmured.

I coquettishly smiled back, and with a deliberate sex-kitten breathy tone, whispered, 'My parents had high hopes for me, you know.'

'What've your parents got to do with it at a time like this?'

'Sometimes, I can't control my thoughts or my body,' I cooed.

I lied. I knew what I was thinking and what I wanted, and it was lying close to me.

I rolled on top of him and wriggled my body, making sure my best bits were rubbing on his best bits. Sebastian squirmed back differently.

I was happily surprised by his ingenuity, especially at 1:00 am, and after being woken up after only a couple of hours sleep.

'Where did you learn that?' I asked.

'University,' he replied in his usual mischievous way. 'I went there to fulfill my dreams'. He wriggled again, and I delighted in our tight, warm body lock.

I playfully tutted. 'Since when did universities teach porn in film studies?

Sebastian framed my face in his masculine hands, holding his nose inches from mine. It took all my effort not to giggle or take him right there and then. I decided to keep the bliss for a little longer.

'You're determined,' I purred in my best Brigitte Bardot voice. I knew I always got him with that, and he responded how I wanted.

We locked lips in a deep French kiss. It lasted as long as Sebastian's blocked nose allowed it to, and he came up for air about half a minute later.

'I like that in you,' I said.

'Such integrity.'

'Integrity? That's for another time.'

We spent the next couple of hours making love until, at 3:00 am, I fell into a deep sleep.

There's nothing like the love of a good man to recover from a bad day at work.

———

My sleep was profound and vivid. I dreamt of a gorgeous osprey soaring high above the sea and parallel to lofty sandy cliffs. *The Lark Ascending* by Vaughan Williams played as he explored his domain. The osprey delighted in using the cliff's updraft to glide higher and higher in the salty air. I watched him from a dilapidated raft a hundred metres offshore, yet I could see him smile blissfully, letting the wind do the work for him. He hardly moved his body, and his eyes fixated downward. Only a tweak of his wingtips now and then to change direction signalled any effort. Flying was easy for the osprey, and when I noticed his chubby belly, I imagined life must be easy for him too. I envisioned minutes before his flight, he had proudly strolled through a beautiful floral garden with his chest heaved outwards. At the same time, he had picked off insect upon insect as if his surroundings were a free buffet.

Then, as we noticed a sparkle of sunlight shimmering off the top of a wave, our eyes met. The osprey flew towards the brightness as I paddled to reach it too. Of course, I was no match for the osprey's majestic flying skills. I had barely splashed my hand in the water before my bird companion had reached his target. Quick as a flash, he dipped his head in the water before flying out with his catch held firmly in his beak, a gleaming fish hopelessly writhing and trying to escape. The osprey then flew above the cliffs again before disappearing over the horizon and out of sight.

I continued to sit on the raft while my body calmed and stilled. Waves lapped over the edge and onto my feet, and I thought more of the osprey. Was his life really so easy? He looked fat, and he flew quickly, despite his girth, seemingly without a care in the world. Life for him was like the proverbial avian beer and skittles. Jealousy filled my mind. I had all the mod cons of society and more. My life should be comfortable, but it wasn't, and I didn't know why. For both of us, life meant survival of the fittest, but in my eyes, he was higher up the food chain than I. The natural order of things felt topsy-turvy and all wrong.

Suddenly, water started gushing over my raft. Its force was too powerful for me, and I began to sink. I tried to stay afloat, but my efforts seemed futile. Before long, I was struggling to balance, too. Water quickly poured over me, first over my ankles, then over my knees, hips, tummy and chest. I couldn't comprehend what was happening. Although it seemed obvious I was sinking, I wasn't sure if it was actually happening.

As I descended into oblivion, musical instruments flashed before my eyes: violins, double basses, trombones and timpanies. I yearned to see a bassoon, but it didn't appear.

Then, after what seemed forever, a bassoon finally made itself known, this time strapped to my back. But I wasn't underwater anymore. I was rushing along a busy city street. Around me, people argued, traffic ground to a halt, and car horns hooted angrily. At the end of the road stood a vast office building, and I reached it in my hurried state, albeit fatigued. I traversed the outside of the tower, looking into its windows. At the same time, another me could see myself from the top of the building where I was sleeping below. I didn't know which Cecelia, the napping or the peeping-Tom Cecelia, was the real Cecelia. Through that confusion, I woke up.

Laying there, as my senses awakened with the morning sun, I didn't know what to make of my dream. For the most part, I didn't believe in dreams anyway. I considered dream analysis as some sort of debunked Freudian theory. To me, they were simply our minds putting random thoughts and events from our lives into a convoluted sleep-time story. If anything, they were merely something fun to talk about with Sebastian. I didn't give the osprey as much thought as it deserved. Besides, Sebastian was already up and around, so our chats revolved around preparing for the day by the time I saw him a few minutes later. Before long, my dream was all but forgotten and usurped by another concert I had that evening. With all the busyness after breakfast, the day flew by faster than a Concorde.

CECELIA

12. CRACKS

The concert's start was only a few minutes away, and I sat backstage admiring my bassoon. Its chrome keys and polished wood glistened under the lights, and I fell in love with it again, as I often did just before a concert. I thought love was a powerful emotion, and in my playing, it gave me the strength to bring out the beautiful sound intrinsic in my instrument. Then, before I fully comprehended it, a sense of sadness filled my body. I wasn't sure why at first, but then I began to understand. I realised once more that I loved the bassoon as much as I loved Sebastian, and I didn't ever want to part with either of them. I'm not sure why the thought of loss came to me at that particular moment. Perhaps it started as a fleeting thought, a random one, as ideas often do before growing and multiplying like seeds grow into trees.

In previous years, thoughts of loss sometimes occupied my mind, and in the few weeks up until that night, those thoughts became more frequent. I guess if you love something so much, you understand the consequences of it not being in your life. As corny as it sounds, the bassoon was part of me. When I touched it, when I held it, when I carried it, when I played it, it felt as natural as my hand was to my arm, and metaphysically, my bassoon felt attached. Sometimes, my mind would play tricks on me when I was holding something else like a fork or knife. I would absentmindedly look at my hand or make adjustments to my posture as if my bassoon was there. I believed I was holding my bassoon, even though I actually wasn't.

Often that resulted in spilling objects such as cups of tea or shopping bags, and I became deft at making up excuses for my clumsiness. I think Sebastian knew what was going on, and he playfully joked about it. He was a bit of a klutz himself.

The other musicians had left the green room, and I was the only one left before I realised I had to go too. I still had a couple of minutes, so I decided to do one last quick bout of practice. Still feeling enamoured by my bassoon, I ran my hands tenderly and lovingly over it, the moisture from my fingers giving the wood and chrome a slight polish. I was feeling good and ready for the night ahead.

My practice went well, but I grimaced slightly as I brought the reed to my lips. I blamed the pain on my chair. It wasn't my usual one, and I sometimes had to wiggle my bum to get comfortable enough to play specific notes. I noticed it made my neck twitch a little, but nothing a rub and scratch from my warm fingers couldn't cure. I played on, and within seconds, my bassoon sang just as I wanted it to and, as a result, my face beamed with smiles between notes.

Feeling in the zone and determined for perfection, I kept going. During that time, an insect caught my eye, its wings reflecting sunlight filtering into the room. It reminded me of the osprey in my dream the night before, and I stopped. Like the osprey, the insect's flight looked effortless as he let the room's drafts do the work for him. I smiled, noticing that his body floated. He circled in front of me, and I played just for him, giving him a mini-concert of 'The Teddy Bear's Picnic.' He was my audience, and therefore he deserved my talents. I finished, bowed, thanked him for his interest (while imagining he used his tiny wings to applaud), and walked off to the stage. I felt even better about my playing and at being one with nature.

The stage was packed when I arrived, except for my waiting seat, so I quickly took my place. As a result, I was out of breath, which is not ideal for a woodwind player. I closed my eyes to relax, imagining the insect and the osprey flying off into the sunset together. The osprey shouted, 'Come on slow-coach!' back to his new bug friend.

My eyes were opened in a jolt, though, when the audience enthusiastically started to applaud. I looked at Annie sitting next to me. We smiled at each other in readiness before we noticed Christopher making some last-second adjustments to his reed.

The conductor tapped his baton and made his usual over-the-top gesture for us to play Dukas' *The Sorcerer's Apprentice*. Annie, Christopher and I joined in with our very recognisable tune, and after a while other sections took over and did their thing. It gave us a short rest before we had to play again.

Then suddenly and unexpectedly, Christopher dropped his reed, and he fumbled helplessly under his seat trying to find it. Instantly, our momentary respite turned into panic. Annie and I glared at him, as did several other musicians. The reed rolled under Annie's chair, and she quickly picked it up and handed it back to Christopher. It didn't stop there, however. Christopher fumbled again, trying to attach his reed to his instrument. Feeling stuck between a rock and a hard place, all I could do was scowl at him. He needed discipline, but I also needed to concentrate and play without attracting attention from players or the audience. Even though I was mad at Christopher, I had to control myself. I looked at him sternly and whispered, 'Focus on your music, Christopher.'

A few nervous moments went by. I needed to refocus, so I listened to the music intently and took a few deep breaths. Counting the beats in my mind, I engulfed the reed with my lips again, ready for my following note.

Then it happened. Something every professional musician dreads very quickly became a reality. I went to blow the note, but nothing happened. Nothing came out. No noise. Nothing. Each time I exhaled, my lips moved away from the reed and no air would enter my bassoon. When I tried to play other notes, the same thing kept happening over and over. Somehow, my head kept moving away from my instrument without my permission.

The orchestra played on while I sat there confused. Now people glared at me. The conductor had fury in his eyes. My turn quickly came again to play my notes, and I willed my facial muscles, lips and tongue to do the right thing. With intense concentration, I forced my lips to engulf the reed and my lungs to exhale the air they needed— still nothing. No noise or notes again. Suddenly, my neck pulled my head over and over to my left. The pain each time was excruciating. I couldn't control what was happening. I tried with all my might and all my consciousness to bring my head back to its natural centre, but I couldn't. My mind raced with panicky thoughts, and I grimaced with discomfort. I couldn't explain what was happening to me.

The music heightened. Fleur moved more and more wildly as she led her violin section, and I managed to force some deep breaths and relax as best I could. At least I had some relief, I thought, but then Christopher glared at me harder than I had to him.

'What the hell are you doing?' he mouthed.

'I don't know!'

Even Annie got rattled with the commotion. She lost her place in the music, having to turn away from us to regain composure.

The music heightened again. I simply *had* to control myself. I knew I was in a fight or flight situation again, and I needed to dig deep to get myself out of the mess. My mind churned over what to do. Suddenly, the notion of me being an Olympic weightlifter entered my mind, and I imagined a tiger was about to maul me. Somehow, in a way I didn't fully comprehend at the time, that gave me the strength to play.

Eventually, the music ended, and my body slackened, knowing I had fought an unknown monster and survived to finish the concert. It was finally over, and Annie and I ran off stage as fast as we could, even before the audience had finished applauding. I told Annie I needed to go straight home, so there was no time to face my colleagues after what had happened to me.

Later that night, I stood in front of the bathroom mirror, gazing at myself for what must have been an hour or more. My mind still sprinted, and I felt confused and distressed. My head was straight and still. Why now? Why couldn't I keep it still during the concert? It was a simple task that hadn't required any thought or effort before. I didn't understand or have any answers. All I could do was come up with simple theories that didn't hold much credibility. The most obvious explanation was that my neck probably had a strained or stretched muscle. But I had sore muscles before, and they didn't move involuntarily. I wasn't sure what was going on. Just like my dream the night before, I was all lost at sea.

As I looked at my reflection, I considered seeing a doctor, but my neck and head were now still and pain-free, so I decided that the best thing to do was wait and see.

I paced nervously to my bed, where Sebastian was in a deep, snorey sleep. I slipped under the covers quietly, not wanting to wake him up, but my stealth was in vain when my knee accidentally pressed against his buttocks. He stirred, groaned something inaudible, and then went silent.

I lay on my back, silently staring at the ceiling, desperate to get to sleep. My mind still raced with thoughts of the concert and its consequences. With my body resting flat on the mattress, my neck seemed to be better than ever. It felt normal. It felt unobtrusive, and if I weren't thinking about it, I probably wouldn't even realise my neck was attached to my head. Besides, the soft pillow took the weight off my head and shoulders. After a while, the rest of my body eventually began to relax.

Still not asleep, however, I tried distracting myself with objects and sounds around me. I listened and hoped something would help, but the room fell silent, except for Sebastian's rhythmic breathing that, thankfully, redirected my thoughts towards what I needed. I slid over, wrapped my arms around him, and gave him a long warm cuddle. He woke slightly.

'Hello, my darling Sebastian,' I whispered.

He exhaled a pleasurable groan and mumbled in a Chicago-gangster drawl, 'See ya baby ... when I wake up.'

With his words, I fell in love a little more. It reminded me of his strengths. Even though he was oblivious to what ailed me just then, he was always one to make light of a situation. No matter how serious it was, he could use humour to deal with whatever was happening at the moment. I was the worrier in the relationship, and he had an acute radar for it. When I agonised over global warming, for example, he used it as an excuse to go to the beach for a swim. I had him to thank for my healthy blood pressure, as well as my healthy-looking tan.

I played along with him as I brushed my fingers through his hair, whispering, 'You're in this speakeasy, in this two-bit ant-hole city, and not anywhere else?'

'*Escape from North Africa*, 1944. Humphrey Hedding, Brigit Berlington. I know that film,' Sebastian whispered drowsily.

He started to fall asleep, and I heard him mumble, 'When does the train arrive in North Africa?'

'I don't know. All clocks have stopped,' I said, still playing along, citing words from the film.

Sebastian grunted.

'Sebastian?' I asked.

He started to drift off to sleep again, muttering barely audible words I only just fathomed, 'Sweet dreams, my love.'

I didn't know what to say. I felt torn. I desperately wanted to talk to Sebastian, but he looked so peaceful falling asleep. I mouthed the only words I could think of, 'Good night, darling.'

I cuddled him closer, and with clenched teeth and a busy mind, I lay awake for another three hours. Finally, mercifully, for no other reason but exhaustion, my eyes shut and I drifted off to sleep.

CECELIA

13. VELLMERSTON CRAGS

A couple of days later, I felt relieved my head and neck had behaved themselves since the concert, and I looked forward to seeing Annie again. She came over in the early afternoon. It was always good to see her outside the orchestra, and my mood lightened when we met at the door. She tactfully avoided any mention of my nightmarish experience in the concert two nights before. This was usual form for orchestral musicians who played under such high pressure that admitting there was a problem was known to be an out of bounds discussion.

We needed to test some newly made bassoon reeds, so we both made our way to the music room. Annie opened up an old box containing a dozen reeds she had been making. She fixed the first one to her bassoon. As it wriggled on, she glanced at me with a cheeky look she often made when she was about to make a joke.

'Attaching a bassoon reed is as easy as tying your shoelaces. I could do it blindfolded,' she said in jest. 'That's why God, sorry Christopher, wears loafers.'

To release the stress of playing, Annie enjoyed disparaging Christopher, and sometimes I played along, even though I didn't like to put people down.

'Yeah, but who appointed him the great Almighty?' I asked.

'Himself!' Annie laughed.

'Or maybe his alpacas!' I said a little too seriously.

We both giggled like teenagers, fooling ourselves into thinking we were as accomplished comediennes as we were musicians. I kept laughing longer than the jokes deserved, realising I needed a good release from the tension of the last concert. We laughed so much, my sides hurt, and Annie nearly snapped her reed.

'Shhh, we need to keep going,' she playfully scolded.

I nodded. Reluctantly I agreed, but then Annie couldn't stop giggling.

'Take a deep breath. Breathe in, breathe out, in, *out*,' I said.

Eventually, Annie composed herself and played scales to refocus. She then played *Sonatine for bassoon* by Tansman so overtly flamboyantly, Liberace would feel proud. I applauded her in the same way, flailing my arms about, happy to know she was in good form.

She looked at me cheekily. 'I feel closer to God already!' she laughed.

I helped her remove the reed from her bassoon as an encore, and I put it in another box, beautifully lined with velvet. It was a box in which she kept her only-for-the-best-concert reeds. I hadn't seen the box for months, and with Annie playing so well, the reed deserved its new place.

Another eleven more reeds still needed to be examined, so Annie took the next one out of her old box. We both looked at it doubtfully. Its bamboo colour looked darker than the others, and we were sceptical. Still, you never know, so Annie blew a few 'quack, quack' sounds on it before handing it to me.

'Must be Christopher contraband,' she said.

I examined it visually. It wasn't even fit for chopsticks.

'Why don't you give it a try, Cecelia?' Annie asked.

I placed it delicately on my bassoon's crook and played a few scales, with no sign of any difficulty with my neck. This gave me confidence to deliberately make some truck horn sound effects.

'Yep, for the coffin.' I mimed playing a golf chip shot as I threw it into a bin a few feet away. My aim was good. It landed smack in the middle. We laughed again, and Annie turned to me, saying casually, 'Sebastian can use that as a golf tee.'

My laughter abruptly ended. Once I heard Sebastian's name, my mind immediately raced to the day before when I had tried to have a longer discussion with him about the concert. It felt so confusing. Why couldn't I mention my difficulties to him or anyone else for that matter? Sebastian and I were always open and honest about everything, but I froze like a rabbit in spotlights when my moment came. I knew he would be supportive and non-judgemental. Yet, I wasn't communicative enough for him to display his listening skills. All of a sudden, I felt a failure as a partner, as well as perplexed about my neck.

I sighed and gathered my thoughts, wondering when the right time would be to have a good heart to heart with Sebastian. During a tropical holiday on an isolated island, perhaps? Maybe while sailing the South Pacific Ocean? Perhaps if Sebastian were swimming with dolphins about thirty metres from our yacht, I'd shout, 'By the way, there's something I need to tell you about my neck!' Then, of course, once I'd told him, I'd throw him a buoy.

'Cecelia ... yoo-hoo ... we still have a few more to try.'

My thoughts were still south of Fiji.

'Cecelia?'

I turned to Annie, and my heart sank. 'It's Sebastian. I haven't told him yet about the last concert,' I said solemnly.

———

A couple of hours before my next concert that night, I put my body through its paces. I played complex bassoon pieces from composers such as Bartok, Mendelssohn and Strauss. The fingering was challenging, but I thought I handled it well and produced an excellent sound. I took the point of view that anything else would be a walk in the proverbial park if I could run a marathon.

When I first started to practise, I worried how my neck would cope. However, it felt fine. It felt great, in fact, and after a few minutes of playing, I was full of excitement and raring to go. Any thoughts of seeing a doctor floated away like musical notes in the air.

Annie gave me a huge hug when we met backstage. We didn't mention Sebastian or the last concert. Instead, we exchanged meaningless chitchat and a few thoughts about the forthcoming concert. By the time we were walking on stage, as usual, our bodies were loose and ready, helped by a bit of laughter about Christopher.

Annie watched Christopher warm up and turned to me. 'Look, there's God,' she whispered.

'I can see the light!' I giggled.

Christopher saw us smiling and smiled back. 'What are you two laughing about? Not my alpacas I hope?' he asked.

'We just saw something *divine*,' said Annie.

Christopher smirked. 'Can I have some?' he asked.

Annie and I giggled again. 'Oh, you already have!' we said in unison.

Christopher laughed. 'I don't even want to know what you're talking about anymore,' he said, smirking again. I smiled back, happy to know he was in a good mood.

'Some things are best left unsaid,' replied Annie sheepishly.

We sat in our spots and practised a few notes, the three of us in sync.

Fleur looked across the string section and gave us a wink before the conductor entered with loud applause from the audience. He tapped his baton, and we started to play.

The concert began, and it felt like everything fell into place. Every note I played seemed just right. I felt in form again, and the orchestra sounded as good as it had ever been.

As the last applause ended, we didn't speak. Annie and I walked off stage with smiles on our faces which said enough. Annie's grin and soft eyes emanated support and happiness. We both knew that the Dynamic Duo was back.

But in the quiet of my car, my mind was messy. I'd had two concerts where everything fell apart and one where something bizarre happened in my neck, and now this concert was good. How could the strange thing in my neck be there in one concert and not in the next? What did the future hold if my body was so unreliable?

———

I was tired, and wanted to go home and have another go at talking to Sebastian. Even though I had just completed another concert without fuss, I still thought I should speak to him about my neck.

The following day, Sebastian and I went on a picnic to one of our favourite spots we liked to call 'Vellmerston Crags', a gorgeous cliff face overlooking the ocean. Sebastian named it after the place Catherine and David loved to go to in the film *Destington Heights*. It was a movie high on the list of films Sebastian wanted to show me, and after I watched it, I loved it too, and we keenly agreed on the name for our secret romantic hideaway.

We had been there many times. The hike there was a lonely one, which involved climbing over rocks and other large obstructions. In all the times we went there, we never saw anyone or traces of human activity. That was fine by us and, as such, we lovingly regarded it as our sanctuary. It was the perfect place to talk.

I sat next to the cliff face and smiled gently at the serenity. The wind blew through my hair as my eyes followed a seagull hovering in the sky, silhouetted against the sun as he neared the far horizon. I must have been preoccupied, as Sebastian and I had been silent for quite a while.

Sebastian lay on a soft rug quietly reading *Finding Me* by Jackie Towerby. I pondered over words I knew well in the book, in particular, *'learn to follow your heart'*. In the few moments my mind formulated the words I wanted to say to Sebastian, I felt I was following my heart. I was in love and in the career I wanted. Part of me thought I should be ecstatic about it, but in a grander sense, I wasn't happy. Why was it so hard to find that deeper happiness?

Sebastian absentmindedly turned a page and looked up at me, and smiled. All of a sudden, I felt in paradise again, but only for a moment. I smiled again, imagining happiness as a series of fleeting moments. Perhaps that's all we can accept in our lives, I thought, and I chuckled to myself in the realisation of such a priceless little life lesson.

A comical companion had come along for our outing, Wills, our four-legged seagull chaser, also known as a tri-colour Cardigan Welsh Corgi, and I reached out for his ear to give him a cuddle. Wills had started as Sebastian's dog when he was a bachelor. But since Sebastian and I married, Wills gladly and deliberately took me on as his cuddle mistress and scratch-behind-his-ears concubine. It was a role I happily took on, especially as his thick fur felt silky nice when I stroked him.

I stared out to sea and ran my fingers softly over Will's big left ear while Sebastian scratched his right. Wills excitedly rolled around from the double attention.

'Loyal, trustworthy, and he doesn't answer back,' I said, smirking.

Wills responded by licking my nose. It tickled.

Sebastian closed his book and smirked with me.

I looked at the setting sun, then back at Sebastian, and then back at the sun. Its light held me in a gaze.

'The sun's nearly down,' I said lazily.

Sebastian sat up. 'You're following your heart,' he responded.

'Hmm?' I replied, not quite hearing what Sebastian said.

'Jackie Towerby. She says if you follow your heart, you'll find happiness. It's the old adage. That's what you're doing with your music.'

I shrugged my shoulders. 'Oh, I don't know.'

Wills interrupted and parked his face in Sebastian's hands. It earned him a little play from his master.

Sebastian gazed at me admiringly. 'Cecelia, you create transcendence,' he said. 'It's what you do best, and, really, the only thing either of us have ever wanted to do. It drives us.'

I felt flattered and gathered my strength. It felt the appropriate time to say what I wanted to say.

'Sebastian ... I ...'

Wills pushed his nose into Sebastian's hands again, and they looked at each other eye to eye. 'Transcendence and mystique, right Wills? Doggies know how to do it, don't they? Maybe you can teach me?' Their noses kissed.

All of a sudden, my mind started sprinting. I wanted to talk seriously, yet I also felt like I couldn't ignore Sebastian and Wills' fun. They wanted to play, and I suspected I was a buzzkill. I wasn't sure what to do. I took a deep breath and gathered my thoughts.

'Sebastian ...'

'Right, darling?'

They both fixed their eyes on me, and I couldn't help but melt over their cuteness. Seeing a gorgeous human and a gumby corgi, both with doughy eyes, focus so much attention on me was too much.

'I ... I suppose so.'

'We're both storytellers,' Sebastian articulated thoughtfully.

That was it. The brave, ready-to-spill-the-beans-Cecelia-of-Troy took a hike. 'Just made that way,' I answered softly.

The corners of my mouth slowly turned upwards. Sebastian was having too much fun with Wills, and I couldn't help but smile. They were both acting like lovable idiots.

Then, Sebastian stopped playing and Wills started nudging me. With that, I gave in and started patting him affectionately.

'You're both nuts,' I laughed.

I kissed Sebastian, and the three of us rolled in the grass before a gust of wind blew *Finding Me* off the cliff and into the sea.

CECELIA – EARLY YEARS

14. MISS PERFECT

A school bell rang.

'Okay. Lesson over everyone. See you tomorrow!' shouted the teacher.

The students packed up their musical instruments as fast as possible, and they were out through the door within a minute. The room, once filled with music, fell silent.

Except one young girl with curly hair stayed. She was still practising her recorder.

'Can I stay a little longer?' she asked the teacher.

The teacher smiled. 'Don't you have another lesson, Cecelia?'

'Not for another hour. I have a free period.'

The teacher looked a little puzzled at Cecelia, not quite sure what to do or say. 'You know, you can't stay here every day. Yesterday, your maths teacher said you were fifteen minutes late.'

'But pl*ease*!' pleaded the girl.

The teacher looked at his watch, then back at Cecelia, sighing as if to give in. 'Okay, but I'll be back in forty-five minutes to check on you.'

'Thanks, Mr Ravens!'

The teacher left, leaving Cecelia alone, and within seconds she started practising her recorder again. She played scales and pieces of music repeatedly, far above the expected talent for her age.

A few minutes later, without Cecelia realising, a couple of older girls walked past. Hearing the music, they stopped at the music room door. Seeing no one else around, they turned to each other. The bigger girl said, 'Hey, let's teach Miss Perfect a lesson.'

'Perfect idea,' smirked the other girl.

The two girls barged in, banging the door open with contempt.

'Hey, Miss Perfect. How's it going?' said the bigger girl, as she snatched the recorder from Cecelia.

'Give it back!' ordered Cecelia.

The big girl and her accomplice started throwing the musical instrument at each other.

'Give it back!' ordered Cecelia again.

Frustrated the girls weren't complying, Cecelia ran between the girls and grabbed the recorder as it flew through the air. 'Now get out!' she shouted.

'Ooh, Miss Perfect has spunk,' laughed the big girl.

As the big girl laughed, her accomplice moved in and snatched the recorder back from Cecelia.

The accomplice scanned the instrument and shrugged.

'Here, Cecelia, you can have it back now,' she said.

But as she handed it over, she threw the recorder at a wall, the impact smashing it into several pieces.

The two girls then ran out the door, leaving Cecelia alone again.

As Cecelia picked up the recorder fragments, the teacher returned to see the mess.

Anger built up inside him as he scanned the room.

'Cecelia! What's going on?' he ordered.

'What?' said Cecelia quietly, as she searched for an answer.

'You know what I'm talking about, Cecelia! How did the recorder break?'

Still not knowing what to say, Cecelia moved backwards in fear.

'It was an accident,' she stuttered.

Cecelia didn't play the recorder for another six months, not until she saved up her pocket money to buy another one.

And in all that time, she churned and churned over her fear in that situation, concluding that sometimes it just wasn't worth speaking up.

CECELIA

15. VOLVO DRIVER

We all sat around the dinner table quietly, and the silent air around us felt thick. For minutes, the only sounds to be heard were the cutting of rump steak (equally as thick) and the shovelling of food into mouths.

Sebastian and I sat opposite my parents. A large rectangular table separated us, and a lamp beamed its intense light directly into our faces as I leaned back and admired Mum.

My thoughts were interrupted by clinks and clanks of cutlery on plates, and the sounds filled the otherwise silent room. Then, Sebastian made the first noise of note when he put his knife and fork down on his plate.

'Thank you for dinner, Diana ... um ... yes ... thanks.'

'You're very welcome,' Mum beamed. Her smile lifted us all, and when Dad scraped the remaining gravy off his plate with a slice of bread, we were all relieved that the main course was over.

Mum and I acknowledged Dad's end of meal ritual with a mutual wink as we packed the plates and took them to the kitchen. When I walked through the door, I turned back to Sebastian and mouthed for him to say something to Dad. It's not that Sebastian had any problems talking to my father. It's just that he wasn't used to talking to him without me being in the same room. Sebastian preferred to communicate in less formal situations too. Perhaps we should have gone on a picnic instead, I thought.

Sebastian looked at me nervously and gulped his cup of tea a little too quickly.

Dad watched him in puzzlement and asked, 'So, how are your studies going, Sebastian?'

'They're going well, thanks.'

'What have you been studying lately?'

'Movies mainly. Roy Rogers, Monroe, Freud and the like.'

Dad looked a little perplexed. 'Freud? What's he got to do with films?'

Sebastian's confidence grew. Now he was on a familiar topic. 'It's psychoanalysis. There's a whole branch of film theory called Cine-Psychoanalysis. We apply theories from great psychologists like Freud to film. Those theories lend themselves to films by Hitchcock. Maternal Superego, the ego and the id, that sort of thing. It helps us to understand how films work.'

Dad nodded in admiration. 'That sounds impressive.'

'Thanks.'

'And you want to make movies when you've finished?'

Sebastian sat up straighter. He felt happy to talk about his passion to anyone. Having his father-in-law showing an interest was even better. 'Yep. Just like Hitchcock. And write scripts too.'

I overheard their conversation from the kitchen, and hearing the smile in Sebastian's voice brought me back to the table. I took my seat, and Dad turned to me.

'Will you be the breadwinner, Cecelia?' he asked.

'Dad!' I exclaimed.

I was taken aback by his question. It hit a nerve as neither Sebastian nor I cared who earned the most money. I had to speak up.

'Dad, do you prefer *Barbarella* Jane Fonda, or *Klute* Jane Fonda?' I asked.

'Oh, I did like her in *Barbarella*,' he offered.

'What about the *Klute* Jane?'

'By then, yes, she had changed', as his face lit up, imagining her image. 'There was the Vietnam war...and the 1970s, of course,' he beamed cheekily.

Sebastian chipped in, trying to impress Dad. 'What about her exercise videos in the eight—?' He stopped himself before realising he might commit a faux pas.

Dad turned to me. 'Cecelia, I asked the question in a practical sense, not in a gender-equality sense,' he said with authority.

'Dad, it sounded like you were having a go at Sebastian ... and my right to work. You've always been supportive of what I've done, so it seems old fashioned to think Sebastian must be the one to bring in the bacon.'

'Well, then there's been a communication misunderstanding.'

Mum walked in, balancing a delicious looking chocolate cake in her hands. She must have overheard too, and she gave Dad a very condescending look.

Sebastian interrupted. He sensed another argument might ensue, so he tried to calm the waters. 'Thanks again for the meal, Diana. Do you mind if I skip dessert?'

Mum frowned in disappointment. She'd been preparing the meal for hours in between preparing lessons for her school students the next day. 'Oh ... would you like a doggy bag then, love?'

Sebastian and I answered in unintended unison, 'No, thanks.'

Mum frowned again, 'Oh, are you sure, loves?'

Dad interrupted. 'Film's not an easy area to find work in,' he stated.

'Arrgh!' I hid my head under the tablecloth and silently screamed before resurfacing. 'Neither is music, Dad, but you let me do it.'

He nodded in acknowledgement before he focussed his thoughts more directly. 'All I'm saying is that Sebastian should contribute.'

Sebastian straightened in defence. 'There are lots of ways a man can contribute, other than financially. He can contribute emotionally.

He can be honest, open, communicate, and show he cares, for example. He can value the relationship above anything else.' Sebastian winked at me. 'Shall I go on?' he asked.

I winked back.

Dad looked at both of us with a confused look on his face. A hint of a smile on his weathered face surfaced as he realised how much we cared for one another.

Mum looked fondly at us too. 'I bet Sebastian is pulling his weight, even though he skips desserts,' she said, smiling sheepishly.

We all laughed in surprise. Mum, as she often did, lightened the mood.

I turned to Dad. 'See, Dad, Sebastian does contribute.'

Sebastian followed me in a breath. 'I didn't have the luxury of studying when I was younger like Cecelia did.'

A few seconds of silence went by, as we all anticipated Dad's response. He looked very thoughtful, seemingly unaware he was keeping us in suspense. 'I think I'll have some of that cake,' he muttered.

———

After our goodbyes, Sebastian and I sat in his car, a stylish old Jaguar, to decompress. Sebastian turned to me, breathing deeply to still his nerves. 'Phew, that was steak to a lion back there,' he said.

I leant on his shoulder, and our breathing became synced. 'My father is like any father, I suppose. He just wants grandkids and a Volvo for his daughter.'

'Not a Ferrari?'

'Safety first. A Volvo.'

We both giggled. I turned on the radio, and *The Hustle* began to play. I couldn't help but bop along. 'This okay?' I asked.

'I prefer death metal.'

I gave him a playful punch on his shoulder.

Sebastian screamed in fake pain. 'Interior. Car. Night. Girl murders boy!'

'Relax. There'll be no more parents for a few weeks.'

'Phew. Let's get takeaway next time then.'

I started to bop to the music again, and before long, we were kissing.

Without warning, Sebastian stopped. 'Wouldn't it be better if we didn't do this in your parents' driveway?' he suggested.

CECELIA

16. FAITHFUL FRIEND

Like a camper staring into a campfire, I sat in the music room, gazing at my bassoon, captivated by its reflective chrome keys glistening in the artificial light.

I thought about my neck again and how I couldn't produce a sound during that *Sorcerer's Apprentice* concert. Even though I now felt okay physically, a sense of uneasiness crept into my mind. As I dissected my situation, my bassoon became the target for my emotions.

Anger welled up inside me, fuelled by a feeling my bassoon had betrayed me. Suddenly, everything felt muddled. I even began to question whether I could play, whether I was good enough as a musician, and subsequently, good enough as a person. My bassoon was so much a part of me. I liked to think its romantic, warm, mellow, ethereal sounds were those of my spirit, personality and essence. The bassoon was my universe, and I was its sun, and we needed each other to thrive.

I began to catastrophise over my neck issue, even though I had no idea what caused the loss of muscle control. Yet, I inconveniently forgot that point. Instead, I mulled over the possibility that if I couldn't play, my whole self-worth would forever be bruised. I had devoted myself entirely to music over many hard years of study and practice. I had given up so much to achieve success, and my bassoon gave back even more, and now things were beginning to crumble. What did I do wrong? What did I do to deserve such a fate? How could my bassoon do this to me!? I was beginning to lose control of a life I spent a lifetime learning to control. Would I suffer the same fate as the trumpet player in the Netherlands? I didn't know if I could carry on.

Time stood still in the music room as angst built over my relationship with my instrument. Maybe an hour went by. It felt like eons. Eventually, I realised that, due to necessity more than anything else, I simply *had* to reconcile with my bassoon. To play again and dissipate the anger and confusion building inside me was the only option.

I studied the warm maple wood of my bassoon, lovingly collected and sorted by the maker to find the best pieces that would create the best sound. The wood had been carefully moulded and cured in a production process lasting many, many years. Each piece of wood used was different; every bassoon was unique. Many people may have worked on it during that time or just one very special and talented craftsperson. They used specialist tools. The metal parts were then very carefully made and added to the wood. During the whole process, weather and humidity affected the overall sound and feel of the instrument as well. Wonderfully, that is why every bassoon has individual characteristics and specific ways to be played.

I reflected on the long process to create this great instrument and how I wanted to honour that process by giving the bassoon a voice everyone could hear.

Every instrument has faults, I thought, and they give each bassoon its individual character, which we learn to love. So, if my bassoon has flaws, I reasoned, so can I, neck and all. Perhaps then, we two inferior entities can produce a perfect sound? I smiled in the realisation of my epiphany, and the romantic side of me burgeoned. I imagined romance, a platonic relationship the two of us shared, and that we were made for each other.

In all of that, there was something nothing could take from me—my determination. I exhaled some air and slowly picked up my bassoon before bringing its reed gently to my lips.

I played scales over and over, and my head and neck kept still the whole time. The sound was very pleasing too. I put my bassoon back on its stand and wriggled my hands and body to release the pent-up stress inside me, and I felt better.

It was time for another test, so I picked up my bassoon again, inhaled a determined breath, and played a passage from Mozart's Bassoon Concerto in B-flat major. It's a piece of music many professional bassoonists play and it's my favourite. Again, my neck and head stayed where they should be throughout the whole piece. That was when I lost track of time. Music filled the room, and I became joyfully lost in its splendour. I played and played in abandon. It felt so good to be back in form, and when the music reached its crescendo, I had to stop myself in fear of laughter.

I put my bassoon back on its stand and rubbed my neck. It felt up to scratch, albeit slightly sore, but no more than in any other practice session or concert. I was going to be okay, and that felt better than the music itself.

Sebastian heard the music stop and called out from the kitchen, 'Do you want a cup of tea?'

I ran towards him, hoping for a big hug. Instead, he was rolling around on the floor playing stupidly with Wills. He looked up at me and grinned. 'That was a long practice. You sounded great. It must have been a good one,' he said.

I was a little worn out and didn't want to go into specifics. 'Well, I've played it before,' I said casually.

'It's amazing how you're so relaxed about playing.'

I met Sebastian's loving eyes but looked away.

'Come on, Wills, give me a hug,' I asked. He happily obliged, and pretty soon, the three of us were rolling around, even more stupidly.

CECELIA

17. MONSTER

In some ways, the most challenging task about playing in a concert as a bassoonist is getting there in the first place. The bassoon section sits behind the orchestra, so it is easy to think that slithering into one's spot would be surreptitiously easy, like a naughty boy sitting in the back of the class—not so. Bassoonists have to navigate a maze of chair legs, feet, French horns, percussionists, music stands and a variety of other concert paraphernalia just to get to their position. They run the gauntlet along a narrow corridor with musicians on either side, all the while carrying their instrument high in the air, trying not to bang, ding or dent it on anything that may cause damage.

And that's just on stage. The trip from the green room to the concert hall is similarly fraught with danger. There are steps to deal with and all kinds of well-intentioned orchestra managers and back-stage personnel who offer last-second advice. But all the player wants is to focus on the task ahead.

That night, I hurried as fast as I could along the corridor to the stage, knowing that the concert was about to start in two minutes. I was the last musician out of the green room, spending every precious second I could preparing, playing difficult sections over and over again until they felt right. It was probably a good thing I was running late. It took my mind off any other issues that could go wrong.

Various photos and paintings of distinguished artists who had performed at the Festival Theatre hung on the passage wall. The place had a rich history. Many famous actors, singers, comedians, musicians and entertainers of all sorts had plied their wares in days gone by. In each picture, artists were performing on stage or looking directly at the viewer, seemingly saying, 'If you try hard enough, you can be as great as me', in a condescending way. If they were supposed to be inspiring, it was a joke. Maybe on better days. For me, as I ran past them, they felt intimidating.

After tripping over the principal horn's fourteen-inch feet, I made my way to my spot with several 'sorries'. Also, I tripped over my music stand, miraculously catching it in one hand while juggling my bassoon and crook in the other. I felt relieved to finally reach my seat and plop myself on its soft cushion.

Despite my time in the green room, to say I was distressed before I even started playing was an understatement. I recognised my mood and realised feeling such a way was not an unusual thing for a musician. We all have lives, and stuff happens, but nothing else matters in the moment of playing. It's a kind of focus that a sportsperson or newsreader has. It enables them to block out screaming fans and other distractions. I knew I had to concentrate, so I engaged my mind to quieten all thoughts and activities around me that didn't matter. With a deep exhalation and intense stare towards my reed, I was thus ready.

Annie looked towards me and gave me one of her (patent-pending) reassuring smiles. It helped, but I felt I needed a little more to loosen up, so I stuck my tongue out and crossed my eyes back at her. Christopher saw us, and we all giggled silently. My body and mind relaxed even more, to the point where I not only felt ready but excited and enthusiastic as well.

I shook my shoulders and lifted my bassoon, ready to start. Christopher and Annie followed in unison, and we looked like three synchronised swimmers. I giggled a little more, then out of necessity, I visualised playing beautifully for the audience. If I saw it in my mind, I could do it.

The conductor took his place and faced the audience. He bowed, turned back to the orchestra, and raised his baton as a hushed silence filled the auditorium.

Just before the music started, I lifted my bassoon's reed to my lips, a simple act that I had done thousands of times, almost without thinking. It should have been easy, as easy as putting food into my mouth, but I simply couldn't do it. Each time the reed touched my lips, my head jerked sharply left, all the way to my shoulder. I tried several times, up to the point where notes that had to be played were only seconds away. Thoughts whirled chaotically. I had to find a way to play immediately. My body shook in immense agony, and my muscles tensed. I grimaced, trying not to vocalise the pain. A couple of times, it was too much, and I let out muted screams that were luckily drowned out by the loudness of the brass section. Finally, all I could do was to push my chin into my neck tightly, place the reed at the side of my mouth, and play through the pain.

Christopher and the conductor noticed my struggle and frowned at me. Annie looked in amazement, but she was too preoccupied and focussed on her music to do anything. I cringed in embarrassment, hoping no one else was watching me. It was a silly thought. Hundreds of people in the audience and orchestra had their eyes on me.

My music part began before I wanted it to, and my neck pulled my head sideways even more. What happened next felt like a blur, but instinct took over. It was like two sides fighting a war, so powerfully and so thoroughly, they almost forgot what they were fighting about in the first place. The only thing I consciously noticed was that the music, and my neck battle, intensified in unison.

But, somehow and somewhat thankfully, I got through it. I played. I missed notes. I was a little out of tune on occasions. Yet, despite everything, I still finished.

The music stopped, and I didn't even pause to take a breath. I quickly got up out of my seat and ran out of the auditorium towards the backstage dressing room as fast as I could. Along the way, I didn't hear anything except my panic. I didn't see much either, as my head continued to twist to my left shoulder. A couple of times, I tried forcing it back to the centre with my free hand and arm, but that only made my neck fight back more robustly than it did on stage. Luckily, no further damage was done to myself or my bassoon, even though there were several steps and other obstacles to navigate along the way.

At the backstage door, George, the orchestra manager, bumped into me. He looked at me sternly. 'What's going on?' he asked.

'I don't know!' I screamed, awkwardly dropping my bassoon onto the table. Unlike me, it remained intact.

Christopher stormed towards us with Annie pleading behind him, 'Christopher, don't!'

But Christopher ignored her, and his face reddened with rage. 'Cecelia, that was shit!'

I covered my face in my hands before realising that touching my face with anything made my head jerking worse. 'I can't play!' I shrieked.

Annie kicked Christopher in the shins. 'No wonder, with God here breathing down our necks!'

Christopher turned to her, shooting arrows with his angry eyes. 'Screw you!'

In the warring commotion, I lost my balance and dropped to the floor. George, ever the diplomat, immediately put on his emergency response demeanour and held my hand softly.

'Everyone chill. Just chill. Now, Annie, do you know Cecelia's part?' he asked.

'Yes, but ...'

'No time for buts. Christopher, you play first bassoon.'

Christopher's face beamed. 'Already there, boss!'

'Good. Get started.'

Annie interrupted. 'But George, he—'

Suddenly, my head jerked sideways very painfully, and I screamed louder than I had ever shrieked in my life.

It stopped all arguments and abruptly filled the room with silence.

Annie kneeled and stroked my hair, whispering, 'What can I do for you, Cecelia? Can I get you a drink?'

Christopher and George offered their hands to help me up. I accepted George's.

Then, as if he couldn't rub his malevolence in any further, Christopher looked at me with his condescending eyes tutting, 'Don't worry, Cecelia. I'll do it right this time.'

My whole body trembled in shock. Christopher's words were amongst the most hurtful and humiliating words I had ever heard. Still, I was in excruciating pain, with my head twisting wildly and my mind paralysed, unable to do or say anything about it.

George held my hand tighter. 'Shush now. It's okay. It's okay,' he whispered, as he helped me stand.

I trembled even more, with pain shooting through my whole body. I mustered the only words I could. 'I'm sorry.'

'It's okay,' whispered George again.

'I've never missed a concert in my life.'

George forced a smile. 'Do you want me to call an ambulance, Cecelia?'

My body tightened. 'No,' I said abruptly.

'Are you sure?'

'Yes.'

The concert hall end-of-break bell tolled, and Christopher headed for the stage entrance. George's eyes darted between Christopher and me. I could see he was torn between going on stage or staying with me. Eventually, he had to go, so he stood up and left, turning his eyes back towards me as he reached the door. 'Go home, Cecelia. Take a taxi, then take a bath. Try to relax. We'll talk about it tomorrow.'

Annie gave me a cup of water. With all my shaking, I barely managed to hold it. 'You know Cecelia, I played pretty badly out there too,' she said softly.

I took a deep breath, and the concert hall bell tolled again.

Annie gazed at me. Her fingers slipped slowly off mine before she left the room with a tear rolling down her cheek. 'I have to go,' she cried.

Now all alone, except for my bassoon, I dropped my cup of water. And descended into a panic attack.

CECELIA

18. ALL IN THE MIND

After about twenty minutes, George came back and arranged a taxi for me to get home. My body and mind still felt in overdrive, and I was still shaking, but at least with his help, I could get up and get in the taxi.

On the way home, thoughts of my time in the Netherlands invaded my mind. I remembered the orchestra I played in where I thought it would be a permanent gig, but they didn't renew my playing contract after six months. I remembered how devastating it felt, and the awful times the trumpet player had gone through and how he lost his job too. He became a pariah in the music world. It was too soon to leave for both of us. Any time felt too soon to leave an orchestra.

I leaned against the taxi window, rubbing my sore neck, angry at myself for not seeing a doctor sooner when my neck first became a problem. I had visited doctors for other ailments, even ones that turned out to be as minor as a common cold, but why not for this?

The truth came down to one undeniable fact. I thought I was the problem. I thought my mind was the problem. It never occurred to me that it was physical, and I blamed my anxiety for my muscle spasms.

In the end, I'm not sure if it was fear or plain common sense that stopped me, as incredible as it sounds, from throwing my bassoon out the taxi window, never to see it again.

CECELIA

19. SECRETS

Over those past few days, or possibly past weeks or years, I chose to avoid an uncomfortable truth. It was a way of lying to myself. In the back of my mind, I knew there was something majorly wrong with my neck. Still, I ignored it, rationalising my symptoms as little more than a niggling feeling. I tried to tell myself there was nothing wrong, or I blamed it on something else. But deep down, I knew there was something going on, and I couldn't face the truth. The chasm between feeling a physical symptom and interpreting it as anxiety bound me up in knotted ropes of inaction.

I continued to chastise myself over and over again for not seeing a doctor sooner. It would have been the rational thing to do. It would have saved me from a lot of heartache and pain. What the hell was I thinking?

My bassoon turned into the target of my blame once more, and in a way, I blamed it for my feelings. I kidded myself that I only had a sore neck. That was easy. The hard part was the concept I had a condition that may end my career. Dealing with that was way too uncomfortable and disturbing.

In the orchestra, musicians kept quiet about medical problems. A stigma hovered over someone's head if anything hindered their playing. It was a sign that they were unfit for the job, a belief no doubt associated with the *'show must go on'* maxim. That was true to an extent. A player couldn't afford to have a day off for any reason. Replacements on short notice were challenging to find.

Even if the orchestra managers could get someone, the proxy musician didn't benefit from rehearsals to ensure their playing was to the quality needed. Usually, during the concert, replacements had to 'sight read', where they played the music as they read it on the sheet music, similar to how a reader would skim-read a book. Sight-reading didn't allow for any nuance or deep understanding of the composer's intention, or any practice time. The quality of musicianship lacked a certain amount of professionalism as a result, unless a top notch player who knew the repertoire backwards could be located, but, of course, they were generally booked-up well in advance.

For classical musicians, music is their life, and the orchestra is their world. It is a world never left by choice. They usually retire at an old age, having led a successful and inspirational career before their tired bodies can't move as they should. If a musician leaves an orchestra for any other reason, they may as well be hanged for heresy. Colleagues treat them like lepers and make them feel ashamed and guilty. It's like being a magician floating in a glass tank of water, wrapped in chains. You know you have the magic skills to get out any time, but somehow, you're stuck in the tank.

Although there was overwhelming evidence that I had an issue with my neck, ignoring it reduced my anxiety in the short-term. However, it presented a much bigger problem in the long-term. I failed to comprehend, of course, that ignorance is the crucial ingredient in the unhealthy-ways-of-dealing-with-problems recipe. I was blind to the fact that I had to face my situation and open up to challenging opinions. I also needed to form new habits and coping mechanisms if I could play again. Even all that might not be enough. I had to get to the bottom of my neck dilemma, and that was the strangest and most disturbing thing.

———

When I stumbled through my lounge room door, Sebastian was watching a comedy show on television. I could hear him laughing even before I entered the room. His laughing did not affect my mood, as I was still suffering from my panic attack symptoms. My mind was racing, and my body was shivering so much, I dropped my bassoon just inside the door. Luckily, its protective case saved it from damage. It was another story when it came to me.

Sebastian seemed not to hear my noise and continued watching the cat program. With his head turned away from me, he absentmindedly said with a smile in his voice, 'You're early'.

I couldn't get any words out of my mouth, and a few seconds went by before he noticed something was up. He twisted his body towards me and, at that moment, his face dropped.

I fell into his arms, and we hugged and hugged.

'Are you okay?' he asked.

'I ... I—'

'It's okay, darling. You're in my arms now.'

My body continued shaking. Even with Sebastian's body heat and comforting rubs radiating through me, I still couldn't talk.

All I could think about was the book, *Finding Me*, that Sebastian had read the day it blew off the cliff.

Just like me, it was all at sea.

CECELIA

20. OBLIVIOUS

As I lay in bed that night, in the back of my mind I had disturbing feelings I was a failure or not a real musician. I felt like a fake. My last concert was a testament to that. I had to resolve any negative thoughts, any negative judgements, and be at peace with a decision to take time off from the orchestra to get better. The Beatles, Beethoven, and Glenn Miller all had time away from their careers, so why couldn't I?

Many more uncertainties whirled around my mind like flying daggers. What about the side effects of prescribed medicines? What about practical stuff? I couldn't drive, and simply getting around was hard. Could I enjoy the things I used to enjoy before my neck spat the dummy? Yes, I was scared, not only for my future and my job but also for the treatment I urgently needed. I didn't know what I was getting into or what I was about to endure. I knew I needed to be strong, but I wasn't sure if I could be. In all that, there was one undeniable fact staring at me in my mind's eye, and it helped me decide what to do, and that was the comfort in knowing that courageous people seek help.

So that's what I'd do, seek help, even if I had to fake being a courageous person.

I sat in an empty, stark doctor's room staring at the exit door, knowing Sebastian was on the other side, waiting for me. He'd been fantastic, driving me to see my general practitioner and being as supportive as he could, especially during my meltdowns.

As I waited for the doctor, sunlight beamed through a small window straight into my face. When I moved to avoid it, light from the globe above caught my eye. It annoyed me that I couldn't escape the distractions, and I felt caught in the middle no matter what I did. What made the whole experience worse was that the chair I sat in felt overly soft and, as such, I sunk into it unevenly. My neck and head turned more forcefully to one side over and over again, and my vision blurred. Very quickly, I had sore muscles in the upper half of my body.

During a brief moment when my neck kept mysteriously still, I noticed two (or was it one blurred into two?) diplomas hanging on the wall from unknown universities. I also saw a fern that was in obvious need of water. A doctor who couldn't take care of his plants didn't fill me with confidence, and I felt things were off to a bad start even before they began.

A man who looked more like a film star than a doctor walked in and introduced himself as Dr Stewart before sitting behind a large desk. I fidgeted nervously, thinking the desk wasn't the only thing between us. He stared at me, examining my involuntary movements for what felt way too long. I had to break the silence.

'You can see why I'm here,' I said.

'Yes, how long has your neck been doing that?' he asked.

I put my head between my palms to steady myself, but it didn't help much. 'In recent days, it's been worse.'

He nodded, and I felt a pang of envy, seeing him do that simple move without thought or effort.

'Yes. Are you currently taking any medications?' the doctor asked.

'No.'

'So, we can rule out any side effects.'

I tried to copy his flawless nod but failed. He knew what I meant, though.

'Have you had any trauma to your neck? An accident or anything like that?'

'Not really. I was only playing my bassoon.'

His eyes lit up, and he leaned forward. He looked like he just won the patient lottery. 'You're a musician?' he pressed.

'Mmhmm.'

'Has it caused a problem like this before?'

'No.'

'We can rule out something physical then. Let me have a look at some notes.'

The doctor turned to his computer and checked my health history. As I hadn't been to the doctor for a long time, there wasn't much for him to read. I waited in silence for what seemed several minutes before he turned back to me. I wistfully stared at the fern, imagining a big dark rain cloud hovering above it. If the doctor wasn't going to water the poor thing, at least I could in my mind. Besides, I had to distract myself with something. This guy wasn't Mr Chatterbox.

I turned back to him with my eyes, a little startled, as he began to speak. 'Cognitive Behaviour Therapy can change your thinking, Cecelia. I'm interested to know your thought patterns and how you learnt to think the way you do.'

He printed a diagram on a sheet of paper for me and slid it across the desk. It showed the relationship between thinking and body movement. It also looked like a bowl of spaghetti.

He continued. 'When we have a thought, it makes us experience a feeling: sad, happy, calm or nervous, for example, and a resulting body movement.'

I heard the doctor's words, but I didn't take them in completely. The fern's dilemma was still in my mind. Its state of decay fuelled my scepticism, along with the fact that the doctor was stating the bleeding obvious. I was also taken aback. Three sentences had just rolled off his tongue. Maybe he was Mr Chatterbox after all?

'Are you saying my neck movement is some sort of nervous tic?' I asked.

Dr Stewart leaned forward again, almost knocking his glass of water over in the process. If only he could give it to the fern instead?

'I'm saying, let's delve into your past and see what we can find. We can train your internal dialogue to talk in a better way. I believe your symptoms are merely a defence mechanism to avoid painful memories from your past.'

On that, my neck suddenly twisted badly. It hurt, and I grimaced from the pain. I could have yelled out, but I didn't want to give away too much.

'What was your thought just then?' he questioned.

'I don't know. My mind is kind of blank.'

'That's okay. Humans have hundreds of thoughts a minute. Many are so fleeting, and we don't even notice.'

'But I would have noticed that thought.'

Silence filled the room again. The doctor smiled to lighten the tension between us. He was correct on that point. Things were tense. My body sat rigidly, and my neck and head felt like they were going haywire. Pain shot through my arms and upper torso, before releasing its torment into my legs and feet. It was all I could think about, and I wanted desperately to go home.

'Do you have any unpleasant memories associated with music in your past?' he asked, not acknowledging my distress.

I paused in thought as Dr Stewart waited patiently for an answer. How can someone answer a question like that? I, like anyone, had many experiences in life. Picking a bad one out of thousands on such short notice felt harder than finding a boat in a used car lot. I let out a large gush of air from my lungs and said the first thought that came to me.

'I pushed myself hard. I was focused and stubborn. That's what made me. And I got there.' I laughed awkwardly at what I thought was an overly direct retort. 'I'm a successful and prominent musician.' Satisfied with my answer, I retreated into my chair.

I surprised myself in summarising my career so briefly, which made my neck and body move even more crazily. I didn't say it proudly. I didn't beat my chest or toot my trumpet in any way as the words came out. Instead, I was like a scolded dog who had stolen some chicken. The thing is, as I struggled to make sense of everything and speak, I felt I *deserved* to say it loud and proud, especially after all the hard work I had done to get where I was in my career. Why did my body betray the words I had the right to say? I wasn't sure what to think.

'You must have put up with a lot to get there?' he asked.

I squirmed, still not sure of what to say, and my body moved further backwards in retreat.

'Good. Good. It's okay to do that. What's on your mind?' the doctor probed.

Suddenly, I was getting fed up, and thoughts of going home grew more substantial. My eyes darted around the room as much as my head and neck would let them. On the wall to my far left hung a captivating photo. For a moment, I chastised myself for not noticing it sooner. It was a mesmerising and stunningly beautiful portrait of an ageless woman posing behind a see-through silk white curtain.

Dr Stewart was waiting for my response, intensely watching my reaction to the picture.

I looked back to him, upset that he took me away from something so lovely, and in defiance, I said, 'Every woman gets harassed.'

'Tell me more.'

I tried to shake my head but couldn't. It didn't stop my intention to, though. 'Let's not go there,' I said tautly.

The doctor moved back into his seat. I hoped he felt defeated. 'Maybe we can come back to it in another session?' he asked.

I looked back to the photo, not answering his question. It didn't stop him from continuing to probe my thoughts.

'So ... is your neck movement worse when you are playing?'

'Of course.'

'I imagine playing in front of so many people is stressful.'

I rolled my eyes at his obvious comment.

'People who aren't musicians think that, but there's more to it,' I said.

'Yes?'

I paused my train of thought, not wanting to go further. I didn't want to explain the many insights and revelations of music. Music is a wildly personal experience between the player and the listener. Opening up at all to this felt very vulnerable. 'It's a way to communicate something special to large groups of people. It's very emotional', I ventured.

'Sounds like a lot of pressure.'

This time, my eyes didn't roll. They blinked instead.

'Ha! That's music for you,' I laughed.

The doctor leaned back to scratch his Roman nose. For some reason, it made my nose feel itchy too, but I resisted the urge to rub. I didn't want him to feel like we were making any connection.

Then, without warning, I thought about the many hours I had put into music and the challenging pieces I had needed to learn, even if I didn't particularly like them. The relentless pressures to perform dredged themselves into my mind, including, in some cases, the pressure to be someone else on stage, like playing a deranged character with my bassoon in Bernard Herrmann's *Psycho*. Suddenly, I wanted a less stressful career that would make life much more comfortable. My eyes began to moisten. Not quite tears, just ... wet.

Dr Stewart handed me a box of tissues. It was the nicest and most caring thing he had done for me, and I gave him a wry smile as a small thank you. But I didn't want his help, so I shook my wobbly head and pushed the tissues away. He looked at me, surprised and a little hurt.

Still, I wanted to take home some knowledge of my condition, so I asked him, 'Have you got any more information you can give me?'

Grudgingly, he went on the attack. 'You seem to be changing the topic,' he said. I sensed he felt hopeless as a doctor who couldn't do anything for his patient. He felt a little ineffective for me and my situation. Even so, I couldn't answer his question.

I put my hand under my chin and pushed my face upwards to look at the clock. 'Time's nearly up,' I said.

I got up out of the uncomfortable chair. It felt good to stand, especially as it put me in a higher and more powerful position than the doctor, who was still sitting and crouching down in comparison. 'So, that information?' I asked again.

The doctor rolled his eyes (now it was his turn), and reluctantly he retrieved a thick book from his bookcase. He opened its cover, and as he flicked through its pages, my focus returned to the photo of the woman. It really did capture my imagination. I saw myself in a similar image, looking down the camera lens. I thought of the audience looking at me and enjoying the music I played, seeing and hearing what I did as a kind of romantic musical experience. I compared it to the way watching a bird in flight enhances listening to 'The Lark Ascending'.

The whir of the doctor's photocopier brought me back to the room and the task at hand. He offered me a few pieces of paper, and as I scanned them, my eyes lit up. On the front of one piece, I read:

> *Tics: ... can look like nervousness; movements can be controlled for a short time by voluntary means ...*

> *Dystonia of the neck (spasmodic torticollis): ... involuntary twisting movements of the head ...*

My face reddened. 'The second one sounds like me!' I exclaimed.

The doctor shook his head. 'No, no. Your movements are *clearly* voluntary, believe me.'

CECELIA

21. TWISTED

Without meaning to, I shut the doctor's door a little too hard. For a second, I thought of opening the door again and apologising. Instead, I said my sorries to the poor receptionist, who looked perplexed by my behaviour.

Sebastian gave me a most welcome hug, and we rushed to our car. The receptionist saw us with our arms around each other and smiled. Her days must be hard, I thought, having to work with the quack who just wasted my time. Seeing me embracing a man must have brightened her day almost as much as it brightened mine.

Later that day, I lay in bed with my eyes facing upwards towards the ceiling. It felt good to relax, and I was tired already, even though several hours were still left in the day. My neck and head had been moving since I woke, and they used up much more energy than they should. I envisioned eating energy bars all day, just to keep my muscles happy. At least that would give me an excuse to eat more chocolate and tiramisu.

My pillow felt extra soft, and my head buried into it rather deeply, to the point of keeping my ears and cheeks warm and cosy. When I lay down, everything in my body remained relatively still. Yet, when I was standing or doing any activity, my neck and its immediate attachments went bananas. It was one more thing I didn't quite understand. When particular objects touched my head, such as a hand or hairbrush, the result would be a very abrupt and painful jerk to the left. Yet, when a pillow touched my head and neck, the movement felt subdued. The fanciful notion my neck had a mind of its own and the ability to decide how to react when different objects came into contact with it seemed absurd. It added to my confusion.

I looked up towards the ceiling, and with my head relatively still, I enjoyed the simple pleasure of being able to run my eyes along its cornices. It wasn't easy. My eyes were tired, the product of the struggle to focus on objects as my head moved.

My pleasure in being able to look at something was short-lived. I attempted to look more widely around me, and my eyes refused to focus. Before long, it made me despair for all the beautiful things in this world: sunsets, art, nature and stars, to name a few, that I would struggle to see in the future.

I needed to look at something joyous to rejuvenate my soul. The warmth of sunlight filtering onto my face gave me the magic pill I needed. I got up and tucked the pillow under my arms.

'Wills! Where are you?' I called.

On cue, Wills appeared, tail wagging, and we headed outside. We plonked ourselves on the cool grass on a blanket and I lay back. Wills snuggled up into my arms.

'You're such a good boy, Wills.'

I stroked his back.

'Sometimes.'

Wills pushed himself tighter up against me.

'Now Wills. How about we play a little game of 'What shape is that cloud?'

I looked up to the sky towards the white floating balls of fluff above me, and I saw or imagined all sorts of shapes. It was such a delight.

'Look Wills! That one looks like a dog.'

Wills actually looked upwards.

'Sorry, Wills. It looks more like a bulldog, though.'

I continued looking. Another cloud appeared like a mountain, another a tree. Suddenly, I couldn't stop laughing. It felt absurd to compare shapes in clouds, and I felt the sting of the doctor's diagnosis soften a little.

Stepping back inside, I smiled at Wills who seemed to sense my happier mood.

I went back to bed and rested my back on the headboard before grabbing my computer from the side table. As I opened the computer to view its screen, my head and neck began to move without permission and I struggled to focus, yet I managed to type the words:

Twisted Head.

Thousands of search results came up. Mesmerised by what was before me and by the flickering light of the screen, I scrolled through the most popular ones.

They all mentioned symptoms of what seemed to ail me: muscle spasms, muscle aches, stiffness, nerve pain, headaches, reduced range of motion, and more. As I read, a checklist went off in my head, tick, tick, tick, tick, tickety tick. It was as if someone was telling a blind man they couldn't see.

Next, I read causes: whiplash, muscle strain, disc problems (degenerated, herniated or slipped disc), various other degenerative conditions, and posture. Unlike the list of symptoms, it took a little longer to identify whether those causes pertained to me or not. Posture and muscle strain were the hot self-evident favourites, as holding and playing the bassoon put my body in a very unnatural position. My head and neck twisting no doubt compounded muscle trauma. I ruled out whiplash, as I couldn't identify anything that may have caused that condition.

The possibility of having a disc problem and a degenerative condition did worry me, though. Those were unknowns. I had a sore back, but I put it down to excessive movement higher up in my body. If my back were painful because of a disc issue, it would probably be much more painful. Still, I couldn't rule that out without further investigation. The idea of having more tests didn't excite me.

In the end, my symptoms were wide-ranging. As they matched nearly all of the medical conditions I read about on the internet, I simply couldn't self-diagnose. It felt very disappointing. If I was to find out what was going on, I had no choice but to seek more professional help.

Staring into space and thinking about what I had just read made me even more tired, so I put my computer aside and lay back again. It wasn't as relaxing as earlier, however. My head jerked to the left again, and my mouth and nose buried in the pillow. It became hard to breathe. I tried digging my head deeper, hoping the pillow would give more support, but that didn't work either.

Just at that moment, Sebastian, from the lounge, cheered. It angered me to think he might be cheering at my misfortune. How dare he! But I had more important things to ponder. I still struggled to breathe, so I pushed my hands into each side of my face and held my head tightly. That didn't work. My head jerked even more strongly to the left. So much for respite. I had to stand up just to get air into my lungs, which I did with urgency. Once up, I punched my pillow angrily. It was met, once again, by a whooping cheer from Sebastian. His lousy timing was perfect, and I stormed into the lounge to rebuke him.

It was then I realised he was watching golf. Someone, I don't know who, as I didn't follow the sport much, had just got a hole in one. I watched the replay and realised that there was no hope in heaven I would be able to swing a golf club so sweetly and elegantly as the player on television. Even though the sport wasn't a thing I played, it saddened me to think that I could never take it up if I wanted to.

I thought about how my new world would be if my neck refused to settle down. Most people define a fulfilled life as doing things we have to do and things we want to do, and that is enough. But nature is wonderous, and the choices within it are endless, especially if we dare to get out of our comfort zone. Now, for me, however, the planet looked to be a finite place with limited possibilities. Before my neck problems, I liked to think that something like golf was there for me, even though I would probably never take up its challenges. My neck had taken the choice away from me, and suddenly my world felt a very dull and uninteresting place.

Still, if I couldn't play golf, I could enjoy watching it. So I sat down next to Sebastian and joined him. It wasn't clear who got the hole in one, other than the Australian flag was flying. It certainly was a great moment for sports fans, but how was it for the incapacitated? The fact that someone else did something I could never do, or more importantly, I could never even try to do, didn't warrant celebration as far as I was concerned. Golf and all other sports for that matter were going to be challenging to appreciate. Anything was going to be challenging to enjoy, but what choice did I have?

'Who's the golfer?' I asked, trying to savour a moment of Sebastian's joy to get me out of my funk.

'Adam Scott. He's a dead set legend!'

I didn't reply. I was too busy trying to stop my head from moving, using my hands as a barrier. On top of that, my lips were dragging sideways towards my ears. It was as if someone had a hook inside my mouth, like a fish, and was pulling it behind me. I squinted, trying to focus on the television screen. I must have looked like I had rabies or something (they shoot dogs with rabies, don't they?). If I was with anyone else but Sebastian, I most likely would have felt very embarrassed. Eventually, my head dropped, and I couldn't lift it again. It was all too much.

Sebastian noticed and stood up abruptly to help. 'Would you like an emergency massage?' he asked.

He stood behind me and, in silence, massaged my shoulders slowly. Boy, it felt good. I felt my tight muscles loosen with each knead, and my strength returned a little, enough to lift my head closer to its rightful position. Minutes went by without a word. I thought of things I could say to Sebastian, how I felt, how much I was sorry this was happening, and how much I appreciated the massage and his support, but I felt weak, so nothing came out.

Thankfully, Sebastian didn't seem to mind the silence. He just wanted to give. I could sense he wanted to say something, though. Eventually, he did, blurting out a little too loudly, 'Cecelia, why didn't you tell me about your neck earlier?'

'Umm, it only happened when I was playing. I didn't know what it was back then,' I exclaimed even louder than Sebastian.

'If I realised, I would have helped you.'

I turned away, feeling very guilty about compromising my own and Sebastian's high standard of communication. Usually, we were good together, waffling on about anything and everything. Yet now, the room fell silent on a subject that meant so much to both of us.

Not only that, I had thrown a concert by playing poorly. I let down other players, the audience, and the person that mattered the most to me, Sebastian. I was the wife I didn't want to be.

'I'm sorry. You know musicians. They blame everything on themselves,' was all I could say to Sebastian's offer of help.

'There's no blame, Cecelia.'

'That doesn't make it any easier.'

'Yes. You're right.'

I could hear Sebastian still trying to help by the tone of his voice. What he said next, however, had a less confident hue about it.

'Cecelia. There's been no formal diagnosis yet. It could be something simple and easily fixed.'

'I hope so,' I said, the words not matching my racing thoughts.

Sebastian nodded in acknowledgement and continued the massage. He didn't need to say anything else. His kindness and dextrous hands lifted a little weight from my shoulders in more ways than one.

Suddenly, my head dropped even more, and I screamed in pain, 'Ouch! Not so hard!'

'Sorry. Sorry!' Sebastian apologised.

I pulled away and tried to make my way back to the bedroom. When I got up, I realised it was too hard to walk with my head collapsed, and for a few seconds, I didn't know what to do. Neither did my body, so I fell to the ground. If it weren't for the soft arm of my chair and Sebastian's catching skills, I would have hurt myself, inflicting even more damage to my delicate body.

Eventually, with Sebastian's encouragement, I managed to crawl to the bedroom. He reassuringly whispered, 'You can do it,' the whole way. It was only about twenty metres to the bed, but the journey felt like a marathon. It felt like my head and neck were so limp, they could snap at any second. When I finally made it to my destination, I collapsed on the mattress with a big thud.

I then tried to sit up, but my head felt like a lump of cement. I couldn't move. Sebastian sat next to me and gently stroked my hand, but even his support and comforting words weren't enough.

'I can't lift my head!' I screamed.

Sebastian brushed the hair away from my eyes and leaned forward to hug me. I could see the panic in his eyes too.

'It's too heavy!' I exclaimed. 'I'm paralysed!'

My mind started to gallop more with panic, and my beating heart felt like it would explode. Lying in bed, feeling so unwell and with my body in complete pain, I forgot that I hadn't received a final diagnosis yet. Instead, I worried that my world had caved in. It felt like the worst my life could get. Would I even survive, I thought? If I did, maybe my weak neck would break and leave me a paraplegic or, worse, a person with quadriplegia? A world inside, in bed only, without sunshine and fresh air, would leave me at the mercy of disease or a multitude of other ailments. Life like that would mean atrophy and slow, painful death.

Sebastian held his gaze on me. He looked shocked and powerless. I wanted to help him but couldn't. All I could think about was rest. Sleep was the only way to get me out of this nightmare.

'You go back and watch television. Let me get some sleep,' I whispered, my voice croaky and spent.

'What can I do? Sebastian asked.

'Water, maybe. Then let me sleep.'

'I'll be right back.'

Sebastian stroked my hand one more time and made his way to the kitchen as fast as he could.

As he made his way through the door, a tear ran down his cheek.

SEBASTIAN

22. RIPPED

When Cecelia crawled to the bedroom, I encouraged her as much as I could while I held back tears. No real man wants to see his wife hurting, and there she was in unbearable pain. It was far from our old life full of sunny days and hugs. With her body as it was, I couldn't even wrap my arms around her without inflicting some damage, and I craved her touch.

The only light was hope, but dark clouds stretched ominously on the horizon. The future felt uncertain, and I didn't have the confidence to face what may come. At least Christians have faith, I thought, but I'm not religious, so that wasn't an option unless I had a quick-fire baptism or something. I asked myself, what can I do? It seemed like no mere mortal held the power to fix Cecelia's medical condition. I wasn't a miracle worker, and with my mind operating faster than a formula one driver, I probably wasn't seeing every option either.

As Cecelia lay in bed, I looked at her one last time before making my way to the kitchen. It was lucky I knew the directions so well, as I barely managed to keep myself together. I could easily have tripped over furniture or collided with walls.

I leaned against the fridge door, out of sight and sound from Cecelia. Then I let it all out. Tears welled up in my eyes, and before long, a full-on bawl took over. My body shook and my face soiled with salty waterworks until my eyes were dry and empty. I reached over to the kitchen bench to get a tissue, and it was then that anger welled up inside me.

My fists clenched, and I noticed the calendar on the wall. Like a hungry lion eating a carcass, I ripped it apart, month by month, each month containing reminders of film events and concert dates, including a concert with Luciano Pavarotti.

SEBASTIAN – EARLY YEARS
23. HOLLYWOOD OR BUST

It was the 1970s, and an excited young boy relaxed back on a carpeted floor. His primary school teacher had just hired a sixteen-millimetre movie from the state library. As the teacher prepared it for screening, his eager students, including the young boy, cheered, anticipating the break from lessons.

The kids loved the whole experience, so before long, movies became a tradition with the students watching at least one film per week. Australian films and travel logs were the leading choices, and afterwards, the students discussed what they liked and didn't like about what they had just seen.

Outside school, the young boy's mother often took him to the cinema. A seminal moment came on his eighth birthday.

'What film would you like to see for your birthday, Sebastian?'

'*Charlotte's Web*, thanks, Mum.'

'Okay. Let's go!'

During and after that film, the boy's love of cinema rose exponentially. For him, seeing a movie on a huge screen, more extensive than a white sheet on a school wall, was like an adventurous journey into outer space.

Of the hundreds of films the boy watched, he loved *It's A Wonderful Life* the most. In the movie, George Bailey, a highly moral person, played by James Stewart, yearned to travel the world and do great things. Instead, he was stuck in the small town he grew up in. After his dad died, he was trapped into managing his father's business, a small building and loan company, which ultimately prevented him from following his dreams. Later, he married Mary, and they started a family. Responsibilities to George's new family were further hindrances to his wanderlust. By the end of the film, George slowly came to see that family and friends were actually more important than his freedom.

The boy didn't have many role models in his life and instead connected with George and his character, particularly in the early parts of the film. The boy believed life was about travel and the pursuit of what makes your soul, and other souls, happy. Being stuck in a dead-end job was the antithesis of that and to be avoided at all costs. It was a belief that later played out in his experience when, after working in boring office jobs for years, he left and decided to go to university instead.

It was natural that he would choose to study film in this new free part of his life. He desperately wanted to be a film director, following in the footsteps of his heroes such as Alfred Hitchcock and Richard Linklater. Studying was easy as he had already read movie books and watched lots of old films. During his education, though, an aspirational shift happened within him. He still wanted to direct films, but he found something else he enjoyed even more—scriptwriting.

The jackpot came in his third year when he was able to do subjects dedicated only to scriptwriting. Each week, students wrote short film scripts, and he received high distinctions for every one of them. One teacher, a successful scriptwriter herself, even took him aside one day and said he had particular and exceptional talents for scriptwriting and writing in general. She certainly encouraged him to keep going and follow his dreams.

One night, after he had met Cecelia, when he was feeling some-what safe, he opened up the most he ever had about his lack of mentors and his tough journey early in his life. Cecelia listened thoughtfully and tried to wrap her arms around him, saying gently, 'I understand.'

At first, he resisted. Cecelia tried again and he softened. 'I under-stand,' she said again.

He replied with a tear in his eye and a 'Thank you.'

It was just what he needed to hear.

Cecelia also empathised with Sebastian's aspirations very deeply. In music, she had the courage and determination to follow her dreams as well. It was why she was Sebastian's biggest cheerleader and why they were exceptionally close.

Shortly after he married her, Sebastian felt deep contentment. They were doing well, financially and relationship-wise. He worked as a scriptwriter on an old-fashioned style of television show that centred around reading books to pre-schoolers. Unfortunately, the show didn't last long. The network axed it and replaced it with something more modern. As a result, Sebastian lost his job. Still, he hoped to write more scripts as a career, so he went job hunting. Some producers were interested in him, but because networks had cancelled their shows due to an industry downturn, he struggled to find work.

Things were tough for Sebastian, apart from a few small gigs and time studying a further scriptwriting course at the University of California in Los Angeles. He earned a little bit of money, enough to contribute to the household, but by no means could Cecelia and he live solely off his income. She was terrific about it and Cecelia became the primary breadwinner in their home. She remained supportive of his writing and efforts to sell the several feature film scripts he had written.

And nothing was more important to Sebastian than Cecelia's happiness. If he could not provide for her financially in a traditional sense, he could provide for her emotionally. It was a role he took on wholeheartedly. He may not have been directly responsible for her heart, but he could make it sing as much as she made her bassoon do the same thing.

SEBASTIAN

24. SHREDDED

It seemed impossible to keep Cecelia happy when I saw her struggling with her body not operating as it should. As her friend, her partner and her husband, it was hard to watch, not knowing if everything would fall into place.

At times, I noticed Cecelia's mind racing. It was as if she wasn't there. My mind raced, too, as it didn't know what to do. I hoped to be able to do something huge, something magical, like clicking my fingers together to make it all okay again. But all I could do was little things that I wished, when added together, were big enough to help. I offered her patience and understanding, as well as healthy doses of compassion. But I could not push her to improve. All that did was make things worse, especially with her neck, which seemed to respond when anything touched it negatively. In all of that, I trusted Cecelia felt a quiet acceptance that I would always be there for her.

I grieved for Cecelia, and I could see her grief. It kept me awake at night and my mind away from my writing. I needed to write every day, and I hadn't written for far too long. My projects drowned a little further with every passing sunset, and with it, my career gradually disappeared into the dark.

But I didn't blame Cecelia. She hadn't done anything wrong.

CECELIA

25. BE THE CORGI

The next day, I woke up feeling confused and dizzy and, miraculously, no longer paralysed. Somehow, my body slept, and to my relief, it slept deeply. It wasn't pretty, though. Having woken many times during the night, my nightie was drenched in sweat and the sheets were all tangled from my distorted neck and body. In my pain and panic, time passed slowly. At the same time, I worried about everything on Earth *to* worry about, including that morning would arrive before my eyes closed. Around midnight, I realised sleep would take up half of my day. That meant less time to enjoy the dwindling number of activities I was still capable of doing. It was only pure muscle exhaustion that enabled me to eventually close my eyes. I slept for six or seven hours. Usually that would feel enough for anyone, but in my body's new hypervigilant state, I felt like I needed ten to twelve hours or more to feel adequately rested and repaired.

I reflected on Wills, blissfully and peacefully dozing on the bed. What a carefree life he had, sleeping for more hours than awake, happy just to lay on anything soft and watch the world around him. For him, it was simply an honour to be with his humans. He enjoyed his meagre possessions, his toys, his master and his cuddle mistress. Three things. That's pretty much all he needed for a fulfilling life. As long as he got his regular walks and meals, and we loved him, he would give us what we foolishly believed to be unconditional love. I cuddled Wills, and opened up his big floppy ears to whisper, 'I wish I were you,' before he stretched his paws and offered a cute canine, 'Mmmmm' as a thank you. Seconds later, he went back to sleep, unaware of the night I had just had.

Once I was awake in the morning, my neck kept relatively still and comfortable, and I didn't know why. Pain still reared its ugly head, but it had a lot less bite. It was more of a gnaw than a chomp. While still in bed, I rubbed my neck with my palms to soothe away the pain. It made my head turn slightly to my left, but only by about thirty degrees, instead of an uncomfortable ninety degrees as it had the day before. The warmth of my hands radiated through my neck muscles like a hot pack, and I relaxed into it.

I shuffled into the kitchen, rubbing my eyes along the way, still sleepy and yawning. Being somewhere between an alpha and beta state seemed to make my neck muscles calm, and that made me feel a little hopeful. I wondered what would happen if I were to take up meditation? However, I wasn't sure how far to go with it. My neck seemed to be okay when I slept, yet it often went crazy during the hours I was awake.

I tried to decide at what point on the sleep-wake spectrum my neck did settle down? Maybe I could bring my mind to the point where it was almost asleep, yet aware enough to notice my surroundings and when my neck behaved itself. Perhaps to help my neck, I needed to go deeper into transcendental meditation, into the world of theta and delta mindsets. Along the way, as a bonus, maybe I could tap into some deeper collective unconscious? All of a sudden, being a Tibetan monk seemed to be an option for me.

When I reached the kitchen, Sebastian was devouring a big bowl of porridge. His eyes were locked heavily on what appeared to be the information Dr Stewart, the GP, had given me. His face looked intense, similar to when he was in his writing zone, and he didn't even notice me entering the room. I didn't mind. I knew how important writing was to him, and I appreciated that the medical material captured his attention too.

'Good morning, sunshine,' I whispered. I wondered how loud I would have to talk before Sebastian heard me.

Nothing.

'Goooo-oood morrrrrr-ning sunshine.'

No response.

'The world's on fire.'

Nope.

'Let's have sex.'

Still nothing.

I tip toed up to him and lightly kissed the back of his neck. Anything heavier than that would probably have made my neck do cartwheels. Sebastian started and grinned when he saw me.

'Feeling better, darling?' he asked.

'A little.'

He sighed in relief. 'Me too, just a little.'

Sebastian pointed towards Wills. 'Shhh, we have to let Wills sleep.'

'Oh, he's all right. He slept through the world when it was on fire,' I laughed.

'Huh?

'Never mind.'

I gave Sebastian a peck on his soft lips.

Leaning over Sebastian's shoulder, I began reading what he was reading, and he looked at me lovingly.

'Things always seem better in the morning,' he said brightly.

'So they say.' I smiled and kissed his forehead.

Sebastian turned over a page of the photocopied material the doctor gave me, and brought it to my attention. 'It says here a movement disorder neurologist might still be an option. Have you thought about seeing one?'

My face darkened. 'No. That stupid doctor waylaid me.'

Sebastian nodded. 'Who starred with Bing Crosby in the *Road* movies? Bob ... umm ... Bob ...'

'Hope,' I answered.

'That's the spirit!'

CECELIA

26. CUCKOO

Over the next few days, I thought about Dr Stewart's last comments to me. 'Your movements are clearly voluntary' rang in my ears and it wasn't long before I began to question my lucidity.

Was it dystonia, or did I really have a nervous tic as the doctor suggested? Perhaps my neck movements *were* voluntary? I looked back to the time only several days before, just before the concert, when my neck was relatively okay. Right now, it wasn't. Perhaps something in my mind *made* my neck movements go in and out of control? I didn't know the answer, and I wasn't sure the doctor, or myself, were confident in our opinions either.

I also examined my behaviour during the doctor's appointment, and I could see I had problems with concentration and memory. The photo seemed more important to me than my neck. My apathy, frustration and distrust must have been evident to the doctor. The whole time with him felt overwhelming, and the icing on the cake of sanity was that I couldn't hold down my job with my wobbly neck condition. That sounded like someone who was a nut job to me.

In addition, my mood swings over the last few days had been erratic, from intense love for Sebastian to severe panic and just about everything in between. Happy, sad, angry, overwhelmed, guilty, frustrated, anxious and confused. They were all there and more, and I flicked between each one wildly. Were those erratic emotions part of life, part of living, or was I going insane? A fine line split sanity and insanity, I thought.

The doctor had honest and good intentions. He was trying to help, but I didn't accept it. I thought I knew more than the doctor, even though he had more qualifications in health, albeit from unknown sources, than I had. Everything was at stake for me, and I failed to reach out properly for help. As a result, I was angry at myself. I needed calm, urgently.

Sebastian and I were sitting lazily in the garden stroking Wills, and I tried with all my might to keep my head and neck still. I reasoned if I could just keep it still for a moment, then it most likely would be a nervous tic. If I couldn't keep it motionless at all, then dystonia, or something else, would most likely be the diagnosis.

'Sebastian, just give me a chance to try something, okay?' I asked.

'Sure. Go for it.'

I smiled at him as he turned to stare at the flower bed, and I closed my eyes. My body and mind still needed soothing, and it wasn't going to be easy. I needed a step-by-step meditative approach starting with the parts of my body I could control, such as my toes and breathing. Forget my neck for now. I would work up to it later.

With my eyes closed, I became increasingly aware of my active mind, still chatting to itself about the orchestra and the doctor. Not to worry, I concluded, just imagine each thought sailing off into the sunset. Focus on your breathing. Move your attention down your body to your toes. Visualise them. Visualise my nails and skin. And notice the rhythmic movement up and down of my diaphragm as I sent it messages from my brain. Easy. Now to my legs. I imagined them to be very heavy, almost as if they were being pulled down to the ground by a mysterious force.

I then pictured my stomach rising and falling with every slowing breath. As I exhaled, my torso, shoulders and arms slowed as well, and soon I felt relaxed. My mind stilled, dominated by its observations of breathing and respite, and I felt like I was floating on a puffy cloud.

Now was my chance. Now was the time for me to quieten my neck. I acknowledged that it was still moving, so I imagined it was heavy too as if a gentle weight pulled it towards the bottom of a clear water lake.

Then something so small, so minuscule, yet hugely miraculous, happened. My neck stopped moving. Not for a long time. Not even for a whole minute, but just for a few seconds. I opened my eyes quickly in delight. Instantly, my neck started rotating, but it didn't matter. I could control it *and* learn to control it again, and that was all that counted. I smiled from ear to ear like a marathon winner.

Then the realisation of bad news hit me. If I could control my neck, I could rule out dystonia, so I must therefore have a nervous tic. There was no room for celebration. I concluded that I must be crazy.

When my head involuntarily turned to Sebastian, he stared at me in shock and confusion. 'Did I just see what I think I just saw?' he asked.

'What?'

'Your head. It stopped moving.'

'Uh-huh.'

He turned to me so that he could face me directly. 'But how? What? Why now!?'

'I'm not exactly sure, but I felt relaxed. I still do a bit.'

I smiled meekly, still a bit dizzy about what just happened. Visions of a funny farm began to swirl around in my mind, and my happy face transformed into something more serious.

Sebastian blinked, unsure as to why my grin left me so quickly.

'So, we should be happy, right?' he asked.

'No. I'm thinking of Dr Stewart. He thinks I'm crazy, and he may be right.'

Sebastian heard the doubt in my voice and shrugged, 'So what? Freud thinks we all have maternal superegos and oedipal complexes with penis envy.'

I couldn't hold back a laugh. All I could think to say was, 'Probably.'

Sebastian gazed at me softly and cheekily. 'You're not crazy, and if you are, I like it.'

I made a crazy face and crossed my eyes. It gave me a slight headache for a second.

'What does he know anyway?' Sebastian continued. 'He's a GP, not a psychologist.'

Frustration began to build in me. 'This is so stupid!' I exclaimed abruptly.

Sebastian held my hand to reassure me. 'Stupid's not crazy,' he whispered softly.

'But I am,' I said.

'Crazy thoughts don't make muscles spasm.' Sebastian looked at me cheekily again. 'But they make Cecelia crazy, though,' he said adoringly.

'The doctor thinks they do.'

I re-examined my time in the doctor's room and wondered if I understood what he said. Did he say thoughts *or* moods make our bodies move? I imagined both were connected. Either way, the nagging issue was that lately, I had too many wildly differing thoughts and attitudes for my liking, and I didn't know what to make of them.

Sebastian stared directly, and a little sternly, into my eyes. I gazed back into his big, blue irises and wide pupils and felt comforted. I knew he was about to speak from his heart.

'Cecelia, you know yourself better than anyone, and you're the most sane person I know,' he said.

I grinned a little.

'Thank you,' I whispered.

'Maybe it's something else?'

'You think?'

'Yep, and it's time to take control. Remember the Meg Ryan movie, *You've Got Mail*? The scene where she shadow-boxes? She was trying to be determined and tough, but she was also adorably cute. Those two opposites made her boxing kind of funny.'

'This is no time to bring up your young man crush, Sebastian,' I scolded.

'Yes, but ...'

'Oh. I get it,' I replied.

I smiled and punched the air with my tight fists. 'Pow! Pow!' I laughed, left-hooking Sebastian's chin. He play-flinched in response.

'You're crazy too,' I joked.

'Takes one to know one.'

CECELIA

27. A WINDLESS SAIL

It was a torturous wait, to say the least, to finally get an appointment with a movement disorder neurologist. He was all booked up, and I was lucky to get an appointment in a month's time following an urgent request. I didn't work or play my bassoon during that time, and I didn't know what to do with myself. It felt strange to be at home and have so much free time. Usually, orchestra members only had leave over the Christmas holidays unless they faced an emergency. Even then, it was approved reluctantly.

Annie visited often, but sometimes I had to postpone our meetings as I just wasn't feeling up to seeing anyone. After two weeks without eye-to-eye contact, she complained, albeit sympathetically, when we finally had a chance to meet.

'It's getting harder and harder to see you,' she said, as her arms wrapped around my shoulders.

'I know. I want to keep seeing you, but I have all this medical stuff, and my neck is like a tornado sometimes.'

Annie frowned. 'You're still the cat's miaow, Cecelia. But right now, the bassoon section is like a bunch of pussies chasing laser beams. We need you back!'

'But I'm not the cat's miaow anymore. I'm the cat's smashed paw.'

'Oh, Cecelia,' she lamented. 'Never fear, Annie's here.'

I smiled and gave her another hug. 'Thank you,' I said softly.

As we embraced, in my mind, I wanted to talk to her about how things really were, about what was going on, about how I felt afraid, and how no one seemed to understand what I was going through. But all I could manage was a simple, 'Anyway, how are you?'

'Let's just say, I've been popping more pills lately.'

'Christopher?'

'Yep.'

To my relief somewhat, as it took our discussion away from my neck, the mention of Christopher led Annie to talk more about workplace matters. She made a point to mention that George, the orchestra manager, apparently did see my situation as an emergency. Thus he promptly appointed Christopher to first bassoon. Annie said that Christopher was okay to work with at first, but then he started to enjoy gloating over his new role. It didn't take long for him to consider members of the section as little more than his minions. He even had the nerve to order Annie to make him coffee before every rehearsal, as if she was his personal assistant or slave, instead of the well-travelled and respected professional musician she was. She obliged the first time he asked but then added a healthy dose of saliva in his second cup. The third time, Annie threatened to take the matter higher, whereby Christopher backed down.

Just as bad, one of Christopher's students won the temporary third bassoon role. It felt very unfair. Instead of the position being up for grabs on merit, his student appeared to get the job based on nepotism, not talent. It saddened me to know that the bassoon section, which I once loved and presided over, quickly became an unfair and unhealthy workplace because of its new boss. I felt unwanted too, and that, perhaps more than anything else, added salt to my wounds.

As for Fleur, she called once. 'How *are* you?' she asked in her excitable way, a little too loud so it hurt my ears. Still, I felt thankful to hear from her and glad she asked about my wellbeing.

'I'm not doing so well ...'

But instead of listening to me, Fleur interrupted and launched into a big tirade.

'... Oh, you poor thing. You won't believe what's happening in the orchestra!'

I was taken aback, not sure what to say except, 'What?'

'There's *division*!'

'Division? What sort of division?'

'There's some who do, and some who don't!'

'What are you talking about, Fleur?'

'Well, the good news is that some people sympathise with your, umm, neck situation. They see it as an involuntary physical thing, and what happened to you could happen to them. They're living in fear.'

And what about the others?' I asked.

'Well, umm, they don't.'

There was something in Fleur's 'umm' that filled me with reservation.

'How about you, Fleur? What do you think?'

'Well,' she paused. 'You know how busy the orchestral programme is and how we all feel overworked?'

'Of course, I do.'

'Well,' she paused again. 'We think what happened to you could happen to us. You know, if management pushed and overworked us to the limit. So, I organised a protest!'

'Wow!'

'Wow, yes! But management protested too. They were very strong about it. They said the music program had been set in stone at the beginning of the year, blah, blah, blah. Changing it would not only mean rearranging musician's timetables but also cancelling venues and refunding ticket sales, blah, blah. And that was an enormous logistical operation and bad publicity for the orchestra. So management held onto their position and didn't budge.'

'That's very, umm, brave.'

Fleur agreed, then she suddenly changed topics, and we went on to talk about trivial things. But as we spoke, in my mind, I kept doubting what side Fleur was on. Yes, she did a brave and supportive thing standing up to management, and I was thankful, but to whose benefit? Hers or mine? She didn't really answer my question. I still didn't know if she saw my situation as physical or mental.

I wondered if I was selfish thinking that way. If I had a selfish nature, I could have rejoiced about the orchestra's demise without me as a member. Instead, I was sad, and I felt for Annie and Fleur. I understood the predicament my fellow musicians were in, who were undoubtedly struggling to play at their best under increasing pressure. Not to mention the hungry audiences who missed out on hearing classical music played in its highest form. For all our quirks, the orchestra was a team, and I was letting them down. In sporting terms, we were once at the top of the ladder. Now the finals were out of reach, and I had something to do with it.

―――

At the start of my unwanted sabbatical, my neck felt better, and I still held onto a small amount of hope. I spent a significant amount of time swimming and found that treading water and letting my head float in the sea eased the physical pain. My days were relaxing, and a little healing, especially as Sebastian joined me in the water too. Often though, I got the impression his mind was on his writing, so we didn't talk as much as usual.

I spent a lot of time exploring transcendental meditation. It must have looked like a comic novelty for Sebastian when I sat in the garden, surrounded by a circle of candles and potpourri, repeatedly chanting the classic 'Om' for hours on end. The lotus posture was very painful and uncomfortable at first, but it became relatively easy after a week or so. I hoped it would help me become one with the universe, and I would experience an epiphany. Instead, I became one with flies and ants, and subsequently, I moved inside. More importantly, meditation didn't help my neck much.

In the second week of my sabbatical, things took a rapid turn for the worse. One lazy morning, I was floating in the seawater, absent-mindedly thinking about the osprey in my dreams, when a massive wave crashed over me. It jerked my head to the side abruptly and painfully, and by the afternoon, my neck moved side to side without control again. It wasn't long before I needed to spend hours in bed each day, as well as at night when I struggled to sleep. It all knocked my confidence, and before long, my whole body felt in the doldrums again.

I descended into a depression from there. The week before my neurologist's appointment was spent with me very much in a funk. Disappointment filled me with each passing hour, as well as any hope I might grow to become a world-famous bassoon soloist. My heart felt empty, not being able to play the bassoon I loved, and at times, I even regretted ever having taking it up all those years ago. Sebastian tried to cheer me up with silly jokes, and he helped keep our household going, but all I could do was manage a sad smile at best. I questioned my resilience, or more precisely, whether I had any at all.

As Sebastian would say, like Obi-Wan Kenobi, the neurologist was my only hope.

CECELIA

28. END OF THE ROAD

In the late afternoon, Sebastian and I sat inside our car in silence, staring at the front door of the neurologist's office building. With its minimalist and angular construction, it would have been easy to think cold and heartless people filled its interior. Instead, its modern construction made me feel that the neurologists inside would have access to the latest practices and medication.

Sebastian stroked my hair slowly as we waited. 'Do you want me to come inside with you?' he asked.

'I can do this alone.'

I tried to kiss Sebastian goodbye on his lips, but a sharp neck movement thwarted me, and I only managed a light peck on his cheek instead. 'One more thing I hope to do properly,' I said ruefully, stepping out of the car.

Sebastian gave me a cheeky grin. '*The French Connection*,' he said.

'What?' I asked, confused.

'1971. Gene Hackman. It's a classic film.'

'What's that got to do with things?'

Sebastian grinned sheepishly. 'That kiss reminds me of the movie. It was nice, but I look forward to a deep Frenchy later.'

I smiled. 'It's a deal,' I said.

———

As I introduced myself to the receptionist, a rather handsome man with chiselled features smiled at me. 'Ah Cecelia, come through,' he said, leading me along a thin hallway to his medical room. I didn't say much other than, 'Hello'. He introduced himself as Dr Hayworth and asked me how I was in a formal yet caring way. I immediately felt at ease in his presence. My wild neck movements gave him the needed answer. I wasn't very well indeed.

The inside of the room looked the opposite of the outside of the building. Instead of being stiff and sharp, it was warm and cosy. The light was subtle yet effective, and the furniture was Victorian rather than modern. It looked more like a lounge room.

'Please take a seat,' suggested Dr Hayworth. I sat in the middle of a soft Chesterfield, and it made me feel the most comfortable I had been for a long time, as well as feel like a queen. I rested back and exhaled a profoundly relaxing and needed breath.

Dr Hayworth sat in a French recliner, and for a second my thoughts brightened. I thought he might offer me a martini.

'So, your neck?' he asked, as he read some notes. 'I see you're a musician with the Weistar Symphony Orchestra.'

All I could say was, 'Uh-huh.' I wasn't sure how to elaborate, even though people had asked me that question many times before.

'How long have you had these symptoms in your neck?' he probed.

'It's been bad for quite a few weeks.'

With the sudden attention on my neck from the neurologist, I couldn't help but rub it a little with my palm. Dr Hayworth observed me intently.

'What about before that?' he asked.

'My neck was tight sometimes, like anyone I suppose who's had a sore neck. Sometimes it affects my playing,' I said.

'Sometimes, or most of the time?'

'Most.'

He nodded without giving anything away, other than his understanding nature. I appreciated his calmness and support, and he made me smile again. It was just what I needed. Only Sebastian and Annie had supported me previously, and I needed all the support I could get.

'You play principal bassoon?'

I nodded my head the best I could. Dr Hayworth could see how much of a chore it was for me.

'Let's get to the bottom of it, shall we?' he said, referring back to his notes.

I nodded again, trying to read what he was reading. I quickly realised that it's impossible to read words when they are upside down, and your head is jerking around madly, so I gave up. All I saw was a blur of black on white paper.

'We need to rule out a few things first. Mind if I do a few simple tests?'

'Okay,' I said quietly.

He led me to his examination table. 'Pop up here, please, Cecelia,' he asked.

I sat on the table silently. As I waited, my neck and head began to move in ways I thought they could never move, so I tucked my head back into my chin. It helped a little and kept me relatively still. In my mind, I chastised myself for not thinking of using that idea outside the orchestra before. The last few weeks could have been a lot more comfortable if I had.

Dr Hayworth moved in front of me. 'Let's see. Are you able to straighten your head?'

'Not at all.'

'So, you're holding your head that way to stop it moving to the side?'

'I guess so.'

'Okay,' Dr Hayworth continued, 'Could you try purposefully

moving your head to the right? Uh-huh. I see that looked very difficult.'

It was true that my head moved more in a circular motion than a horizontal one when I turned to the right, but it did move, and that felt like a small victory.

'And the left?'

'Good. Let me check your neck muscles.' He moved behind me and touched my neck in different spots. Each time his finger touched my skin, my neck twisted a long way to the side.

He stepped back a little.

'I'm sorry if this is uncomfortable. Do you want a break?' he asked.

'No, I'll manage,' I said stoically.

'I'd like to ask you now to subtract seven from one hundred, and then continue subtracting seven from each figure you arrive at.' Dr Hayworth seemed serious as he waited for me to commence, although I was secretly wishing I had more talent for maths as I felt the absurdity of his request.

I gave it my best, and managed to move slowly backwards from one hundred in my responses, but I felt increasingly distracted by the movement in my neck and found it hard to concentrate. Dr Hayworth's face remained concerned as he watched my head move.

'Right, now let's try this. Touch your index finger to your nose, if you can,' Dr Hayworth asked.

As I carried out the instruction, my head flipped to the side, but I kept my eyes on Dr Hayworth.

He continued, 'Now touch my finger here ... and ... here.'

He moved his finger into different positions, seemingly to trick me, but I managed to keep up.

Dr Hayworth shone his torch into my eyes when I finished, and looked deeply into them.

'Can you make a fist? he asked. 'Good. And how about tapping your thumb and index finger together? Great. And could you please hold your arms out in front at chest height?'

I managed to do all the tasks he instructed, but my head and neck movements made them harder than they should have been to complete. Afterwards, the rest of my body stiffened heavily. I shook my arms to release the tension.

'How was that?' he asked.

'As hard as it looked,' I replied.

He nodded gently.

'Okay, then I need to check your reflexes.'

He reached inside his pocket and removed a tiny hammer before tapping it gently below my knees. Each time I reacted with a bit of a kick.

'Good. No problem there.'

I let out a deep sigh of relief.

'Okay, can you wriggle your toes?' he asked.

'Yes.' I moved my big toes up and down before wriggling the others.

'Perhaps we should stop now. Do you mind if I check your gait as you walk back to your chair, in a straight line?'

'No. That'll be okay.'

I quietly walked back to my chair and sat down, as naturally as I could, feeling pleased that it felt like a fairly straight line.

'Thank you, Cecelia. You walked in a very straight line, although your neck and head were at an angle along the way.'

'It was hard to see exactly where I was going,' I acknowledged.

Before the appointment, I imagined that I would score a zero for any challenge he set me, so it felt good to succeed, no matter how small the tasks would have been without the twisting neck. In the seconds it took me to get back to my seat, I self-diagnosed based on the neurologist's tests, thinking that an unnatural relationship existed between my eyesight and neck. Perhaps all I needed was new glasses? I held out that hope, trying to ignore the sombreness of the situation. However, in the back of my mind, I knew things could turn out to be much worse.

I fidgeted while Dr Hayworth referred back to his notes. He was maintaining his calm physician demeanour, even though his brain must have been churning over with a diagnosis. Watching him read felt like an hour, even though he probably spent little more than thirty seconds.

'Cecelia ...'

He paused.

My mind rushed. After all I had been through, this was the moment. Yet the neurologist certainly didn't seem in any hurry to tell me.

'... it's obvious you have a movement disorder ... and I'm certain it's cervical dystonia, dystonia of the neck, also known as spasmodic torticollis.'

I was stunned at this complete reversal of the GP's diagnosis. I squeezed out the only noise I could muster.

'Oh.'

Silence filled the room for a few seconds as my mind tried to understand what he had said and how it would impact my future. But his words were too much to take in and fathom. My face went blank.

'It's a disorder of the brain,' he continued. 'We don't know what causes it. It may be genetic. It undoubtedly would have been aggravated by your music.'

My mind whirled over what he was saying. All that I took in properly was the word *music*. Whether I had a future in music or not was the burning question that had plagued me ever since my nightmare began. 'Will I ... will I still be able to play?' I asked.

Dr Hayworth sat silently for a few seconds. He knew the gravity of my question, and in his face, I could see he was preparing himself to answer my question. 'There's no easy way to say this, Cecelia,' he said.

I sat up in anticipation.

'I'm afraid it is unlikely you will ever play music again.'

My eyes welled up, but I didn't cry. I should have cried, but my body hadn't been acting like it should for a long time, and there, in the neurologist's rooms, it continued to have a mind of its own. There certainly was enough to cry about and, as I sat stunned into silence, it angered me that I felt empty after hearing such devastating news. Any other person would cry, but not me.

For a moment, my mind searched for a reason to explain my numbness. Perhaps it was a mental block in having to process too much in the few words the neurologist had just told me? Maybe it was that, as an orchestral musician, I had learnt to keep my emotions to myself? Perhaps it was that with this news, in addition to all the sorrows I felt for the world, there simply was no more room for tears, even if they were for me? The truth was, in any event, my emotions were worn out after all I had gone through. I had been in and out of overdrive for so long. Even so, it didn't stop me from fearing that perhaps I was emotionally unhealthy for not shedding tears.

Dr Hayworth stared at me, waiting for my response. I gathered my thoughts and considered his diagnosis. 'What about ... is there any chance of remission?' I asked.

'Only in a very small number of cases. Usually, it's permanent. Even remissions generally don't last.'

He opened up a drawer in his desk and passed me brochures about dystonia including a treatment option called Botulinum toxin type A (Botox), which I thought was used for cosmetic purposes. I skimmed through the pages and noted several types of dystonia: blepharospasm (eyelid dystonia), spasmodic dysphonia (dystonia of the larynx), writer's cramp (a kind of forearm or hand dystonia I hoped Sebastian would never get), psychogenic dystonia (dystonia due to psychological factors), generalised dystonia, and mine, cervical dystonia. As I read about each one, my mind cartwheeled. I had almost no knowledge of such conditions, yet I felt a Pandora's box open as I turned the last page. I needed to learn about my newly discovered disorder, and it felt overwhelming to take it all in.

Dr Hayworth interrupted my thoughts. 'I wish I had better news, Cecelia. Have a further read of those brochures, and feel free to ask me more questions. Dystonia symptoms can be lessened with Botox when injected into muscles. How about I see you next week, and we can get started?'

I struggled to release words, still taken aback by everything.

'Okay,' I murmured.

Dr Hayworth stood up. 'I'll lead you out and see you next week then?'

'Yes. Thank you.'

'Botox can be very successful. We'll see how it goes,' he said gently.

He walked with me to the door, and as I left, he smiled at me. At the last second, though, I saw him drop his head in sadness.

I could see that he understood.

I was more than just another person living with a chronic medical condition.

CECELIA

29. SHADE OVER THE LIGHT

Still stunned, I stepped outside the neurologist's office and looked upwards. Even though the birds chirped as always and the sun shone as it had for millennia, the world seemed different.

Now I knew what I had, I should celebrate. Instead, I felt in limbo. The old healthy me was gone unless my Botox treatment was successful, and the future me was uncertain.

Along with the tidal wave of information the neurologist gave me, new questions with no answers surfaced in my mind. Foremost was Botox. Even though I understood it to be for my own good, the idea of sharp needles jabbing into my muscles still scared me. How beneficial was the treatment? What were the side effects or risks? Maybe there were other options, perhaps dietary or alternative medicines?

I didn't want to hurt my neck anymore. It already had suffered too much, and I thought about how to protect it. What precautions should I take? What activities could I or could I not do? I didn't know if Botox could get me back behind the wheel of my car. What about my sex life? I didn't feel attractive to Sebastian with my head bobbing about. Those were just two activities. What about the countless other undertakings I needed to do just to live, let alone thrive? And I didn't know how or if I could accomplish any of them.

The other thing concerning me was the neurologist himself. He seemed confident, but to my mind he reached his diagnosis rather quickly. The whole appointment took around thirty minutes, and in that time, he gave me a life sentence. Maybe there were more tests, such as blood tests or lab tests, that conclusively could prove that I really did have cervical dystonia? The best trained and most well-respected neurologists could be wrong sometimes. Perhaps, even if it was a minuscule perhaps, the possibility remained that something else may be responsible for my uncontrollable neck movements. I didn't know what it could be, but I would have at least felt better if the neurologist verbally ruled out other medical conditions.

It all felt overwhelming again, but there was a sense of relief that the neurologist, and I, to a certain extent, knew what it was that ailed me. At least I knew dystonia could be treated. I looked up again to the sky, and the light at the end of my long dark tunnel shone a little more brightly, just like the sun above me.

———

Sebastian saw me and stepped out of the car. I ran into his arms, and we embraced for what I wanted to be forever.

'He said I have dystonia!' I exclaimed.

Sebastian pulled away from me so he could look me in the eyes. He tried to speak, but nothing came out, and he looked more shocked and puzzled than I would have thought. After a few hard blinks, Sebastian offered some words I didn't find all that reassuring. 'At least ... at least we know what it is now,' he said.

I took a deep breath and kept my mouth shut, wanting to hug in silence rather than talk. Talking was the hard part. Hugging was the easy part. The urge for me to say something burned inside me none-theless, and I exclaimed loudly, 'The neurologist said I'd never play music again!'

Sebastian held me tighter as tears ran easily down his cheeks. 'What about the Pavarotti concert?' he asked.

At that moment, being reminded of something I looked forward to so much, that I was now unable to do, didn't help me at all. I looked into Sebastian's eyes in desperate disbelief, wanting more from him, but all we could do was hug in silence as he buried his head in my hair.

When we arrived home, the sun had just disappeared over the horizon, and early night felled everything before it. I looked at my bassoon through the music room door, sitting on its stand. It was barely visible in the dull light.

CECELIA

30. PUNCTURED

Strangely, my neck felt and looked a little better after seeing Dr Hayworth. Sebastian put it down to the placebo effect. He assumed I must have felt reassured and therefore better with the newfound knowledge of my condition. My brain, according to Sebastian, sent endorphins and dopamine around my body, especially to my neck, which in turn helped it behave itself. He was right to a certain extent, but other uncertainties remained, which indeed would have cancelled out any benefits a placebo may have given.

I concluded that my lift in health was just a result of luck, or perhaps the result of a few nights of exhausted sleep. After a few days, I found that I didn't need to spend my days in bed, and I could do some activities. Unfortunately, improvements in my physical condition also gave me a kind of temporary brashness that made me forget that too much exercise actually made things worse.

Shortly after receiving my diagnosis, Annie came over.

'Cecelia, I'm your new head cheerer-upper!' she declared. "First up, a good run on a treadmill will iron out any kinks in your body, especially your neck!'

I cautiously agreed. 'Okay, but slowly at first, then let's see what happens if I push myself harder.'

We drove to the gym, and along the way, Annie made me laugh by talking in a kind of punch-drunk boxer's accent in the hope it would motivate me.

'You cannot fail. You must succeed!' she said several times, each time making me laugh. Her confidence in me was empowering, and by the time we arrived at the gym, I felt ready for almost anything.

Once inside, we stepped on our respective treadmills and stood side by side. Initially, I set my pace to one kilometre per hour, which literally would have felt like a walk in the park if trees surrounded us. Next, I put it to three, then a brisk five. We walked for ten minutes at that pace without any issue, other than one brief moment when my neck pulled to the side by about twenty degrees, without pain, which was far less than what it was at its worst. My confidence increased, so I set the treadmill to a moderate jog speed. No significant problems there either.

Then, something in me decided to test my limits further. I can only explain it as a rush, similar to what teenagers may get when they perform extreme sports without assessing the risks beforehand. I set the treadmill to the maximum and ran as fast as possible. All I wanted to do was to push my boundaries and get to an unknown place as fast as I could.

It worked for a while and felt fantastic. I felt free. Annie kept up too, and we both ran and ran, dripping with sweat and grinning all over. She was correct. The kinks were dissipating, and I was going to be all right.

Then the worst happened. Suddenly, my head and neck jerked severely to the left again.

'Cecelia, slow down!' Annie pleaded.

I fell over, banging my arm on a metal railing as I hit the ground.

Annie stopped running abruptly and knelt to help. 'Are you okay?' she asked.

I lay on the floor, not knowing the answer. I tried to get up but fell back on the ground in exhaustion. Annie offered me her hand, and I used it to lever myself up again. Smarting, I stood up and checked my arm. Thankfully, it was the only thing damaged, except maybe my pride.

'I think so,' I responded.

Annie handed me a towel, and I wiped it down my forehead. It was a struggle, but I managed to do it.

My neck shot painful arrows throughout my body, so I hid my face in my hands for a while.

'Let's go sit down for a minute,' I said.

'Sure.'

We sat in silence while Annie rubbed my back gently. It calmed my neck a little.

'Cecelia, you're stronger than you think,' she said.

'I hope so.'

'Good. Shall we try something easier then?'

'Okay.'

'How about the mats?' she asked.

I wiped some more sweat from my brow and gasped in some air. 'I could do with a lie-down,' I said, still feeling tired.

'Excellent,' said Annie.

She retrieved two padded mats and an exercise ball and lay alongside me. The time she took gave me enough of a break to get my wind back.

Annie looked at me and smiled cheekily. She had 'coach' written all over her face.

'Let's try something easier,' she asked, before promptly shoving the ball into my chest.

I grabbed it awkwardly and tried to lift it, but it dropped from my hands.

Not to be perturbed by my weakness, Annie cheered me on. 'Try again. Give me a C, give me an E, another C, another E … gosh, your name has lots of Cs and Es … an L, an I, and an A!' she sang.

'Yes, coach,' I said dryly, as I used all my remaining energy to attempt another lift of the ball. But it was simply too heavy. My neck thwarted me again, seemingly affecting my strength, and I dropped the ball. Annie patiently retrieved it for me.

'Never mind,' she said sympathetically, as she kicked the ball away.

I took a deep breath, trying to relax, feeling like I had dropped the ball in more ways than one. I covered my face with my hands once more. I didn't want Annie to see me in my pathetic looking state.

It didn't work. Through my fingers, I could see Annie studying my neck muscles, and she looked shocked. My muscles were twitching wildly.

'Cecelia, your muscles look really wasted. It's amazing how you can hold your head up at all,' she said anxiously.

'I'm trying to!' I exclaimed.

'Let me rephrase that,' Annie offered apologetically. 'You're holding your head up, in many ways, so to speak, except your muscles won't *actually* hold your head up?'

'Is it that obvious?'

'A little. Your muscles look like they need strengthening.'

I offered a little smile to her. 'But Botox weakens muscles,' I said. 'It's a catch 22 situation.'

Annie looked at me patiently. 'Remember when I was in Germany, and you were here in Australia a few years ago?' she asked.

'Uh-huh.'

'Well, I injured my finger after about a month. It took me the whole year to recover, and I played like a swordfish the whole time. It was amazing I kept getting gigs.'

'I didn't know that,' I said, surprised.

Annie shrugged her shoulders. 'I did tell you. You must have forgotten or something. Never mind. You've been through a lot.'

I tried to get up again but lost my balance. Annie caught me and stopped me from falling. She embraced me, and we hugged.

'We're a team, Cecelia,' she whispered. 'I got better. You can do it too.'

I looked at her and smiled.

I wanted her to see the tiny glimmer of hope in my eyes.

————

The next day, Sebastian and I sat inside my car, pensively looking out the window again towards the neurologist's office. Wills sat between us, panting as if he sensed our nervous mood.

In my mind, the old what-ifs came back to haunt me. What if the neurologist was wrong? What if Botox didn't work? What if I still couldn't do the things on my wish list, even after the injection? I felt like my confidence had taken a colossal hit, and with my neck how it was, I felt like I couldn't do or cope with much. Botox, and the neurologist's plan, suddenly felt way outside of my safe space.

As I sat with my head resting against the window, Sebastian looked at me, and I could tell he saw the paralysis in my mind.

'I'm not sure I can do this,' I mumbled.

He gazed at me with his reassuring blue eyes. 'If you don't have Botox, you'll risk losing so many life opportunities, and that's much worse.'

'But this is so out of my comfort zone,' I said.

'Think of *The Forest of Being*.'

'What?' I asked.

'Take the less trodden path through the forest, Cecelia.'

'But there's still a chance it won't work.'

Sebastian ran his fingers through his hair and exhaled an exasperated breath. 'Then the alternative is to accept yourself as a disabled person,' he said.

I gasped and pulled my body back, and the hair stood up on the back of my stupid neck. It was his last two words that got to me more than the others—a *disabled person*. That wasn't who I was. It was what I had, if anything. It wasn't all of me, just part of me. Yet, hearing it from someone who I loved and respected fuelled doubts. Maybe Sebastian was right about me—I was a disabled person?

On the other hand, I thought, maybe he suffered from a kind of ableism himself? I looked at him in shock. He retreated and slapped himself on his forehead. 'I'm sorry. I didn't mean to say it that way,' he said apologetically.

'No. You're right,' I said. 'Saying it does me a favour.'

Sebastian smiled apologetically again.

I opened the car door and leaned over to give him a kiss on the lips, but when I was about three inches from his face, my neck jerked my head sideways. I kissed his ear instead.

He laughed. 'See, your aim's improved already.'

I couldn't help but laugh with him.

'Remember our French kiss later,' he winked.

———

It felt like I was walking in slow motion through a movie set when I entered the neurologist's office. I greeted the receptionist, and within minutes I was on a medical table. But those minutes went by slowly. To say I was nervous would have been an understatement, and my head and neck let me know about it in no uncertain terms. They went crazy, to the point where Dr Hayworth even considered rescheduling my appointment to a later date, hoping that things would settle down by then. Sebastian's comments about me being a disabled person ran through my head again. I wondered if I was worse than the neurologist's other patients if he couldn't even treat me.

I also wondered if my head would need to be restrained in a cage to keep it still, and I pictured myself having to wear a helmet or upper body enclosure. At least it would mean I didn't have to see what was about to be inflicted on me by the neurologist. However, even that idea felt futile, as a helmet or brace touching my head would only worsen my dystonia.

Dr Hayworth felt around my neck. His fingers prodded my muscles in a way that settled them down for a few moments. It gave him enough time to inject the Botox.

'This will hurt, Cecelia,' he said, his words contradicting his reassuring tone. The large needle closed in on my neck, and I squirmed. Maybe I did need the body enclosure, after all, to save me from what was about to happen? I squirmed again, albeit knowing it was too late to escape.

'Turn your neck to the side, please,' he asked, when the needle was inches away. 'Ready?'

'I think so,' I muttered, not sure if I could comply.

He injected me with the Botox, and I screamed, 'Aaaaah!' in pain as the needle punctured my skin.

Seeing my distress, the neurologist took a step back and paused. 'Shall I continue?' he asked.

'Yes.'

'Try breathing out as I inject. That will make it easier, and may help the pain.'

I followed his instructions, but my whole body tensed and grimaced when he continued with the needle. Sweat poured profusely from my brow. Dr Hayworth wiped it off with a tissue so he could continue.

He withdrew the needle, and I breathed out heavily in relief.

'Do you want a break?' he asked.

'No. Keep going.'

'I'm sorry. There's no other way to make this less painful.'

It's then I realised that I was in it for the long haul, for better or worse. It was a fork in the road moment. The only other option for me was to walk away along the path of never-ending dystonia symptoms. I *had* to stay and keep going with the Botox. I had survived one injection, and I realised I could survive another.

'Best to get it over and done with,' I said.

I braced myself, white-knuckling my hands, as my fingers wrapped tightly over the side of the table.

Dr Hayworth continued injecting Botox into my neck muscles. It must have been at least seven injections in all. I distracted myself by thinking of silly stories involving Wills chasing the osprey before he developed wings himself and flew away. It worked, at least temporarily and got me through. A flying corgi was a fantastic antidote for pain. If only I could patent it.

Dr Hayworth straightened. 'All finished. I'll give you a couple of minutes, okay?' he said, seeming satisfied with his work.

I tried to respond, but the pain returned, and I couldn't answer.

Dr Hayworth smiled reassuringly. 'Well done, Cecelia.'

He walked out, leaving me alone and staring at the ceiling. I still had blood trickling down my neck.

CECELIA

31. ENDEARING

As I lay on my back, waiting for the neurologist to return, I thought about my future and how well Botox would work for me.

Things were still uncertain, but even with all the pain of the Botox injections, at least I felt proud of myself for taking the first step. It was a relatively small gain in the grander scheme of life, but a first step nonetheless. It felt good to know that the decision to see the neurologist was ultimately mine and that in itself was something I could own. It was something dystonia couldn't take away from me, even though it had stolen nearly everything else. Finally, I was beginning to take back control of my life. Instead of questions haunting me as they had been, there was now an element of excitement in answering them.

I reflected on how time has an interesting way of passing. When Dr Hayworth returned, it seemed like he was gone for less than a minute, when in fact, he was gone for around ten. When I was in the throes of dystonia, and everything looked bleak, time seemed to work the other way around. Every minute felt like an hour. With renewed hope, I was happy to see the neurologist again, despite the discomfort of the Botox injections.

'Let me take care of that blood,' he said, as he grabbed a wipe and wiped my neck clean. 'Sorry I took so long.'

'I hardly noticed,' I replied.

A slim and graceful lady followed him. She had green eyes, dark hair, a soft face and long slender limbs. We both smiled at one another, seemingly in recognition of an unspoken similarity in gentle determination.

Dr Hayworth scrunched the bloodied wipe and placed it in a bin. 'Feeling better, Cecelia?' he asked.

'A bit.'

He turned to the lady, then back to me. 'Cecelia, this is Indira. She's a neurological physiotherapist who specialises in retraining the brain and muscles.'

I nodded to her, which made me wince. The blood was gone, but the consequences weren't, I noticed.

Indira held out her arm, and we gently shook hands. 'Hello, Cecelia. Dr Hayworth tells me you're a musician. I used to be a dancer,' she said politely.

I smiled softly. 'You're a performer too?' I asked.

'I was.'

'So ... you had to give it up?'

Indira shrugged her shoulders. 'Uh-huh. I suppose I wanted to do something else,' she said thoughtfully.

'Would you be okay if I made a few gentle assessments with your neck?' she continued. 'I'll avoid the areas that have just been botoxed.'

'I guess so,' I ventured cautiously.

She moved behind me, and I didn't know what to say next. It didn't matter, though. Indira held the conversation.

'Cecelia, are you able to move your head from side to side as I hold your neck?'

The thought of another person touching my neck again made me recoil, but Indira held it anyway. It felt unusual to have her barely imperceptible touch on my skin. It was even more strange that she placed her fingers in a configuration I thought nearly impossible. But, whatever she did, it worked, and I was able to move my neck more easily than I had in a long time. I couldn't help but smile again as Indira comforted me.

'Good. I must have hit the right spot. Shall we try some other exercises?'

'Yes.' I gave Indira my full attention.

'Now. Try to make your nose follow the lines on the ceiling.'

I slowly did as she instructed.

'Great. Now rest your head on the pillow. Let it take your weight, and very, very slowly move your head a tiny bit from side to side.'

With effort, I completed her challenge. A momentary burst of excitement spread through my body. I squeezed my fist and said to myself softly, 'Yes!'

Indira glanced at Dr Hayworth, then looked at me. I could see them both smiling. 'That'll be easier when the Botox kicks in,' she said.

Indira stood up confidently, looking like she had just painted the last stroke of the *Mona Lisa*. She walked over to the sink and washed her hands, engaging in some chitchat as she rinsed. 'How's your neck feeling now, Cecelia?' she asked.

'Tired.'

'That's to be expected. With your permission, I can give you some more exercises, very straightforward ones at first, then more challenging. We'll start with exercises lying down, then sitting, then standing up.'

'But I've tried that sort of thing before,' I said.

'Okay, but let's give it another shot, shall we? It'll be important to do the exercises extremely slowly at first. It will take a lot of work, and progress will be slow. How does that sound?'

There was only one answer, and it was a question.

'What about playing music?' I asked.

Indira gave me another confident smile, and it filled me with unimaginable joy. 'I'd like to think we may get you back to playing,' she said.

CECELIA

32. PHOTOSYNTHESIS

Having things bad for so long before the medical appointment made Indira's good news feel even better. The previous time I stepped out of a medical room, I had just been diagnosed, and this time I had just been treated. The difference was immense. Maybe it was increased levels of dopamine that gave me rose-coloured glasses. Even so, the world seemed just brilliant. Right then to me, as I shut the door and stepped outside, the birds chirped louder, and the sun shone brighter. If it was a scene in a television rom-com, I'm sure it would have been rather corny.

I liked Dr Hayworth and Indira, and not just because they helped me and gave me some much, much needed good news. If there wasn't the sacrosanct doctor/patient relationship between us, I'm sure we could have all been good friends. I felt they showed me a kind of empathy I had been missing in my life a little, even though Sebastian and Annie had shown me quite a lot over the last few weeks. There was always room for additional compassion and understanding, and I felt understood and valued, and not just for being a well-known musician either. It motivated me to appreciate what was around me, and just as importantly, I could laugh, which I hadn't done much in a long time.

My whole body felt less stressed, including my neck, even though the Botox hadn't waved its magic wand yet. I felt the wind was back in my sails, and I punched the air in relief before running back to the car. As I opened the door, Wills jumped on me and wanted to play. I happily indulged him, and I rolled around on the front seat with him trying to lick my face while I tried to scratch the back of his enormous ears. He certainly sensed my upbeat mood, and he wanted to exploit it for his pleasure.

I ended up lying on my back, with Wills on my chest. He looked happy as if he had just slurped me on the tip of my nose with his wet tongue. I grabbed his muzzle between my hands and looked into his gorgeous eyes. 'Well played, maestro!' I said, playfully chastising him. It's then I noticed a tiny grey patch of fur on his right ear. I grinned, realising that I hadn't been able to notice such small things like that for a long time. It felt like another victory over dystonia.

Sebastian watched us play, giggling the whole time and egging Wills on. He often took Wills' side for fun, even to my detriment. 'Good news?' he asked.

'Finally!' I said, punching the air with my fist again.

Sebastian joined in with a heartfelt, 'Yay!'

'Uh-huh!' I nodded gleefully, if somewhat crookedly.

Suddenly, Sebastian looked puzzled. 'Wait, what am I yaying about?' he asked.

I beamed with a huge grin on my face. 'I found my genie,' I exclaimed excitedly.

Sebastian looked around the inside of the car. 'Where's the bottle? I have a few wishes of my own.'

'No, silly!'

'What, you found Pavarotti?' Sebastian asked.

I shook my head, thinking for a second he had lost his mind.

'Sick 'em, Wills!' I ordered. With that, Wills jumped on Sebastian and played his favourite I'm-going-to-lick-your-face-if-it's-the-last-thing-I-do game, coming out the champion in less than five seconds.

'Blurgh', Sebastian coughed. 'So, Pavarotti?' he asked.

'As good as,' I beamed.

———

Indira gave me an exercise regime, and at first, it didn't look like exercise at all. Most of the tasks she set for me people do every day without effort or conscious thought. They were movements I had recently been unable to do or had forgotten how to do. It's amazing how things that I once took for granted needed relearning. I felt like I was back in preschool.

Once I started, I followed her instructions to the letter. For three months, ten times daily, I did exercises such as moving my head to the side one degree at a time, moving my eyes around, and touching my face or neck very quickly and softly for less than a second (first on my forehead then around my face until I reached my chin). I also focussed on objects at different distances from my eyes. I read books, first one word, then two, then three, etcetera, before stopping. Initially, I sat down in a comfortable chair to do the exercises, but that became a little boring. After a while, I started doing them while doing other things.

It was more than a happy surprise to find that the exercises were more comfortable than expected and had little effect on making my neck worse. Perhaps the Botox offset any muscle interference the activities may have caused. Still, either way, I improved, slowly at first and by the third week, exponentially. I felt so good, I even considered running a marathon, as, before long, the exercises felt like a breeze.

In the second month, I phoned Indira to give her the good news. She was chuffed and subsequently gave me additional workouts, which she laughingly called 'punishments'. The 'advanced' exercises included turning my head very slowly to each side while laying down or sitting, through to standing and raising my arms into various positions while moving my neck. They also included strapping a headlight to my head to follow its beam with my eyes (Indira called it the 'miner' exercise) and watching a basketball as I bounced it up and down and around. Sebastian even dusted off his bicycle, and one day we went for a very shaky ride around the neighbourhood. None of what I did felt like punishment at all, and as a bonus, it gave me an excuse to go outside and enjoy the sunshine while doing something healthy.

There were good days and bad days, but Sebastian was a real trooper. Just about every hour on the hour, he offered me a massage. Of course, I gladly accepted each one.

On a few occasions, Annie came over, and we would do the exercises together. Sometimes she would bring extremely light weights and workout balls, and we would use them to measure progress. Annie also used them to do her punch-drunk boxer's accent again.

'You are GONE, dystonia!' she said, before lifting the weights and play-acting as if they were too hard for anyone else to raise above their heads. To even the score, I'd squeeze Annie's biceps to show that she was really relatively puny.

After many months of gradually increasing the difficulty of my exercises, the big moment came on the day I could lift twenty kilograms with no adverse consequences to my neck. Annie and Fleur were with me cheering me on, and as soon as I accomplished the task, I ran to get my bassoon. I found I could easily take its weight, and just as remarkably, hold it as I did before dystonia came into my life. Fleur and Annie must have known my readiness, as they had their instruments with them too, and we spent a short time playing trios and duets of our favourite pieces.

They gave me rounds of applause and pats on the back after each piece, and afterwards we hugged and hugged. Later, I was a little sore, but nothing a little muscle cream couldn't fix. I expected some body discomfort. It had been a long time since I had used my muscles in such a way. So the moment when Annie and I finished our last piece of music before taking the reeds away from our lips as we collectively took a deep breath felt very, very special.

Once I established a regular bassoon practice routine, my journey back into the orchestra happened quite quickly. Annie came with me with her bassoon to see Dr Hayworth and Indira. We played our instruments for them in the hope that showcasing some of our favourite music pieces would give them a better understanding of how beautiful a bassoon can sound, which in turn would help them form an opinion about my orchestral readiness. Not only were they convinced I was set to play back in the big-time, they were also happy to receive a private orchestral concert.

Of course, I was super keen to play my bassoon in the orchestra again. Even so, the neurologist and Indira asked for more information. They probed me with all sorts of questions about music, such as the stamina required and the mental capacity to handle the pressure. They gave the big thumbs up for everything, feeling confident that I had the nerve and talent to carry it off.

Still, caution was the option over valour. Indira wrote a detailed letter to George, the orchestra manager, stating that I was ready to try again, recommending a graduated return to work. That meant playing just one piece in one concert to start with, before playing full concerts as required afterwards.

A few weeks later, with more encouragement from Sebastian and my friends, as well as lots more practice, I was about to play my first concert ... in what seemed like forever. Through what felt like a whirlwind, my impending return to the orchestra caused several nights of restless sleep.

CECELIA

33. AROUND THE WORLD

It's one thing to play a musical instrument at home in front of a corgi, and another to play in front of two thousand people. One has the danger of being licked to death, and the other has the threat of being 'licked' thoroughly by being drowned in a sea of 'boos'. The latter has more pressure than an earthquake-prone tectonic plate.

To say I was nervous would be an understatement. The weight of expectation felt heavy on my shoulders, and my body responded in overdrive. Rapid pulse, sweaty palms, dry mouth, nausea, they were all there, this time more severe than in any previous concert. Usually, I harnessed my nervous energy into my playing. This time, it took most of my energy just to suppress it.

———

The night of my big return concert had arrived, and all the other orchestra musicians were onstage and ready to go. Yet, I was still backstage in the green room, pacing around in circles. Memories of my previous exit from the orchestra fought their way back into my mind again. I imagined the colleagues who wanted to end my career were the same people who expected me to fail on my comeback. I had to prove more than what many players were capable of, even to musicians who had never played in senior positions such as myself. It suddenly felt like the rank and file violin players, for example, who had never done a solo, were like hungry lions in a gladiator arena. Unrealistic expectations were the name of their game, and I didn't feel like a willing participant. What I wanted was to perform something I loved for the enjoyment of the audience. That was the primary weapon I used to overcome preconcert demons, as well as walking to shake off any jitters. The knowledge I had eaten a healthy meal beforehand to see me through helped too.

The Festival Theatre's two-minute bell chimed, telling me I needed to be in the wings, pronto. George met me as I arrived at the stage entrance. 'You'll be fine. Break a leg,' he joked.

'If a broken leg were my only problem!' I exclaimed.

I turned my back on him at the point-of-no-return spot on the stairs and walked towards the stage, but George interrupted me before I could take any more steps.

'Cecelia?' he asked.

'Yes?'

'Welcome back.'

I smiled. 'Thank you,' I said.

They were two words I needed to hear, and my body relaxed.

Everyone was there, including the conductor, and the theatre erupted with applause as I walked on stage. To my surprise, news had disseminated around the music world that I was back, and the show of support was most welcome. My face reddened from all the sudden attention, and it showed in my astonishment.

However, the support I thought I had waned when I looked around at the faces in the orchestra. Some had big smiles, and their appreciation felt genuine. Others seemed to have fake smiles. One or two even glared at me. Christopher was a mix of all three. He seemed happy at first, but I saw him roll his eyes when he looked away.

The conductor stepped off his podium, took my arm and led me to my soloist spot in front of the orchestra. I had negotiated to perform a small solo as my first comeback as I argued that it would be easier to have the extra space on stage and flexibility in movement and nuance that a soloist enjoys, rather than attempting to squeeze into the small space at the back where I'd need to fit in with everyone else's playing. This way everyone would be fitting in with me. I hoped I'd made the right choice.

The audience applauded again, and I bowed as I had done many times before. I felt warm from all the adoration, and the affection from the audience gave me confidence.

In the crowd a few rows back, one particular punter, Sebastian, gave me extra attention. He garnered my interest cheekily, firstly by wearing a bright shirt so he would stand out amongst hundreds, and secondly by blowing me a big kiss. To calm my nerves, I imagined playing just for him. It washed my cares away and lifted my spirits. I smiled back, stretched my neck, and examined my bassoon one last time. Check, check, check. Finally, I was ready to play.

After that, my time on stage was similar to my dreams of an osprey in full, glorious flight. I hardly remembered the intricate stuff, such as fingers on keys or notes themselves, just soaking in the experience as a whole. The music started, and I played intensely, gushingly and profoundly. So much so, I couldn't help but sway vivaciously during some moments. Occasionally between notes, I'd look back and see Annie following my lead. She had a big grin on her face. The piece lasted fifteen minutes with myself and the conductor in front of the orchestra, setting the playing tone and delivery for all musicians involved. In all respects, the concert felt simply ... magnificent.

I finished playing and took the bassoon's reed out of my mouth, as a wave of relaxation flowed through my body. Just as importantly, my head and neck kept still. I surveyed the audience. For a second, there was silence, and I wondered if I actually played badly or lost a strap on my dress or something, but then the theatre erupted. My eyes were drawn to Sebastian once more, who blew me an even bigger kiss. It made me laugh, not only for the kiss but for the fact that a tall guy sat next to him, shaking his head at Sebastian as if he unwittingly sat next to a crazy person. The applause continued, and as I looked around, I saw Dr Hayworth, Indira and my parents in the front rows clapping. Annie and Fleur applauded as well from the stage. It was Sebastian, though, who clapped the loudest.

Triumphantly, I kissed my bassoon and bowed graciously. Over and over, the applause continued, spurred on by the conductor. I bowed humbly again and skipped off stage. 'More, more!' people cried, and back I went. I bit my lip and held back tears as I continued to bow and thank the audience.

All I could think was, 'I'm back, world!'

———

Naturally, after the concert, I was on a triumphant high, so Annie, Fleur and I decided to go out for drinks. For me, that meant a cold lemon squash with ice, but drinks nonetheless. Sebastian nearly attended, but he realised in his excitement to get to my concert, that he might have left the side gate open and let Wills escape. Instead, he gave me a big hug and rushed home, promising 'something amazing' when I joined him later.

My body felt so energised, I could have travelled around the world in a heartbeat. I didn't care if that meant I was looking around me through rose-coloured glasses again. Everything seemed to go right at last, and I was on a high. But interestingly, feeling so rejuvenated made me reflective and, as I downed my second squash, visions of the osprey in my dreams returned. It annoyed me slightly that he came back to me at that moment, but in my mind's eye, he flew high as I flew with him. We both circled a fire below us that had appeared in a previous dream. I didn't want to think about the osprey anymore, though, so I envisioned him flying away into the sunset, where he disappeared to let me join my friends.

Annie interrupted my thoughts to give me a huge hug.

'I could say how thrilled I am for you, but this is just a start. A new door has opened,' she beamed.

Fleur chipped in, starting a three-ringed ring-around-the-Rosie dance while we all celebrated.

'You'll be great. You star you!' she sang.

I smiled at Fleur, then looked back at Annie. 'I'll take your door and will happily walk through it,' I said cheerily, as we all hugged again and again.

———

That night, as I lay in bed quietly snuggling Sebastian's chest, the soft light of a full moon cast its shadow through our bedroom window. Sebastian leaned back into the bedhead as he typed on his laptop, working on his film script. I cuddled in closer, hinting for him to put his computer on the bedside table. He stopped and looked softly into my eyes.

'Your face paints a picture,' he whispered.

I snuggled even closer. 'You didn't tell me you have psychic powers,' I whispered cheekily.

'Psychic or psychotic?' he probed before I planted a kiss on his lips.

'I was thinking,' I said. 'I've found new ways to interpret music.'

Sebastian's eyes glinted, and he rolled over on top of me.

'Interpret this,' he whispered, planting a kiss on my lips in return.

It was very sensual, but I pulled back a little once we finished.

'Can't you be serious?' I exclaimed.

'Cecelia, your face is like a Picasso,' he continued.

'No. No!' I exclaimed again. 'I see things in music I never saw before.'

Sebastian pretended to paint my face like a possessed artist. I smirked and gave in. 'My very own groupie,' I whispered.

Sebastian pressed himself against me. 'Groupie with benefits,' he said, before making love to me.

Exhausted, hours later, we fell asleep. As my eyes closed, I imagined the theatre's seats slowly filling with an audience, one by one.

It beat counting sheep.

CECELIA

34. EXAM TIME

It didn't take long for my playing peak to morph into a life of routine once more. The next few months were pretty much like how they were when I played in the orchestra before my dystonia. I settled back comfortably into my role as principal bassoon, and the orchestra went through their set repertoire of much-loved composers. Beethoven, Mozart, Vivaldi, Grieg, Debussy and more, we played the concerts audiences wanted to hear and the types of concerts we had already done several times. My comeback concert proved to be the last one for a long time when I had the privilege of playing in front of an orchestra. However, I still had many solos from the vantage of my seat in the woodwind section, so all felt good.

The most remarkable thing was that my neck behaved itself and felt better than it ever did. I played without hindrance, and I was able to play in top form, winning over one or two Cecelia doubters in the process. I was happy in a familiar way, like resting on a much-visited beach on a warm sunny day. All in all, it felt good just to play. That's what mattered the most on the many days that seemed to meld into one another.

During that time, Sebastian immersed himself heavily in his

scriptwriting. Like any writer, sometimes he seemed a little distant, especially when his mind contemplated words to be put on the page. It was something I had grown used to and even more familiar with when, since my comeback, I had immersed myself into music in a similar way. I was happy to leave him alone to concentrate and do what he loved, as that's what he did for me when I needed to practice or play in a concert. Even so, we still made time for each other, just not in a spectacular way. Stolen cuddles were the order of the day, and our free times together were spent with quiet picnics and gentle walks on the beach, just not trips to the moon or swinging from chandeliers. The best thing was that I felt healthy instead of ill with dystonia, and I soaked up my time with Sebastian all the more.

———

The orchestra finally reached our end of year concert, and Annie, Fleur and I were looking forward to our Christmas break immediately afterwards, consisting of six weeks' holiday from late December to early February. By Christmas, we were all exhausted from a full year of playing without much of a break, and we needed the time to recover. For me, I was relieved that I made it, and my neck held up well.

An air of excitement filled the air as we sat backstage preparing our instruments. Two more hours of playing and we were free to do whatever we pleased. Summer beckoned. Sand, sea and lazy days called our names. Yes, our minds were on the musical task at hand, but they were also on holiday activities, as well as the following year's orchestral programme.

Fleur bounced around excitedly, talking about a tropical holiday she had booked, while Annie read a booklet outlining future concerts.

'Looks like the concert programme for next year is lighter,' Annie said. 'I guess they don't want to overwork us.'

Fleur and I sighed. We didn't like hearing the word *overwork*. Fleur stopped bounding around like a deer, and her demeanour changed instantly.

'They don't want us to end up like you, Cecelia,' she said in a worried tone.

I almost choked on my reed. 'End up like what, Fleur?' I asked.

'No. I mean, I've seen it before. After the Ring Cycle a few years back, we dropped like flies.'

Annie butted in. 'That was fatigue.'

Fleur retorted. 'Call it what you like, Annie. It still happened.'

Fleur shrugged her shoulders and headed for the stage. As she departed, she linked arms with the cellist and looked at him lovingly. It then occurred to me why she seemed so happy. They had been in a relationship for several months, and Fleur was about to jet off with him, probably to an island full of palm trees and coconuts. She just hadn't told me that they were going on the trip together.

I shrugged my shoulders and turned to Annie. 'Looks like she might come back with more than a tan next year,' I joked.

Annie laughed. 'She's had her mind on other things for weeks.'

'I'm just glad she's happy,' I said.

'Me too.'

We smiled. Annie and I really did agree on almost everything.

Just as Fleur disappeared through the stage door, she turned back to us and winked. 'Come on, cripples, we have a concert to do,' she called out.

I rolled my eyes and shook my head. Annie tut-tutted. 'Ignore her, Cecelia.'

'I know,' I said determinedly. 'I have to sometimes.'

Annie smiled and blew some notes on her bassoon to lighten the mood. I smiled back and joined in, and we played a short, upbeat jazzy duet together.

George came in, leaning over a couple of violinists as he spoke.

'Time everyone,' he ordered.

Annie and I stopped playing and began to adjust our reeds in preparation for the concert. It was something we had done hundreds of times, but as I moved my reed, it fell off the crook and landed on the floor. I bent down to pick it up, stretching my back a little too much in the process. The pain quickly moved to my neck, and I winced sharply.

Annie saw my discomfort and picked my reed up for me. 'Pesky little things,' she joked.

I wryly nodded in agreement. It was no joke.

It was the first time my neck had hurt in a long time.

Annie and I arrived on stage with a couple of minutes to spare, and we sat down in our respective seats. My neck pain had settled but my intuition told me something was still wrong. My stomach felt woozy, and my body had stiffened. It was more than just preconcert nerves.

All of me needed to relax, so I took some deep breaths. They didn't help much, so my mind churned over, trying to discover what was wrong. As I looked around, Christopher turned to me and gloated as he was preparing his contrabassoon. Maybe it was Christopher who filled me with doubt? He loved the contrabassoon for many reasons, not just because it was his principal instrument and one I rarely played. I shrugged my shoulders to ignore him, even if he got under my skin a little. Maybe it was the theatre itself? The place looked a little darker and emptier than usual. Maybe, maybe, despite my neck feeling okay at that moment, my dystonia had come back to haunt me? Before I was able to explore all those possibilities, the time for me to play had fast approached. I had no choice but to brush them off. Maybe the scenarios my stressed-out mind painted weren't real at all? Perhaps I was too sensitive?

The music started: *Saint-Saëns Symphony No. 3*. The first movement began softly and then became faster. I gained confidence as I played, and there were several breaks when I didn't need to play, which gave my neck and mind respite. My neck was holding out, so I relaxed and navigated through the piece in a relatively straightforward way. I even managed to put a little extra flair in a couple of notes, to Annie's excitement and pleasure.

The second movement was slow, and I felt exposed. As I played and my threshold neared, however, my body moved like a finely tuned leopard. The notes came out easily, and they purred like a cat. Nothing else seemed to happen in my body except the music. In the corner of my eye, I saw Annie smile. Her solidarity lifted my playing even further. We were like a pride of lions running through the Serengeti. I was going to be okay. I was going to be okay.

At about the twenty-seven minute mark, the music slowed—the calm before the storm. Twenty-eight minutes in and the organ behind me fired, almost deafening my ears. I played as loud and powerfully as I could, and my neck obliged obediently. The end was near. The cymbals and timpani thundered as I performed my last notes. Then, during the finale, all the concert required of me, and the rest of the orchestra, was one long, drawn-out last note. We all stopped and collectively exhaled. We had made it. I had made it. If I could play that piece, I could play anything.

The smile on my face was so wide it hurt. Annie grinned too, showing off her admirable pearly whites.

'Phew!' she exclaimed. 'Double phew!' I retorted. Annie continued. 'Triple ph ...'

'Wait,' I interrupted. 'I get the message. Let's get out of here.'

'Like a couple of thieving bandits,' she joked.

'Okay. Let's go!'

Annie and I held our bassoons tight and rushed to the green room. Unbeknown to us in our excitement, Christopher had even beaten us to it. He was almost packed up and ready to leave altogether. 'Nice concert, you two. I always feel like a better player with you around,' he said.

Annie looked at him in slight confusion. 'Thanks,' she said.

Christopher shut his big contrabassoon case and casually walked to the door. He was rarely one to stay after a concert for chitchat.

'See ya,' Annie and I said in unison.

I thought Christopher played to standard for once and wanted to let him know. Credit where credit was due. 'Well played, Christopher,' I said. 'You played beautifully.'

'Thanks. But I gotta go!' Christopher nodded. He picked up his bassoon and the latest alpaca book he was reading, a thick one titled, *Alpacas – Specifics of Breed and Breeding* and tucked them under his arm. Without saying another word, he was gone, leaving Annie and me together.

Annie looked at me, and I could almost see the cogs turning around in her brain. 'You know. That was a backhanded compliment,' she remarked.

'What was?'

'The fact that he feels like a better player when the three of us play,' Annie said. 'I think he feels like a better player because he thinks we are worse players than him.'

I shrugged my shoulders. 'Maybe.'

Annie shook her head. 'If I had a dollar every time I heard Christopher give praise, I wouldn't have enough to buy a cup of coffee.'

Still, I gave Christopher the benefit of the doubt. It was necessary sometimes, or the woodwind section would collapse. 'Maybe he's saying we lift his playing because we're good too,' I said.

'God knows he needs to. You know, *lift*,' Annie joked.

I began to laugh even before I said anything and then blurted, 'But I thought he believed he *was* God.'

———

I left the concert hall and started to drive home, eager to see Sebastian. Along the way, I stopped at traffic lights. Some fans in a nearby car grabbed my attention as they called out to me through their window. As the lights turned green and I accelerated, suddenly my head swung to the side and the view ahead disappeared.

The next thing I remembered was being hauled out of my car by paramedics and taken to hospital in an ambulance.

CECELIA

35. LUCKY OR UNLUCKY?

I woke up and saw a blurry man walking towards me. He wore a lab coat that seemed to glow in a heavenly white colour, and for a second, my own religious beliefs were challenged. I wondered if I had reached the afterlife. But, as I focussed my senses, I realised the man was a doctor. I smiled in relief and exhaled, knowing I was still alive. Then, without warning, I felt a shooting pain down my left side. The agony was intense, and it hurt more than my neck. I leant back and examined my body. Someone had plastered me in thick bandages, from my left armpit to my hips. As I moved, I also noticed my left wrist wrapped in gauze. 'Can I still play my bassoon?' I instantly thought.

The doctor spoke. 'Hello, Cecelia. I'm Dr Novak. How are you feeling?'

'Where am I?'

'In a hospital.'

I sat up with a start and yelped in pain before falling back into my pillow. 'Where's my bassoon?' I asked.

Dr Novak looked to a chair near my bed. 'It's over there. Safe and sound in its case.'

'Is it damaged?'

'Not as much as you are. But I think both of you will be okay.'

I smiled fleetingly.

'What about my Renault?'

'It's at a crash repairer.'

Then, in my mind, an image of the crash scene appeared. It was the last thing I remembered and the shock of it made my heart beat faster.

'What about everyone else? Are they okay?' I asked, as I gasped for a breath. 'There was a dented and twisted truck.'

'They'll be all right. The truck driver was asking about you too.'

The doctor smiled and rested his hand on my forearm. It felt comforting and my body relaxed a little.

'We'll keep you in here overnight, Cecelia, and tomorrow you should be able to go home. Okay?' he asked.

'Yes.'

'You know, you were quite lucky. Things could have been much worse.'

I removed my eyes from his gaze.

'I don't feel lucky,' I said with a lowered voice.

I tried to move my fingers. They felt very stiff. 'What about my fingers, my wrist?' I asked.

'Yes, they're not broken, but they are strained and bruised.'

My mind filled with dread. 'But I need to play my bassoon!' I implored.

The doctor gave me a reassuring smile. 'You'll need to rest for a few days. Then we'll see.'

My neck twinged, and I immediately felt fearful. It reminded me of something I wanted forgotten. But I needed to know.

'What about my dystonia?' I asked abruptly.

Dr Novak looked at my chart and nodded. 'Yes. Your dystonia. I spoke with your neurologist.'

I looked at him, my dread growing, and my body tensing. I imagined the future and pictured myself with dystonia again. In addition, I realised I would have to talk about my dystonia everywhere I went. I was not too fond of either prospect. I wanted to be known as Cecelia, not Cecelia with dystonia.

Then, just as my body tensed even more, my neck jerked my head wildly to the left, and it wouldn't stop moving. It was back. My dystonia was back.

'I still have it!' I said in a panic.

'Is it any worse since the car accident?'

'I'm not ... not sure.'

'You'll let me know if it changes?'

I sat there quietly, unable to answer.

Seeing my discomfort, Dr Novak tried to give me an uplifting smile. 'Well, you need more rest. I'll go see about more painkillers and leave you for now. I'll check on you later, okay? Rest your head back on your pillow as best you can.'

'Okay,' I trembled.

'I'll be back in a few minutes to chat some more, Cecelia. See you soon.'

As he walked out, my mind desperately replayed previous uncomfortable dystonia moments. There were many. I couldn't believe it. It *was* back. All I said to myself over and over was, 'No, no, no!'

CECELIA

36. MONSTER RELOADED

I'm not sure how long I remained in that state of dread. It must have been a long time. Eventually, when my thoughts slowed a little, I calmed myself as best I could and rested back on my pillow, mentally examining my body. I realised all of me felt very stiff. I also felt exhausted and thirsty, so I leant over to get a drink sitting on the bedside table. That was a mistake. It hurt a lot, and by the time I could hold the cup and bring it to my lips, I felt even more exhausted.

Just at that moment, Sebastian walked in. He looked very shocked and concerned.

'Are you all right?' he gasped.

'Not really, I guess.'

Sebastian sat on the bed and held my hand. He took a deep breath outwards and scanned the room. He didn't seem to realise what was happening with my neck as it was supported and somewhat hidden by my pillow.

My body trembled with the words I needed to say to him.

'My ...'

Sebastian whispered, 'What was that, darling?'

'My neck is pulling to the left.'

Sebastian stood up abruptly and walked around in a circle like a trapped mouse. Then, after a minute, he turned back to me. 'It could be anything. It could be a one-off,' he pleaded.

I covered my face with my hands. 'I don't want to go back down that slippery slope!' I exclaimed.

CECELIA

37. THE WALL

Once home from the hospital, all I could think about was how I hoped things would be better in the morning.

But things weren't better. They were worse. My neck still hurt, and the pain increased day by day. I knew from previous experience painkillers were not enough, so at night, I hoped and prayed that sleep would be the cure I needed. I had restless nights, groggy mornings, and, more importantly, dashed hopes instead.

I managed to make breakfast some days, settling on a cold bowl of cereal rather than hot cooked porridge. Cooking oats and making a cup of tea were tricky with my uncontrollable head and neck movements, not to mention my wrist preventing me from picking up particular objects. Still, I managed the cup of tea. At least it gave me something warm inside and an opportunity to ponder over things that mattered.

It took several cups of Earl Grey and English Breakfast to conclude that life for me had always been about progression, not regression.

Decisions I made and actions I took were about getting somewhere. I went to school to learn about the world; I practised music to be a musician; and I played in the orchestra to share my love of music with others and be the best I could be. Even the things I achieved along the way, such as love and fame, were a means to an end: more love, more recognition, more of this, more of that. Not in a greedy or selfish way, though. I liked to think of them as rewards for my efforts.

It took so much energy to feel like I had put dystonia behind me for good. Then, once Dr Hayworth diagnosed what it actually was that ailed me, I expelled nearly all my courage to exercise and get back to playing. Even then, except for ongoing Botox injections, it took a year of playing back in the orchestra before my dystonia was all but forgotten. Now, with its dreaded return, I doubted the courage of my convictions.

No one likes to return to a bad place. All it does is bring memories rushing back; in my case, painful memories of feeling like I was going crazy, panic attacks, playing poorly, leaving concerts and shattered dreams. Going back to those dark places and moments meant I was further away from where I wanted to be, in the orchestra.

Also, I realised a sense of ownership. That is, the tough times I had before my diagnosis were the times that were mine, no matter how difficult they were. And the memories associated with them were *mine* —no one else's. No one else was suffering from dystonia exactly like I was, so all the bad stuff felt so unfair and undeserved. No one deserved to go through what I was going through. I felt alone in my experiences and alone in my mind. It was like I was living on a planet all my own, not of my making, and I couldn't find a way back to Earth.

I began to doubt the choices I had made. What had I done wrong for my neck to get worse again? If only I had been looking directly at the road ahead while sitting at the traffic lights before accelerating. Maybe my neck would be okay if I had? Maybe I exercised too hard? Maybe my neck problem was something else? Maybe I should have seen another specialist? Maybe, maybe, maybe. Life was full of maybes.

While I sipped my tea and stared into space, fear of the past gripped my body. Yet, I had to find an answer. I *had* to. It took a while, but eventually, I did. I looked out the window towards the morning sun and realised there was a way out, a path towards the light that would take me away from dystonia darkness, one *thing* and one *maybe* that could move me forward.

It was simple, really.

I had been there before. I had been in a place where my neck was out of control. Then I reached a point, albeit temporarily, where it wasn't a problem anymore. Perhaps I could get to that place again? Of course, things don't come easy, but at least that was something positive I could take from my experiences and feel like I still had some control.

———

I manoeuvred my bassoon strap in readiness to play. Usually, the strap would sit high at the base of my neck, but that seemed impossible. With my head jerking side to side, the lower part of my shoulder became the improvised spot.

I wasn't in a concert hall, though. I was in Indira's treatment room, trying to play my bassoon. She was feeling around my neck while I struggled to play something any professional musician would have played a million times: scales.

Indira had scanned my hospital X-rays before she pressed her thumb around my wrist. I grimaced a couple of times when she touched sensitive spots.

'Can you move your fingers?' she asked.

'Yes, but they feel a little weak.'

'There has been some soft tissue damage, but with rest and then some physio, we'll see how it goes.'

I smiled gently.

'Now, what about your neck?'

Indira moved behind me and prodded a muscle just above my right shoulder blade.

'Sometimes a traumatic event can bring on dystonia,' she said. 'Did you have an MRI at the hospital?'

'Yes,' I answered anxiously.

'And did they find anything?'

'No. I don't think so. They mentioned it looked normal.'

Indira's face filled with concern. 'How about your left side? Does that still hurt?'

I prodded the skin below my ribs a little. The bandages had been removed a few days earlier, and it felt okay to touch around that area. 'It feels fine. Not one hundred per cent, but okay.'

'Hmmm, and when did you last have Botox?' she asked.

'About a month ago.'

Indira nodded. 'Looks like it hasn't worked as well this time.'

I slowly put my bassoon down, laying it to rest over a soft seat.

Indira observed me intently. 'Do you think you could play right now?' she asked.

My head dropped uncontrollably, signalling my disappointment.

'There's no way I can play any more notes. I'm exhausted.' Panic began to well up inside me, and I began to shake.

Indira saw my reaction and tried to calm the situation. 'We could try more exercises,' she said, as she felt around my neck again. 'But I'm not sure if there's much more I can do.'

I almost dropped to the ground and pleaded with her, 'I have a Pavarotti concert in a few weeks!'

Indira stepped back. 'Have you thought about another type of therapy?' she said, seemingly unsure of what to do or say.

I turned my back to her. I didn't want her to see any more of my panic.

SEBASTIAN

38. GENTLEMEN PREFER BLONDES

I'd always thought that writers were observers. They have vivid imaginations to call upon to understand people and problems, and Cecelia was drawn to those qualities when we met. But I'm not sure if Cecelia realised at the time that writers have a peculiar ability to create unrealistic worlds to escape to when real-world troubles become too much.

I admired Cecelia immensely. She went through more than anyone deserved, and she had a lot of strength, more than she realised, and more than me. Yet, I worried about her health and my own.

I wouldn't say I liked to use the word 'disabled', but in truth there were some things that Cecelia now couldn't do. On a personal level, Cecelia couldn't love physically or emotionally like she used to. So I felt it was my role to fill in her gaps.

It wasn't easy being a carer. I took on a lot, dealing with her personal needs as well as household needs, all the while putting my own to the side. On some days, my altruism felt like an all-encompassing, unrewarding chore, especially when there didn't seem any cure in sight.

I felt stuck in a game of Solitaire. It was a lonely business having to put one's emotions aside for another. Being a writer was lonely enough, without having someone to talk to about it. I suppose I could have spoken to Cecelia, but she was too busy coping with her lot. It felt like she wasn't the woman she used to be, and it was my challenge, as we both dealt with dystonia, to accept that. Even more so, it was my challenge to not be angry at her for having to give up on my dreams, especially when she struggled to hold onto hers.

So, in all that hullaballoo, I found myself in my favourite café, a downtown, always busy, speakeasy kind of place where creatives loved to wallow. It was a rare moment of solitude, stolen while Cecelia spent time with her orchestra buddies. My mission wasn't alone time, however. It was to delve into the science behind dystonia, hoping that my studies might find something helpful to us both. I had magazines and science books strewn all over my table. Some of them were bookmarked for further reading, and some I put aside, assigned to the useless pile. The task was enjoyable, but made more challenging by the busyness and loudness of my surroundings. People were everywhere. It was the antithesis of a writer's secret den, but I still loved it as I had the opportunity to observe so much. Occasionally, I'd look up from my books and watch other customers, imagining all sorts of stories and scenarios about why they were there and what they were doing. I also congratulated myself for just surviving and taking in the information I was reading amongst such noise and commotion.

As I buried my head in a magazine titled *Discoveries in Brain Science*, a blonde woman walked past me. At first, I didn't notice her, but she demanded attention, not only from her looks but from the plate of mouth-watering food she was carrying. It almost fell to the floor as she tripped over my chair.

'Wherever I turn my head ...' she said.

I looked up from my page, jolted from my concentration. 'Huh?'

'Oh, I was just saying ... I can't find a place to sit. Mind if I ...'

I looked around the café. It was full. 'I'm rather busy now,' I said.

The blonde slid some of my books aside anyway and sat opposite. I looked at her momentarily and returned my focus to the book in front of me. My mind was still firmly on Cecelia, and I didn't want to talk. 'You don't mind if I keep reading, do you?' I asked.

'Sure, go ahead.'

I returned to my reading, and for several moments, the air between us was filled with an awkward silence, interrupted by the blonde's sips and gulps of her coffee. She finally put down her cup, and the clang of it hitting the saucer made me lift my head.

'Must be interesting?' she asked.

'It is. Thanks.'

I lowered my head and began reading again, but suddenly the words on the page just weren't sinking in. It was hard enough with all the noise around, and now with the blonde seemingly intent for a chat, my focus was utterly broken up.

The blonde took another sip of her coffee and leaned forward to look closely at what I was reading. 'Have you heard the 'Brain in a Vat' theory?' she probed.

I raised an eyebrow. 'Yes. That's philosophy 101.'

The blonde smiled and nodded. 'Some people believe there's no reality. Apparently, we live in a kind of simulated universe made by an evil dictator who prods our brains and controls our thoughts.'

I tried to ignore her again, but the blonde kept going. 'Personally, I'd rather be a brontosaurus ...' she said. Then, she pointed to her forehead and put on a baby-doll voice, 'You know, not enough grey matter to think.'

I laughed a little too loudly before spending a moment studying the woman opposite me. In my mind, she seemed like a caricature of someone. It was almost like she wasn't real, yet she was playing someone once very much alive, someone I had loved all my life. I felt like I was dreaming, inside another world and another time, in Hollywood in the 1950s, looking at, and admiring, Marilyn Monroe.

Not that Marilyn was a dumb blonde of course. She read books such as *Ulysses* by James Joyce and *The Prophet* by Khalil Gibran. She also read *The Brothers Karamazov* and books by John Steinbeck, Tennessee Williams, F. Scott Fitzgerald and Ernest Hemingway, not to mention books about philosophy, art and psychology. Without a doubt, Marilyn was the movie star who captured my attention when I was younger and had ever since. My friends would say our names in the same breath. Cecelia liked Marilyn too. When we first met, she owned a book about Marilyn, which earned her some serious points.

I believed Marilyn was beautiful in every way, inside and out. She had an ethereal, captivating way about her. It fascinated me from the first time I saw her in the movie *The Misfits*, written by her then-husband Arthur Miller. I was attracted to her strength and how she rose above her troubled past. Marilyn's sensitive nature seemed similar to mine too. She certainly flamed my love of everything Hollywood, and I would credit her, in part, for my decision to be a scriptwriter.

While my mind compared the blonde and Marilyn, the blonde was laughing and shimmying in her seat. 'Although we'd be extinct,' she continued.

I shook my head to bring myself back to the present, unwittingly putting a downer on the situation.

'Perhaps it would be better if we were,' I responded gloomily.

The blonde shook her finger at me, in a mock telling-off kind of way, the same way Marilyn did in several of her movies.

'Oh, come on. It's not that bad,' she scolded.

She frowned playfully. 'Are you a scientist?' she asked.

I leaned back. 'No, I took a vow of poverty and became a writer.'

'No way!' she beamed. 'A writer! So am I. Well, I want to be one anyway.'

We continued talking.

After all, I thought, what man could resist Marilyn Monroe?

CECELIA

39. STRAWS

When my music teachers taught me the bassoon, they failed to prepare me for when I would no longer be playing. For students, the music school was all about career, lessons, practice and being in top shape for the next concert, not such things as sickness or life away from music.

But truth be told, I relied on my bassoon for my self-worth a little. It was not very *Forest of Being*, but my instrumental mastery and passion for music made me feel like a better person. Without it, I felt like a type of also-ran, who may as well stay at home and watch television all day and every day. A bassoonist was *me*. Doing anything else probably would have made me feel a little like a loner with no genuine friends or life. The orchestra was my life, and the musicians in it were my friends and my soul.

When I first met Sebastian, I was already in the orchestra, and he quickly came up with simple phrases to identify me. Cecelia the musician, Cecelia the bassoonist, for example. What made him special, however, was that he saw more in me: Cecelia, the kind, generous, soft, loving gal, determined for success (his words, not mine!). Sometimes though, I worried for him, or more precisely, worried about what he thought of me. What would he think if I never played music again? Would he still see those qualities in me? Would he blame me? Although I knew he was supportive and loving, the answers to those questions were somewhat unknown during my lowest moments.

After the finality of Indira's words, my emotions were all in a spin. Anxiety, insecurity, helplessness, hopelessness, despair and fear rose again. They all mixed in the melting pot of my mind to create a formidable and desperate cocktail. Would I ever find the kind of happiness the bassoon gave me again? Only one hope remained, pointed to in Indira's last words to me: alternative therapies. I had to try them. I knew I was clutching at straws, but if there was even the slightest chance of success, it was worth a shot. The rewards were too high. Besides, I had an interest in holistic cures and a disinterest in Western medicine. Maybe, just maybe, they would work, and success would be my friend again.

———

Still panicky, I paced around my couch, clutching the Yellow Pages phone directory in my good hand. Wills joined in after a few laps, thinking it was all a game, wanting to play let's-catch-my-mistress-before-she-does-one-more-lap. But instead of playing, I collapsed on the cushions in dizziness and exhaustion. I was in bad shape. My body travelled barely fifty metres and my lungs already burned. Yet, two years before, I could handle that in a heartbeat.

Wills jumped up and landed on my left side. At first, I felt annoyed at him, especially as he ended up where the bandages once were. But his cuteness won me over again, and I cuddled and stroked him. It was the panacea I needed, and soon after, I felt calmer.

My fingers scanned the Alternative Therapies section in the Yellow Pages and hovered over an advertisement for Bowen therapy by Dr Martin. I read on a little and learnt more. Fundamentally, it involved gentle movements of soft tissue. That sounded familiar, a kind of extension of Indira's neurological physiotherapy. It seemed like the best of both worlds; a scientific approach balanced with an holistic one. Once more, it involved no drugs, no side effects, it wasn't addictive, and there was no pain caused by treatment. The doctor didn't use needles either.

I rang the number. A friendly, soft voice answered, 'Hello, welcome to Bowen with Dr Martin.'

His manner relaxed me. 'Hi, my name's Cecelia. I'd like to make an appointment, please,' I asked.

Another phone rang in his office, and I heard voices in the background. 'Yes, I'd be happy to help. Would you mind holding?'

'That'll be okay.'

I sat there swaying in my seat, listening to harp music play. It was so enjoyable, for a second, I wondered if I had chosen the right instrument to play.

Just then, Sebastian walked in with a *Discoveries in Brain Science* magazine in his hands. Realising I was on the phone, he stopped, but hearing the music and seeing me dance, he gave himself the go-ahead to talk. 'The neurologist?' he asked.

'No, a Bowen therapist.'

'A what? Did you say, Bowen?'

'Yes. It's an alternative therapy.'

He shook his head in disappointment, first at me, then at his magazines. 'So much for this research, then,' he said.

He showed me an article, and I skim-read it. Nothing about it seemed surprising, as I had either learnt or heard about the developing science before from my doctors. The magazine smelt like perfume too. I grabbed it and threw it on the couch.

Sebastian looked at me in puzzlement. 'Well, what do you think?' he asked.

I hung up the phone in frustration. The doctor had left me on hold too long anyway. 'Where did you get that? At the perfume shop?' I growled.

'What? I got it at the library.' He picked up the magazine and shoved it in my face. 'What about the article?' he asked again.

I leaned back, trying not to get poked in the eye from the edge of a page. What's more, Sebastian's forcefulness surprised me. I thought he was considerate of my feelings, and he rarely got angry unless he stubbed his toe or something. But not this time.

Then, my whole body started in defence.

'That's life on Mars stuff. I need treatment now!' I pleaded.

Sebastian paced around the room, and I watched him in confusion. I didn't know what to expect with his behaviour. After a few laps, his demeanour calmed, and he looked at me softly like he usually did. 'But there isn't any treatment,' he conceded. He picked up a framed photo of me cuddling Wills and softened even more.

'I can understand you're willing to try anything. Most of us would in your circumstance,' Sebastian said.

It was that last word that got to me. Now the hairs on the back of my stupid neck stood up. 'And what is my circumstance, Dr Sebastian?' I said sarcastically.

Sebastian stopped pacing and looked into my eyes, fair and square. I blinked deliberately, hoping that would be enough to settle the air. It wasn't. Sebastian moved forward and stared at me intently, and I felt a little threatened. Then, as if he realised how he was coming across, his face softened again, and he looked at me pleadingly. 'It's just ... if playing the bassoon can set off dystonia again, even if it's treated successfully, it can come back anytime. I'm just saying ... isn't it time to accept...at least until there is a cure?'

I could see Sebastian trying to hold on, but it was too late. The tables had turned. I was angry, and my body felt like it was boiling over again. I raised my voice and stamped my foot like a child in a temper tantrum.

'Accept what!? That I'm a cripple!? You're calling me a cripple now!?' I thundered.

'No. It's just that this article ...'

I stood up, grabbed the magazine, and threw it on the floor.

'I'm not interested in the article!' I shouted.

Sebastian took a step back and signalled with his hands for both of us to calm down. 'Cecelia. I support you in your efforts to get well. I absolutely do.'

My shoulders dropped, and I shook my body in a vain attempt to put a lid over my hot blood. Steam still escaped like a whistling kettle, however, and my voice hardened. 'This is my health we're talking about,' I growled.

Sebastian nodded. 'Of course. Of course.'

I put my hands on my hips like a prize-fighter. 'Whatever it takes.'

'I know. I'm saying try something else.'

I threw my hands up in the air, which made my neck and shoulders hurt. Now I was in pain, exasperated as well, and my anger was rising to new heights. 'So, it's all coming out! You said yourself, there is nothing else!'

'But if Bowen worked, every doctor would use it.'

My sarcasm rose too. 'And look what happened when I saw the GP?' I said, with my arms crossed.

Sebastian shook his head and turned away. 'Cecelia. It's just ... it's just ... irrational.'

I stamped my foot again. 'No, it's not!'

'To even think Bowen therapy works, it's crazy,' he said.

My whole body tensed tighter than a rope. I had never thought about hitting Sebastian, but at that moment, I came closer than ever before. 'Now you're saying I'm crazy!?' I said sarcastically.

He looked at me a little scared and stepped back, this time in self-defence. 'No ... I don't know.' He turned his back on me again and began to walk away.

I wished I were looking at him in the eyes, though, as he had when he gave me his two cents' worth. I shouted again so he could hear me loud and clear.

'So, what are you saying? You agree with the quack doctor!'

He walked out the back door, slamming it behind him.

I stormed out the front door, slamming it much harder.

CECELIA

40. SATURN

As I fell on the bed in a heap and punched my pillow, I mulled over the time I had spoken to the GP. After that appointment, I had questioned my rationality and erratic feelings and actions, and I had just demonstrated the same things with Sebastian. Of course, it's never nice to argue with a loved one, whoever's right or wrong. Still, we did fly off the handle quickly and easily, and that in itself suggested my anger involved another element. It would have been easy to explain my temper away by saying it was due to difficult feelings over my possible career loss. But love for my job was one thing, and love for Sebastian was another. They had elements in common, but I never felt that just because one was in trouble, the other was as well. Maybe if I wasn't so unpredictable and irrational, we could have discussed the whole thing calmly over a cup of tea and scones?

Nobody in their right mind enjoys fighting or conflict either. Most people, I suspect, preferred to sail through the sea of life under a soft, gentle breeze. For me though, in part, I felt angry and insulted. How dare he call me crazy!? But more so, I felt guilty an argument had just happened and mad at myself for not behaving in a way I liked. If only it had gone differently, the outcome would have been so much better. Alternating between guilt and anger made me feel even more erratic and closer to the loony bin.

Just like I had done in the past, I could have respected Sebastian's feelings and point of view. They didn't always match mine, and I didn't always agree with them. Still, everyone's emotional state of mind, as well as their thoughts and beliefs, were valid to *them*, and I could have recognised that. I realised I didn't listen to him, *really* listen, and I wasn't aware that he felt threatened, just like me, by my potential career demise.

Sebastian and I had always found a happy medium or come up with an agreed compromise plan if we ever had differing points of view. Usually, though, the stakes weren't as high. For the most part, any lack of conflict resolution was something we could both live with, even if neither of us got what we wanted. Suppose one wished to eat chocolate ice cream, for example, and the other wanted vanilla. We'd settle on strawberry or get all three to satisfy our diverse tastes. The stakes were different this time, though, and I wanted to keep talking, but Sebastian was gone.

———

A few days later, Indira gave me exercises and a tennis ball to squeeze to regain strength in my left wrist, and after a week or so it seemed to be working. After a period following her regime, I was able to move my wrist and pick up objects without too much trouble, and I could take enough of the weight of my bassoon in my left hand. It certainly was a relief as I worried that my wrist injury would bring on dire consequences.

My wrist was only one trouble, though. My neck was still another. I phoned Dr Martin again and managed to get an appointment with him. He said he'd squeeze me in, as my condition was 'of the utmost importance,' although there would be a higher fee due to the urgent appointment. Despite my hesitation over his words, he certainly acted much more agreeably than Sebastian had. I hadn't seen Sebastian much since our big argument. That night, he had returned quietly and slept in the proverbial doghouse, or the couch to be more precise. After that, he woke early each morning and left for a run before I had breakfast.

Memories of my solitary mornings became hazy in my mind, though, as I lay on a soft treatment table in Dr Martin's treatment room. As I shuffled to get more comfortable, relaxing, meditative harp music played. It sounded similar to his phone on-hold music, but I didn't mind. My cares and troubles were drifting away like the burning incense smoke in front of me, its potpourri odour permeating throughout my whole body. 'You don't know how much I need this,' I moaned, as my nose squashed into the pillow. 'I'm about to realise a dream. I'll be on stage with Pavarotti.'

Dr Martin, complete with obligatory tie-dyed shirt and ripped jeans, rolled his fingers down my spine and nonchalantly ignored my big statement. 'Don't worry, Cecelia. I've had many patients with conditions similar to yours. It takes a lot of treatments, but I've got them back to amazing things,' he said calmly.

I breathed away my remaining tension. The doctor's voice sounded as reassuring as his hands.

'What sort of things? I asked.

Dr Martin nodded and just said, 'Mmhmm,' ignoring my question. 'Bowen is complementary medicine. It allows the body to heal itself. It enhances the *chi*.' He moved his thumbs up to my neck. 'How does that feel?' he asked.

I thought about what Sebastian would say about the *chi* comment but answered anyway.

'That feels better,' I replied.

Whatever he was doing, it was working. I hoped it was worth the exorbitant cost.

'You need to trust your body.'

Dr Martin switched off the music and stepped back, smiling at his handiwork. 'All finished,' he grinned.

I got up and dangled my legs over the side of the table like a child.

I moved my head from side to side and in a circle. It indeed moved more freely than it had for a while. I smiled. 'It's hard to believe this feels so good,' I beamed.

I left his room feeling a little bouncy and happy and wanting to tell Sebastian all about it. He would like to hear of my successful treatment, despite his reservations and despite our falling out, I thought. But he was lost in his own world when I saw him, deeply absent in his writing, as he pondered the next words for his big blockbuster.

My eyes scanned him from behind, his tall, slender body lit by the soft light emanating from his computer screen. It was a sight I usually adored, a sensitive man intensely in thought, waiting to produce the next world-altering profound idea and write it down. In my book, intelligence was always sexy, but this time, as I prepared to face him after our big row, he looked a little threatening. I had seen a darker, angry side of him, and I both hoped and doubted I was up to the challenge to sort out our problems.

It was necessary to implement lessons I had learned, so I decided to put my good news aside for the moment and focus on Sebastian to win him over again. 'Hello, darling. How are you?' I asked politely.

Sebastian's eyes glanced back at me, then at his computer screen. 'Not bad,' he mumbled. I barely heard him.

'How's the writing going?'

'Not too shabby.' Sebastian looked up at the ceiling to ponder before placing his fingers over his keyboard. 'Just trying to construct a difficult sentence here. You know, for my next Oscar winner. Sorry.'

It was clear my upbeat mood required talking, and I had hoped that would be enough of a start to get words of the exciting kind out of Sebastian. His attitude spoke for him, however. He wanted to write, and that was that. 'I'll leave you alone then,' I said.

'Thanks.'

I headed to the kitchen, chastising myself that we weren't in sync. It was a rare state for both of us. It felt suddenly deflating. Moreover, I still wasn't acting the way I liked. I needed to spell out my feelings more and be precise. Join the dots so he could understand.

'Not to interrupt, but would you like a cup of tea?' I asked.

Silence.

Okay. I searched for another idea to cut through.

'So ... I have some good news.'

More silence.

'The treatment went quite well.'

Sebastian stopped. 'What was that?' he asked hesitantly.

My deflated mood flattened further. Finally, I lost my nerve, turned, and walked away.

'I see,' I murmured as I entered the kitchen.

Sebastian raised his voice. 'Oh. I'm sorry, darling. You know what it's like when I'm writing. Can I give you a massage later?'

I opened a cupboard door to get out a mug. 'I was saying, the Bowen seemed to work!' I shouted.

'That's great,' Sebastian offered back with little sincerity.

I walked outside feeling disappointed, and pondered my relationship with Sebastian.

Perhaps it's not all beer and skittles living with a writer, after all, I concluded.

———

The night sky looked clear, free of clouds and full of bright stars. I struggled to look upwards, wanting to see all the beauty above me. At first I laughed, sure that Sebastian would have had something to say about my green eyes reflecting in the moonlight. But that seemed ages ago. I wondered if he would still see them as soft and dreamy, and my body tensed knowing that I was outside alone, with Sebastian inside and away from me in more ways than one.

Searching for answers in the stars seemed almost vain, like attempting to link my internal self to their external greatness for answers. Then, after a while, one exceptionally bright star grabbed my attention, Saturn maybe. I asked it, 'Why is this happening to me?', hoping it would have guru powers and show me the way. I got nothing back, and its silence spoke a thousand words.

Stupid Saturn.

As I stood there, pulling up my collar to keep warm, my heart despaired. Once I was a real player in the game of life. Things happened to me, and I had control over them and the outcome. In the coldness of the night, I felt like I had control over throwing the dice, but not what numbers came up. I wanted lucky seven but got snake eyes instead.

The Bowen therapy helped the first time, but would it change my life? Would it save me? Rather than be overly optimistic about it, once again, I thought of my future. I asked myself, 'Is this how life is going to be?' Day to day life with dystonia seemed bad enough, and now with Sebastian indifferent and defiant, my synoptic chart looked bleak. I knew what dystonia was like with full-blown symptoms. Having them every day until the day I died appeared unbearable.

I thought about what it was like for just one day with bad dystonia, a whole twenty-four hours with my neck, head and body twisting uncontrollably. From the first waking moment, dystonia hit me like a truck, and that's if I was lucky enough to get sufficient sleep. Then getting out of bed, standing up, and walking to the kitchen for breakfast was the next big hurdle. Walls, furniture, doorways, they all turned into objects of injury if I tripped over them, which was likely and often. Simply cooking my beloved porridge turned into a logistical nightmare. Getting pots and cutlery out of cupboards and drawers was tricky and sometimes resulted in broken dishes and glasses.

Then showering, toileting, dressing, cleaning teeth, etcetera. Tooth decay would be a problem, as the otherwise simple act of putting a toothbrush in my mouth and rubbing the bristles over my teeth made my neck worse. I saw the shower cubicle as a glass cage where keeping balance was like running on a slippery frozen lake. Even sitting on the toilet seat posed a danger as I could easily fall off and hit the floor and maybe do more damage to my already delicate body. Putting clothes on was a massive challenge too. I couldn't stand up to position each leg into my trousers without losing balance, and focussing on a shirt button made me dizzy when my neck moved from side to side. I was lucky I hadn't injured myself more already as a result of dystonia.

And after that, what about the rest of my day? There'd be no driving, no solo outings, no way to leave the house alone to see my friends or to do activities I wanted to do. I couldn't read, watch television, use my computer, cook, or walk without hurting after five minutes. Neither could I run, carry, lift, tie my shoelaces, or do just about anything a non-disabled person could do. The *can't-do* list went on and on, more significant than any list imaginable.

I thought of Sebastian. Would he continue to be my carer? Would he be prepared to help me with the endless list of mundane activities we all had to carry out every day? It was a huge thing to ask, and he didn't appear very enthusiastic about it. We were together for better or worse, and lately, his future and mine looked more the latter. So I could almost understand if he called it all quits.

That's how my future appeared. Every day. Every month. Every year. Relentless and unforgiving. Compassion wasn't an emotion in dystonia's dictionary.

My neck started to get sore, so I held up my head with my hands to watch the stars for longer. At least they were something of beauty I could still appreciate.

Then, after what seemed an hour, it came to me. Finally, the stars did answer my questions.

My trip down memory lane wasn't such a train wreck after all. Funnily enough, after I realised how bad my future sounded, I actually had more impetus to continue. That's because, all in all, I simply wasn't prepared to accept the continuation of my horrible history. I had to change and create a new fate. It was a no brainer again.

I realised that the stars have survived for billions of years. They have outlived disasters such as colliding asteroids and volcanic eruptions. The Earth has survived ice ages, extinctions and climate catastrophes, while humans have endured plagues, world wars, fires, floods and cyclones. So, if all the celestial bodies and life therein could outlast all that, I concluded, I could persist through dystonia too, a much, much smaller egg in comparison. I realised I was just one tiny entity on this busy, crazy planet. And, just as each star above me shone brightly, creating something magical, I wanted to shine too. As corny as it sounds, I wanted to make the world a better place.

So maybe Saturn wasn't so stupid after all.

CECELIA

41. STAR

A lot was riding on my next concert. It was a big one, the first of a short interstate tour to New South Wales where the Weistar Symphony Orchestra would play at the iconic Sydney Opera House. I had played there before, first in a junior orchestra, then casually with the Randhouse Symphony Orchestra and the Reichardt Chamber Orchestra. I also played there in touring orchestras, including one dear to my heart with the German Durchberg Chamber Orchestra, an early gig won soon after my studies in that country. We played Beethoven and Schubert to appreciative audiences. It was the first professional gig I had done in Australia after returning home. The concert earnt little press at the time as, confusingly, I was an Australian playing in an overseas-based orchestra playing in Australia. It didn't change the fact that I loved the Sydney Opera House, though. The place had a magnificent acoustic and atmosphere and was one of the best places to play.

A couple of weeks had passed since the Weistar Symphony's previous concert, centring on a school program, where mercifully and surprisingly, I wasn't required. George, the orchestra manager, took the unusual step of granting me a much-earned break after all I had been through and done. He let Annie take my place and enjoy the opportunity to play first bassoon. I didn't argue and was happy for her. I took the time to do a little Cecelia therapy for myself by immersing more into Bowen therapy. Much to Sebastian's surprise, and mine a little, to be honest, it worked!

Thanks to an early fresh injection of Botox, and Dr Martin's magic, I could move my muscles relatively freely. What's more, when I played, it felt like I was playing in form. Better still, I was back in the orchestra, and preparing for my next concert!

The Bowen treatment had progressed well, and Dr Martin was so happy with my improvements, he wanted to use me for marketing purposes. I declined, even though I felt indebted to him. After all, I had embraced the unfamiliarity of Bowen, hoping my life would become richer for it. It did, but there were bigger fish for me to fry than help an holistic doctor earn more money. I had given him more than enough anyway, considering the thousands of dollars spent, to the point where even I sometimes doubted the value of his services.

Things weren't perfect yet anyway. Sebastian and I still had our differences. We were better, but not tickety-boo. With a concert looming and me being a part of it, we reconciled a little, which was good, and he was happy for me, but I still had trepidation. Was the evidence that I could play enough to persuade him that Bowen worked, or was there something else going on?

In addition, I had been on the neck better, neck worse merry-go-round before, and I felt like I was walking on a tightrope. My neck occasionally got sore, and it worried me. Fortunately, though, it didn't seem to affect my playing. I felt excited mainly because I could play, which was sufficient to manage any doubts about my relationship or my immediate future.

As I warmed up backstage, I didn't realise the orchestra was waiting for me or what was transpiring. In those nervous minutes when my uncertainties were heightening, Annie and Christopher were having a real humdinger of an argument onstage, and I didn't find out about it until later. It wasn't an argument of loud words or fists, as a vast audience would have seen the whole thing, but a dispute nonetheless. Apparently, in his impatience, Christopher seemed to think I wasn't going to show up. So he took the opportunity to promote himself in the section, changing from his third bassoon seat to my empty first bassoon seat. Not only that, he gloated about it, making himself way too comfortable in his new spot.

Having more confidence in me, Annie had other ideas and had no concerns about my absence. She shook her head, angrily signalling for him to return to his place. Christopher ignored her, and then the whole thing took an urgent turn when the conductor stood at the stage entrance and prepared to walk on. The only person missing was me.

Annie noticed, and by that time, even she started to panic. She obsessively looked backstage, hoping I would arrive, but no luck. Eventually, she took matters into her own hands, grabbed the sheet music from my stand, and placed it on hers. Christopher grabbed it back, and a tug of war ensued until the paper almost ripped and fell to the ground.

Of course, being backstage, I was unaware, and to be honest, a little ignorant of time. I was too busy analysing myself in the mirror. It was a moment of introspection I needed before playing on stage. As I looked at my reflection, I imagined how much that particular concert meant to me. It certainly wasn't like any other. It was another last chance. Bowen was another last chance, and I had everything riding on it. If I couldn't play, it could be my last time on stage as a musician. If I could play, hopefully, I could keep playing, which meant even more to me after what I had gone through over the last few months. But, once again, my future was unclear. And almost as importantly, it was a concert I wanted to play more than any other.

My contemplation was soon interrupted when the orchestra finished their warm up. Realising I was way too late, I shook off my nerves, splashed water over my face, grabbed my bassoon and ran out. When I arrived on stage, the conductor was on his podium and the singers were seated next to him. One of the singers turned around and looked at me very sternly. It was a face I knew well. It was Luciano Pavarotti.

Annie looked at me as if she had just immersed herself in a warm bubble bath. She smiled, relaxed, and quickly sorted out the strewn sheet music before handing the pages back to me. Christopher was another matter. He defiantly stayed in my seat. There was only one way to deal with him: more defiance. I stood over him steadfastly, and I wasn't going to move. Finally, he tutted and returned my gaze with an insidious smile.

Seeing our commotion, the orchestra members scowled at us, and that was enough for Christopher to cave in and return to his seat. Annie and I rolled our eyes at him and surreptitiously high-fived each other. Even though the whole thing lasted only a few seconds, it threw my focus off, being so unprofessional. Still, it did give me a boost of confidence, knowing that I could stand up for myself when needed.

The conductor tapped his baton on the podium. Usually, it was a signal for orchestra members to get ready, but it was a telling off for me. I didn't care, but I did care to get ready. There were precious seconds left, and I still remained unorganised. I quickly blew a silent note and steadied my sheet music. It would have to do.

The music started, Verdi's *Requiem*. At first, the music played softly, and the large choir behind me sang, giving me a few moments to get ready. I took the time to look around. It undoubtedly was a grand sight. Hundreds of singers behind me, an orchestra in front of me, and thousands of audience members lapping it up, all while being tucked into a gorgeous auditorium. It was majestic. I felt majestic. But it also felt overwhelming.

I needed to focus on something smaller to gain perspective. Then, by luck or by a sign from something more significant, just at that moment an insect flew in front of me. It was silhouetted by the stage lights and looked larger than it actually was. I focussed on it, closed my eyes momentarily to concentrate, and started to play, going deeper and deeper into the music. It felt wonderful. It felt joyous. So much so, the movement finished before I barely noticed.

After about twenty minutes, my favourite movement started, *Quid sum miser*. It began with a brief introduction by the clarinet section and the first bassoon, then the artist who everybody wanted to hear started to sing, Pavarotti. The music volume lowered, and he sang with his exquisite voice I knew so well. I played along, sublimely and beautifully, and Pavarotti and I danced in a musical duet for what seemed forever. With every note, he lifted me. My playing responded, almost as if the music gods had placed a spell on both of us. As the music intensified, Pavarotti shone brighter than the stars I had spoken to nights before. I was so enchanted, it took all my composure to carry on.

Eventually, the insect flew away, just like the one in my daydreams with the osprey. It felt like only Pavarotti and I were on stage for the rest of the piece, with the beam of stage lights surrounding and sheltering us from the world.

The music ended.

Silence.

Lost in my own world, I closed my eyes, reached my arm up, and embraced my bassoon lovingly.

Suddenly, fervent applause erupted around the auditorium. It included Sebastian's applause, which was the loudest.

Pavarotti signalled for me to stand but I was still lost in my own world and didn't notice. Annie tapped me on my shoulder.

'Take your applause!' she ordered. It startled me, making me open my eyes sharply. I looked around in awe and trembled.

George walked on stage and gave Pavarotti a huge bunch of colourful flowers. Pavarotti radiated his warmth towards the audience, and he bowed several times.

Suddenly, he turned and walked to the back of the orchestra towards me. For a second, I stared at him like a rabbit in headlights.

Then, in a moment when I would have accepted his marriage proposal, he handed me his flowers. We both turned back to the audience and bowed together. From the corner of my eye, I saw Fleur wink at me, mouthing, 'Well done!'

The applause died down, and Pavarotti turned to me one last time. In his eyes, I saw his acknowledgement. I could see he knew the struggle to be a musician, the toil we face for perfection, and the recognition we crave. He smiled at me as if to say, 'Everything's going to be all right.'

Afterwards, I ran backstage and collapsed against the wall. Then, alone and staring at the ceiling, I let out a loud, joyful, ecstatic cry.

I got to play that concert three times. All were more than I could ever have hoped for, and each time Pavarotti gave me his flowers. But it was the first concert I remembered the most.

Along with the time I married Sebastian, it was the most fabulous day of my life.

Still, when the three concerts ended, I couldn't help saying to myself, 'Is this finally happening? Can I rely on this? Is all this too good to be true?'

The truth was, I didn't know.

CECELIA

42. UNHEARD

When Sebastian was in the audience during one of my concerts, it was always a treat. He wasn't like some other orchestra partners who attended every show, so it felt like a Sunday night roast and trimmings feast when he was there. I felt valued as a person and as a player when Sebastian heard me play in the orchestra. He was not only interested in me; he was also interested in my career.

The first concert he ever came to see me in was an opera, *Turandot*. It was a magical night even before it started. I couldn't wait to get on stage and entertain, knowing he was going to be there. He was the person I wanted to be watching and listening to me the most when I played. So, unbeknown to anyone else in the audience, I put on an unforgettable show just for him, giving each note I played additional pizazz. It was a delicate balance between playing what needed to be played and not showing off, but I like to think I pulled it off.

It was early in our relationship, during one intermission, when I looked up towards the top of the orchestra pit. To my surprise, Sebastian was standing there smiling at me. I was taken aback.

'Hi Cecelia!' he said, with a glint in his eye.

'Sebastian! What are you doing!?

Sebastian leant over the railings, making himself get closer to me. 'Just saying hello!'

I gasped. 'You can't do that!'

'What? Say hello?'

'No, lean over the railings! You could drop several metres and injure yourself! It's dangerous!'

Fleur turned to me. 'We have to get ready, Cecelia. We've only got five minutes.'

'Just a second, Fleur.'

I turned back to Sebastian. 'I'll see you later, okay?'

I couldn't help but grin.

Sebastian turned and pointed to the exit, losing his balance in the process. Just in time, he grabbed the railings to stop himself from falling.

'Oops-a-daisy!' he said casually, as if nothing had happened.

From the corner of my eye, I saw a couple of audience members gasp.

Sebastian looked around, dusting himself off. 'I'm okay! I'm okay!' he said to everyone reassuringly.

'Sebastian, go!' I ordered.

He turned away, waved, and smiled cheekily as he headed towards the exit.

'Call me James Dean, a rebel with a cause,' he joked.

I smirked to myself, shaking my head in disbelief.

Fleur tapped my shoulder, tut-tutting me. 'That was *so* against protocol, and a definite *no-no* for any audience member.'

'I know,' I said. 'But it was kind of cute.'

I watched Sebastian leave, thinking about how rebellious he was and how strong his feelings must have been. After all, I thought, as I laughed to myself, he was willing to risk his life to get closer to me.

Fleur looked at me and nodded cheekily, seemingly content that she had successfully completed her match-making duties. 'Cecelia, he's really into you,' she said.

'You think?'

Suffice to say, I couldn't help smiling in the second half of that opera.

———

As we flew back home on the plane the night after my final Pavarotti concert, I thought about many of the concerts Sebastian had seen me in. I snuggled into his shoulder, happy that we had just shared one of the most significant moments in my life, hopeful too that it would bring us closer. The combination of happy hormones and tiredness made me sleep deeply in Sebastian's arms until we landed at the airport.

———

One thing Sebastian and I agreed on was that there was always cause for celebration. For us, birthdays didn't last just one day, they lasted a week. Similarly, Christmas lasted a month, and Easter lasted two. We'd even partied on a Sunday, purely because it was Sunday. So, not doing anything about one of the biggest days of my life was out of the question.

When we arrived home, I went straight to bed and fell asleep again very quickly. Before I closed my eyes, Sebastian suggested we spend some time at a country cottage. In my sleepiness, I promptly forgot what he had said. When I woke the next day, Sebastian had already organised everything. He had even packed for me, and before I knew it, we were off on another fun adventure. All I had to do was enjoy my morning porridge and make my way to the car after a much-needed warm shower. It was a very romantic thing for him to do, and as a result, I couldn't wipe the smile off my face the whole time.

As we drove there, I repeatedly prodded Sebastian. I felt impatient about where and when we would arrive at our destination. Each time, he replied, 'Hold your corgi horses, we'll be there soon enough.'

I laughed, knowing he often said that to Wills, who sat happily on the back seat, responding to his master's voice with a tail wag and an occasional woof. It was Wills who provided most of the entertainment on the journey, making us laugh when he poked his head out of the window to let the wind blow through his big, bat-like ears.

When we reached the cottage, and I walked inside, my eyes widened in delight. The place was gorgeous. It was the ideal setting for a couple; a charming old house built in the nineteenth century containing a wood fire, an ornate clawfoot bathtub and a fridge stocked full of sweet and tasty goodies. Outside, a tranquil garden and nearby woodland beckoned. If it weren't for my skinny cut jeans, I would have sworn I was back in the 1890s and that I was Elise lusting over Richard Collier in one of Sebastian's favourite movies, *Somewhere in Time*.

For the whole time we were there, a joyful three nights, Sebastian was the perfect partner, and I felt we were the perfect pair again. Communication seemed easy for us. We gave each other our full attention, listening when we needed to, and speaking when we had to. Both of us felt understood. We chatted about our careers and our hopes and dreams just like we had done many times before. Sebastian demonstrated that he genuinely cared about my music, and he understood like no other how important it was to me. In turn, I admired his writing, happily becoming his cheerleader, hoping and wishing he would sell his next big screenplay. I had watched him work on his scripts for hours and hours, so I understood his frustration. I knew he was a talented writer, somewhat undiscovered, despite his limited success writing scripts for television. He loved writing much as I loved music and that in itself was enough for us to be kindred spirits.

As we spent many hours walking hand in hand through the nearby forest, I felt reassured about Sebastian's place in my life. He was my support system, the person I went to talk to about my emotions, and to have a shoulder to lean on. And Sebastian always showed a lot of consideration in practical matters, anything from opening country gates for me to giving up his own time so I could practise and play music. Not only that, he was funny, happily telling me joke after corny joke. When we weren't laughing at those, we laughed at Wills, who we both found hilarious.

We spent the time smiling at one another, even if there wasn't anything in particular to smile about at the time. And at night, as we cuddled in front of a roaring fire, it became effortless to get lost in Sebastian's eyes and be physically intimate with him.

By the end of our time at the cottage, my compatibility with Sebastian seemed obvious again. We were both kind and caring people, wanting each other to succeed in our careers and relationship. I was confident we wanted to be with each other for as long as possible. But, almost as important, I felt like Sebastian might give me the benefit of the doubt regarding Bowen therapy. The cottage was a time and space I never wanted to leave.

———

But arguments start over the stupidest things, and they can often spiral out of control before anyone notices. For Sebastian and I, it began with a simple matter of watering flowers. After our three days of bliss, we arrived home, dog tired (including Wills), and collapsed on our bed. Before I went to sleep, I looked up at the poster of Pavarotti above my pillow, and over to the flowers Pavarotti had given me. We had put the flowers in a large vase delicately placed on my dressing table. Their buds and stems were a little wilted after three days without a drink. In our excitement and hurry to leave home on my mystery trip, I had forgotten to water them, or anything else for that matter.

I felt sorry for the flowers, especially as they reminded me of three great concert nights. However, they still made me happy, even in their dilapidated state. I smiled and cuddled Sebastian under the covers. 'I'll bronze those thirsty flowers,' I beamed.

Sebastian kissed my forehead. 'You deserve them,' he whispered. He promptly got up, and without me saying anything, filled a cup of water in the bathroom and tipped it into the vase before coming back to bed. The flowers immediately perked up, almost saying, 'Thank you'. Sebastian turned off his bedside lamp and laid back on his pillow. 'It's been a big few days, for the flowers too,' he yawned.

'It certainly has been. Thank goodness for the Bowen therapy,' I said casually.

Then, without notice, Sebastian scoffed and turned away from me.

Without exactly knowing why, hairs raised on the back of my neck. My tiredness may have contributed, maybe even my jubilation from success? Certainly, my recent history with Sebastian could have been a cause. Whatever it was, my reply to him came without thought of consequences. It was the type of comment I wished I could take back, even before saying it. I said it anyway and unthinkingly added a dose of sarcasm and disappointment for good measure.

'Of course, you know better, Dr Sebastian,' I scoffed. My eyes widened at myself, but I stayed silent, as the words had enough truth for me not to apologise. Anyway, it was too late. I had said them, and I had to own them.

Sebastian's body tensed, and he turned back to me. 'How can you say it works? Botox and physiotherapy work. That's what helped you. Not Bowen,' he argued.

I pointed to my neck. 'Surely, you see the results.'

'But where's the science?'

We both got up out of bed, not wanting to be next to one another anymore.

Wills yelped, having been woken up from his slumber, and ran out the door. Sebastian yelled, 'Wills, here!' to bring him back, but he ignored him. Wills rarely disobeyed his master in such a way. He must have been terrified.

My goat was up quicker than I could imagine, and anger welled up inside me. 'It works!' I screeched.

Sebastian stepped back, clearly not wanting to argue. He seemed shocked, as I was, at how the heat between us had rapidly reached boiling point. 'Let's just cool off for a bit,' he whispered. Sebastian lowered his head and made his way out the door, knocking a framed photo of mine to the floor in the process.

Anxiety rose inside me, and my body tightened. It made my neck hurt more than it had in a long time. 'I'm still the woman you love!' I shouted, as he disappeared from sight.

I walked around the bed, trying to calm down. It seemed impossible. I was angry and felt ignored and misunderstood. I also felt like throwing something. Sebastian was so contemptuous about Bowen. It simply blew my top. If he put himself in my shoes, he wouldn't have scoffed so quickly and readily.

What's worse, I felt angry at Sebastian for not letting me bask for longer in my high from the Pavarotti concerts. Our replay of the Bowen argument extinguished my joy far too soon. I began to question again. Maybe, our time away in the cottage didn't mean as much to him as it did to me?

Suffice to say, I didn't get much sleep that night.

All I wanted was support. That's what partners are for, aren't they?

CECELIA

43. RETURN OF THE BODY SNATCHERS

When I did eventually sleep, I slept alone, with no knowledge of Sebastian's whereabouts. Sleeping with a long-term loved partner was a habit almost as much as it was an act of love. Before drifting off, a regular late-night cuddle ritual was something I craved as a single person and cherished as a lover. Most nights, it relaxed me, taking me into dreamland in a matter of minutes. However, I lay awake for hours that night, still feeling uppity and fearing something else terrible may happen. I wanted sleep and feared sleep, and felt scared the house may be burgled. Even the Boogie monster entered my thoughts.

I felt safe when Sebastian was in my bed. When I realised my dependency on him in such a way, that ironically kept me awake as well. I became angry at myself for not being independent. Wills didn't help either. He was restless, checking the door every few minutes to see if his master was there.

Early the next day, Sebastian walked hesitantly into the kitchen. It had just rained and his clothes and hair were drenched. After our argument the night before, he had tried to start his car's engine but it wouldn't budge. He was therefore denied a much-wanted drive to think things over. Instead, beaten, dishevelled and shivering, Sebastian eventually fell asleep from exhaustion in the driver's seat. When I first saw him, I hoped the rain had washed away some of his attitude but then I looked at him and softened. We both looked like we needed a few more hours of rest and a good, hot shower.

Wills ran to him. His tail wagged so much, he looked like he would take off like a helicopter. They were like two long-lost lovers who hadn't seen each other for a year. I felt a pang of envy, turned my back, and began to make myself some porridge.

Sebastian scratched Wills behind his big ears. 'I'm sorry, darling,' he said, with his tail metaphorically between his legs.

I turned back to him. 'Where were you?' I asked.

'Wishing I was in the tropics.'

In silence, we finished making our breakfasts. The time seemed to pass at a snail's pace.

Sebastian poured some oats into a bowl and began eating them raw. I looked at him in puzzlement. His breakfast missed some key ingredients. 'Where's your milk and golden syrup?' I asked.

Sebastian looked at me apologetically. 'I left them in the fridge ... with my scepticism.'

He put down his bowl and turned to me with his arms open wide.

I knew he wanted a hug. I quietly accepted it, and we hugged for several minutes, again without words.

———

The next night, I had another concert to do. Driving there, I felt good, albeit still a little tired from the recent lack of sleep. I felt cautiously upbeat, too, as Sebastian and I seemed to have resolved our differences. We had both agreed the previous evening that science, or any perceived lack of it, should never come between us. It hadn't before. Science usually helped to keep us close. We often agreed on evidence-based issues and regularly discussed global warming, deforestation and species extinction. Without saying it, we both also seemed to suspect that Sebastian's disappearance was caused by something far deeper, too painful to discuss. Having said that, Sebastian was rather chipper since our blip, and his usual one-liners again helped make me laugh. They went some way to dissolving remaining tensions between us.

I parked outside the concert hall and made my way to the entrance. Once inside, I usually made a beeline to the green room, but on that night, as I was a little early, I decided to wait outside for a minute and take in the surroundings. I marvelled at what I saw. It was a beautiful place, a purpose-built artistic precinct I always enjoyed. People were sipping champagne and enjoying the gardens on the warm, clear night. Those who weren't waiting for the concert were promenading along a walkway surrounded by lovely, grassed lawns filled with native plants. Some were enjoying picnics with yummy looking food. Strategically placed lights highlighted giant trees, and they drew attention to sculptures and tall office buildings in the distance. It looked like the perfect balance of city and nature. The area was a thriving hub.

One thing felt incongruent, though. I looked at the old theatre building again, noting several modern glassed towers surrounded it. For the first time, I realised the theatre looked a little out of place. It looked like it should be in Venice or Freiburg, not in the relatively modern country of Australia. I shook my head, surprised that I hadn't taken much notice of that fact before, which would seem so obvious to most observers.

Annie and Fleur greeted me in the green room, and we gave each other our customary Three Musketeer hugs. We were all feeling confident and ready for what was shaping up to be a relatively easy night. The two rehearsals for the concert had gone well with no interruptions. The difficulty level was only a five out of ten. It was a new concert that excited me. Every so often, the orchestra premiered an up-and-coming composer's work. The pieces to be played were light, short and not too complex. As a result, we hoped to finish early and go for a relaxing drink and chat in the nearby pub.

We rushed to the stage and took our places. Christopher smiled at us as we sat down and prepared our instruments.

Annie winked at me and leaned into my ear. 'I wonder what he's all happy about?' she whispered playfully.

I spoke softly back, 'Whatever it is, it's good to see.'

'Yep. Things are definitely on the positive side, Cecelia.'

The conductor tapped his baton on his podium before I could reply to Annie. The music started, and the rest of the orchestra played vigorously and loudly. I brought my bassoon's reed to my lips in readiness and started playing boisterously.

But, suddenly, it happened again.

My head and neck jerked far to my left, twisting well past my shoulder. The pain was the most pain I had ever experienced—definitely ten out of ten on the pain scale. I yelped loudly, even though I tried not to, and felt my bassoon starting to slip from my grasp. I'm sure some audience members heard and saw me. I hoped the volume the orchestra played at was enough to cover any noise I made.

Annie and Fleur turned towards me with a concerned look I hadn't seen from them before. It took a considerable percentage of my effort just to recover from their shocked faces. Their eyes were wide open, and they appeared terrified as if I were wrestling a shark.

Christopher scowled at me as if he had seen enough. Even the conductor missed a beat when he saw me. I checked that my bassoon had no damage and luckily there was none. Then I shrunk back in my seat like a scolded schoolgirl. The last thing I wanted to do was to ruin another concert.

The music played on, and the bassoon section didn't need to play for a few lines. Annie turned to me in the short reprise, concerned as always. 'Are you okay?' she mouthed.

'I'm trying,' I mouthed back.

The orchestra played on, and I kept missing my cue. I sat there hoping that no one in the audience realised that the concert had no principal bassoon. There were indeed a few notes where I would normally be heard on my own, so those in the composer's inner circle probably did.

There was nothing I could do. I couldn't play.

Christopher and Annie played on without me, and the piece ended. I didn't make any further contribution other than sitting there and looking like I had crashed the party.

The audience seemed to only give mild applause. It was one of the few times in my life when I didn't feel deserving. I hoped again that they didn't see too much.

Christopher nudged Annie during the applause and stared at me condescendingly. He whispered in her ear, 'There's plenty more where she came from.'

Annie glared back at him. For a second, I thought she might hit Christopher. Instead, she retorted, 'Where Christopher? Your planet?'

I stood with the other musicians to take a bow, holding my neck, before rushing off stage.

Annie made an urgent call to Sebastian who met me outside the theatre to take me home. Sebastian vainly tried to comfort me as we hugged in silence.

Words weren't necessary between us at that time.

CECELIA

44. ZOMBIE

My neck had once more become a problem, and somehow life felt like living in fear of being shot, even after doctors had removed the bullet. Life was even more unusual and different than it had ever been. Previously, when I was fit and able, I rarely considered my fears would ever come true, because they never did. However, with each neck episode, the likelihood of something going horribly wrong felt more and more real.

Fear protects you. It stops you from doing stupid things that put your life in danger. We're scared of jumping off a cliff, for example, because if we did, we know we'd probably be gravely injured. But sometimes, too much fear stops us from doing the things we need to do. So life becomes a navigation between taking risks that we believe we can handle if they go wrong, or holding back to ensure we are safe. Knowing my neck history, those sorts of decisions became a tricky balancing act in the orchestra. There wasn't a choice. I needed to play, come hell or high water. After the car crash and my last concert, a train wreck, I felt like high water had arrived in the shape of a big, fat tidal wave.

Fear drove me to see Indira again, as well as a rapid decline in my physical health. After the concert, I had stiffness in my neck, and I had muscle stiffness all through my body. It felt like post-traumatic stress disorder and a deep depression gripped me. My heart continually palpitated and I couldn't sleep. I had memory loss and couldn't think straight. Thankfully, there was enough in my tank to enable me to do something small, instead of curling up in a ball and staying in bed all day.

The sight of Indira made me perk up a little. She smiled and looked positive when she first saw me, although I must have looked like a mess. She had come to feel like a good friend to me and I enjoyed her company. She had a kind, humble way about her, which I admired. Just as importantly, she made me feel acknowledged, making a quick appointment for me after hearing about my latest woe. She was the best kind of friend anyone could hope for, being available when the going got tough and not judging if I did or said foolish things.

When I spoke to her on the phone, she asked me to bring my bassoon to the appointment. That was easier said than done. My bassoon felt heavier than a truck with my body how it was, so just getting it there was a problem. Also, I wanted my neck fixed first before I attempted playing again. But Indira convinced me that the bassoon was necessary for any further diagnosis, so I agreed, and with Sebastian's help, I found myself in her rooms trying to play.

As she watched me intently, I repeatedly attempted to bring the bassoon's reed to my lips. Each time, my head and neck jerked fully to one side again. I couldn't stop it, and just as bad, I couldn't even play a note.

After several tries, I had to take a break, and Indira felt around my neck, expertly prodding and massaging my neck muscles.

'That's okay,' she said. 'That'll do for now.'

Panic rose in me. 'Are there any more exercises I can do?' I pleaded.

Indira stared at her notes while sweat began to drip down my brow. I waited and waited in silence for an answer.

Eventually, she spoke. 'Cecelia, have you considered something else?' she asked.

My voice began to shake. 'You know music is all I ever wanted to do.'

I could see Indira searching for answers. 'Perhaps you can take a break?' was all she offered.

'How did you feel when you gave up dancing?' I asked.

Indira looked at me with a conviction beyond her words. 'I moved on,' she said.

I'm not sure exactly how, but I managed to pack up my bassoon and go home. With my mind stupefied like a zombie, I could hardly comprehend what would happen next.

So that was it. I hadn't fully grasped it yet, but that's all it took for me to know that I'd never play music again.

CECELIA

45. EVERYONE NEEDS A JULIA IN THEIR LIVES

For the next week, on medical leave again, I descended into an even deeper funk. I spent a few days in bed eating tiramisu and other sweet treats, in the vain belief that they would cheer me up. They did, but only for a few minutes until the sugar rush wore off.

But there was a method in my depression. I hoped the rest would help my neck recover, to the point where maybe it would fix itself. In any case, rest is what I needed to mend from all the muscle stiffness. In my mind, that was justification enough for me to try and watch all the daytime movies I had missed over the years. It didn't help my neck much, but it did give me film fodder to talk about with Sebastian, who loved to talk about anything on that subject.

In my brighter moments, I considered what other options there were for my neck: acupuncture, hypnotherapy, massage, Traditional Chinese Medicine and others. They all seemed futile. I concluded that if Bowen didn't have a lasting effect, neither would other alternative or complementary therapies. Maybe Sebastian was right after all. I should have listened to the science. When I did, in the respectable form of Indira and Dr Hayworth, the problem was that they couldn't find an answer or a cure.

In my depression, Sebastian didn't boast about the science. He was pretty incredible, helping me, cheering me up, and watching the daytime movies with me. He didn't offer any solution, just company, and that's what I probably needed the most.

In the second week of my deep hopelessness, the mindless daytime movies and isolation began to feel like torture. After enduring *Santa With Muscles* starring Hulk Hogan, I realised my life was at a low ebb, and that was enough for me to get out from under my quilt and see some friends.

Annie was the friend I wanted to talk face to face with the most, but she was interstate doing a temporary gig with the Robinsborough Symphony Orchestra. I felt happy for her. It was a great opportunity, as she got to play principal bassoon in some very challenging pieces. Still, a selfish part of me wanted her by my side to listen, support and give me all the chitchat about the orchestra.

Fleur was my second choice for support but my first choice for gossip. We arranged to meet in her favourite restaurant in the city, a very trendy and busy place, frequented by musicians, writers, artists and those with money who wanted to hang around with the cool kids.

I found a table near the centre of the restaurant. It wasn't the best table to sit at, but diners packed the place, and it was the only one left available. My body hurt severely from the train trip to get there. I sat rubbing my neck, waiting for Fleur, feeling anxious and hoping she would arrive sooner rather than later. Eventually, after my third lemon squash, she turned up, bouncing in like she had springs on her legs. As she entered and saw me, she shouted, 'Darling! At last, we have a chance to have a one-on-one chat!' Several diners looked around in curiosity at her dramatic entrance.

She gave me an air kiss and joined me at the table. Just as she sat down, a handsome waiter saw us, and he immediately came over to fill our glasses. Fleur winked at him and said flirtatiously, 'Thank you, darling.' I looked up at the waiter, which made my neck hurt even more so I rubbed it soothingly. Fleur noticed, and her upbeat mood dampened. 'How's your treatment going?' she asked. 'I know a good shrink you can try.'

I rolled my eyes. 'It's not that simple, Fleur.'

Fleur looked at me. She straightened with confidence as if she knew all the answers. 'Maybe Christopher or Annie can play your parts for a while longer,' she said.

I pushed away my drink. Fleur immediately retreated and apologised with an embarrassed, 'I'm so sorry.'

'Sorry's not a cure,' I retorted.

Fleur paused in awkward silence. She looked around as if she were about to tell me a secret she didn't want anyone to hear. 'Cecelia ... people in the orchestra have been talking ... things aren't the same anymore.'

'What do you mean?' I asked.

Fleur lowered her voice. 'It's been great to have you back playing principal bassoon and everything ... but ... do you think you're up to it?'

Suffice to say, I was taken aback. I looked at Fleur sarcastically. 'Of course, you're the superstar concertmaster,' I said. 'And what about Annie ... does she feel the same way?'

Fleur ignored my question, intent on making her point. 'What are you doing about it?' she prodded.

'Lots of things.'

We sat in awkward silence again for a few seconds while both of us gulped our drinks.

I fell back in my seat. 'So much for supportive friends,' I whispered to myself.

Fleur heard me and softened. 'I know. I know. And I do support you. I wish this weren't happening.'

'To me, or you?' I asked.

'To both of us, Cecelia. To everyone.'

I felt my lips quiver as I pushed out more words. 'This isn't easy for me, you know.'

Fleur nodded, and as with others around me, it angered me

slightly that she could move her head and neck so quickly, while I couldn't. 'I know. It's just ...' she said.

'It's just what!? I said, interrupting, my voice getting louder.

Fleur turned around and saw an elderly couple watching us intently. She signalled for me to quieten down.

I fell back in my seat, taken aback again.

Fleur whispered, 'It's just ... people are watching us.'

'They always have. It goes with the job,' I snapped.

'I know. We're celebrities. But they're watching for different reasons now. And the orchestra audience ...'

I interrupted again, nearly spilling my drink. 'So, you're a mind reader now?'

Fleur shook her head. 'No. I don't mean ...'

She had gone too far and I stood up angrily. 'You know what? I'm not hungry anymore,' I seethed.

'Wait. Cecelia, I'm sorry.'

I stepped back, knocking the table leg, as well as my drink. It spilled over the floor, but I ignored it. I was too angry at Fleur. 'So many sorries. I'm sorry you don't want to be seen with a damaged person, Fleur,' I said indignantly.

I turned my back on her and stormed out.

————

The train trip home was busy, and the only seat available was near a mother and some young children. Watching the children and their social interactions turned out to be a good distraction, as my tense body and jangled nerves drifted a little to one side in my conscious-ness. I was reminded of my first day at preschool, a big day, as it is for any young child, being the first formal day without a parent or guardian present. Like the other children, I had wandered around the playground, not knowing anyone and feeling lost about what to do. A girl had walked up to me and introduced herself.

'Hi. I'm Julia,' she said.

I smiled because her name sounded similar to mine.

She immediately asked, 'Will you be my friend?'

'Yes,' I answered.

That's all it took. No judgements. No preconceptions. Just friendship, and we played happily every day for the whole year.

My memory failed me as to how or why I parted with Julia, but my mind swung quickly back to think about what to do with Fleur. I was angry with her, and not just because of my dystonia. I felt hurt that she had let me down. She was someone I had let into my life in the most personal way. She knew all about my personality, the good and the bad, including my insecurities about music, love and people's perceptions of me. We made decisions together, from simple choices about what to wear or places to go, to bigger things like how best to approach and play music as musicians. I had devoted a lot of myself to her and a lot of my life.

After our café debacle, however, the possibility of losing her friendship became forefront in my mind. I came to realise that, although we had been through so much together, those times were mainly good times. She was always there for a positive orchestra review, for example, but went AWOL when we were out of form. The bottom line was that Fleur became absent when life got hard. Yet, I was there for Fleur when she had man trouble, needed cheerleading for her playing, or needed a backup as a spokesperson on controversial issues in her role as concertmaster.

I felt sad. Not only was I grieving the loss of my career, but also the loss of my friendship with Fleur. It felt too hard to reconcile Fleur seeing me as less of a person, while I saw myself as just the same old me, if not more.

In my mind, I shouted, 'I'm still *me!*'

Only my neck was different. I just needed to do other things now instead of playing music. Apparently, Fleur didn't see it that way.

I needed time to think.

———

When the following morning arrived, the sun shone into my bedroom window so brightly, it forced me awake after a night of restless sleep. After breakfast, I decided to go to the beach. It was hot and sunny, and the idea of laying on the sand for a whole day instead of being cooped up at home in bed watching television seemed a better option. The choice wasn't easy, though. I had to fight my lack of motivation just to get up and do something.

I packed a simple lunch of sandwiches and lemon cordial, and headed to the sand with a newspaper I planned to read, as best I could, from start to finish. The broader world around me had become less significant since my neck problems started, as I hadn't the energy or inclination, or sometimes the ability, to watch or read the news. Nonetheless, the world still felt important enough to get things in perspective.

The beach was tranquil as I lay down on my towel. I surveyed the scene before me: great surf, lots of sand, bathers, children playing and building sandcastles and a clear blue sky. After twenty minutes of intense thought, something very significant dawned on me.

Even though it was a perfect day, it was challenging for me to take in its beauty. Typically, a faultless day like that would bring me abundant bliss. But it felt hard to recognise what I was *really* feeling that time, even though I knew I was still angry at Fleur.

The coastline didn't seem to have as much colour. The sky and sea weren't as blue, and the sand wasn't as golden. I knew the colour was there, but like hearing termites in the roof, I just couldn't see it. My perception was askew, and my anger at Fleur, and dystonia, and so many things, had eaten away inside me. I knew I needed to express how much rage boiled inside me. I wanted to climb a mountain and shout with all my might, 'SCREW EVERYTHING!' but couldn't. The problem was, I felt like I *had* to be good, *wanted* to be good, but I simply *couldn't* be that way. My fists curled up in a tight ball. I felt sick and tired of being Miss Goody Two-Shoes.

It would have been so easy to give in and run amok over dystonia and so many challenges that had hit me. With Fleur, I could have so easily punched her. Yet, according to my rationale, at that heated moment in the café, I felt like I needed to be the best I could be. It all felt too hard, though, and I walked out.

I lay there in the sun for a while longer with my thoughts in overdrive before concluding my day at the beach wasn't the perfect, stress-free day I wanted, so before lunch, I picked up my towel and walked home.

CECELIA

46. MORTAL

It doesn't take much to be thrown out like an old cabbage. Ever since the very first concert when I lost my ability to make a sound on my bassoon, I knew something was up within the orchestra. There weren't as many smiles or as much small talk. Meetings gradually became scarcer too. I felt left out of the loop, particularly when management didn't invite me to a crucial principal player meeting. It was a meeting I would never have missed, and I would have often chaired. Fewer responsibilities were given or expected of me.

I sensed management had secret meetings about me and my future, even when my playing was fine. Suspecting they were talking behind my back knocked my confidence and self-esteem, affecting my ability to play well. I became scared for my job and my identity. For years, the orchestra had given me structure, purpose, routine and security. If I wasn't to be a musician, who would I be?

The writing was on the wall, though, and it didn't take much effort to know why. I couldn't play my bassoon, therefore, I couldn't play in the orchestra. It was no surprise then that George requested a meeting I was 'required' to attend, just when I had made a plan myself to talk to him about my situation.

It felt surreal to walk down the corridor to George's office, knowing that it would be the last time. Everything seemed to go in slow motion, and my feet felt heavy on the ground. The short journey was a long mental effort, as well as a physical one. By the time I reached his office, I had to wait outside to gather my breath and find enough courage to open the door and walk inside.

To my surprise, Christopher and Fleur were talking loudly in an adjoining office, and every word they were saying echoed further than it should have. Fleur's voice was the easiest to hear as it had a shrieking quality. It was something I had become accustomed to, but she sounded annoying and noisy since our falling out. I knew they were discussing me, and they didn't want anyone to see them, so I hid behind a partition.

Fleur moved closer to Christopher and lowered her voice to somewhat normal levels. 'She needs a shrink,' she whispered.

Christopher nodded. 'I knew it was something like that.'

Fleur stood up straighter. 'Then again, she's always been *better* than us.'

Christopher laughed. 'Ha! Mere mortals we are.'

My blood boiled, and I couldn't hide any longer. I walked past, glaring at Fleur, fighting my neck movements to look as strong and upright as I could. Christopher returned my gaze, looking smug and rotten.

Ahead of me, I noticed Annie and the chief conductor speaking to George in his office. They all turned their heads to look at me but continued talking anyway. Just like Fleur and Christopher, it was apparent I was the subject of their conversation. I sneaked in just as the conductor was leaving. He turned to me and gave me a sympathetic eye. 'I'm sorry, Cecelia. This is difficult for all of us,' he exclaimed.

Annie ran to me and held my hand. 'I tried to sway them. I really did. I'm so sorry,' she said caringly.

I gave her a weak smile. She hugged me tightly and then left, whispering, 'Good luck,' in my ear before disappearing through the door. I wanted to go with her, but George interrupted. 'Come sit down,' he ordered.

I sat down nervously and thought to myself, how do you prepare to hear bad news? It would be the worst news anyone could ever imagine. All I could do was fight for survival like a dying person vainly forcing themselves to breathe. 'I know my playing is affecting the orchestra,' I pleaded. 'I'd be the first one to say I should go, but ...'

George interrupted again. 'This isn't easy for anyone,' he said with precision, as if he had thoroughly prepared and practised his speech beforehand. He slid an envelope across the table towards me. I opened it up and glanced at the contents. It was termination paperwork.

'We don't always get to leave on our own terms,' he whispered apologetically.

And with those ten words, I was never to play again what I loved the most—the universal language that binds the whole world together:

music.

CECELIA

47. TROUGH

But what of life?

Not much more than eating and sleeping became my routine for the next few days, except for thinking. There was plenty of time for that. I felt a deep, deep sadness that wouldn't go away no matter what I tried. It was like the world kept spinning, and I was stuck in the void of outer space, watching it all go around and around.

My body continued to feel heavy when I moved. My body ached, as well as my neck, and life became increasingly uncomfortable. Every part of me was worn out like an old, rusted engine.

If I ever felt suicidal, that would have been the time. But I didn't believe in suicide. There were too many reasons to live: Sebastian, Wills, animals, nature, the beach, to name a few.

Maybe deep inside, something told me there was still a purpose for me to live, even though I always believed there was no purpose in life itself? I began to realise that I was just *here* in this world, and in it, I began to appreciate minor things. Over time, even something relatively simple like how golden syrup runs over a hot bowl of porridge brought a smile to my face. The world still gave me something to enjoy, and that kept me going.

Thinking really did help.

———

One more item of orchestra business still lay in front of me, however. Annie had organised a farewell lunch, and as the guest of honour, my presence was mandatory. Even so, I hardly felt honourable.

Fitting with my mood, rain poured down heavily as Sebastian and I arrived at orchestra headquarters. We made our way towards the largest room, but when we reached the doorway, we could hear Christopher and Annie arguing. Christopher was waving an alpaca book in Annie's face, and she was dodging it, trying not to get swatted.

Not wanting to cause a commotion, Sebastian and I stopped and listened instead of making our presence known.

I could hear the typical condescension in Christopher's voice, but it didn't bother me as much as it had when I was a full participant in the orchestra. His voice didn't seem to shoot the daggers it used to, and my heart lifted slightly, knowing that I would never have to deal with his tantrums and difficulties anymore. I realised he was to become little more than someone I used to know.

He amplified his voice so everyone could hear as he said smugly, 'I've seen this thing before. With the kind of pressure we're under, I'm not surprised Cecelia has a mental condition.'

My face dropped, aghast, and I held Sebastian back. I could tell he was thinking of punching Christopher, or at least giving him a verbal what for and when. For me, I was intrigued. I wanted to know what Christopher, and the orchestra, *really* thought.

Annie had a tone of 'fighting words' to her voice, and for a second, I thought she might do the dirty physical work for me.

'Who are you to talk about performance, Christopher?' she snapped back sarcastically in a quiet hiss.

Christopher retorted. 'The fact is, she shouldn't be in the industry. An orchestra is only as good as its worst player. She's letting us all down.'

Annie raised her voice to match Christopher's. 'She still deserves our support,' she said loudly yet compassionately. 'Or does the orchestra not support its own anymore!?'

At that question, Sebastian and I composed ourselves and walked in. We looked around the room. It was all low-key, and there weren't many orchestra members present. Fleur rushed up to me with her arms open wide.

'Cecelia! Where were you?' she asked. 'You're late, darling. We have to get back to work.'

I looked at her as directly as I could.

'I wouldn't want to keep you, Fleur,' I said dryly.

Christopher and Annie continued arguing, interrupting our awkward moment with Fleur.

Annie baulked at Christopher's lack of response. She turned away to ignore him before she looked at me with softness in her eyes.

'It could happen to any of us,' she whispered gently.

Christopher looked at his watch impatiently. 'Not to me. I guess it's good for you, though. Now you'll be playing more first bassoon for a while, Annie.'

Annie pushed closer to him. 'Cecelia's too nice to say this, so I'll say it for her. Christopher, you're a real WANKER!' Annie then snatched Christopher's alpaca book from his hands, and she angrily ripped it in half. It was quite a feat. The book was a hardcover.

Christopher stepped back, scoffed and turned away. His refusal to admit defeat or wrongdoing was apparent for all to see.

Annie didn't seem to care and walked away from him in disgust before heading towards me. She interrupted Fleur, composed herself, and wrapped her arms around me. 'We were the Dynamic Duo,' she said with pride, as she gave me a tight hug.

My heart lifted. 'I hope we can still see each other,' I offered.

We shared glances for a few seconds in silence. I was expecting Annie to look excited and ask me out for a coffee, where we could plan our days of fun, but instead, her face dropped. She looked guilty like she had just stolen the orchestra's takings for the week.

'I'm so sorry. I wanted to tell you earlier. I haven't told anyone yet ... but ... I got a first bassoon job interstate,' Annie said contritely.

As quickly as my heart lifted from her hug and her fantastic news, my heart sank. But, before any words came out of my mouth, Fleur interrupted. She tapped her glass of wine loudly, which was a cue for everyone to stop, turn around and listen.

'Gather around, everyone!' she shouted. 'I'd just like to say a big thank you to Cecelia. We thank you for your time with us and appreciate all you have done. It's sad to see you go, but we wish you well in the future.'

The orchestra members raised their glasses.

'To Cecelia!' shouted Fleur.

Everyone joined in, calling out in harmony, 'To Cecelia!'

The sound of clapping hands rang through my ears. All I could do was smile sweetly. I was a little embarrassed. Leaving for reasons I didn't want certainly didn't feel worthy of applause.

Annie gave me another huge hug. 'You inspire me, Cecelia,' she gushed. 'I've enjoyed working with you so much.'

I stepped back slightly, not quite knowing what to think or feel. With all the attention, my emotions were up and down like a hopping kangaroo. Sebastian and Annie were the only ones keeping me in the positive. I wanted to say how much Annie meant to me, but with all eyes focussed on us, all I could whisper was a simple, 'Me too.'

Annie slowly drew her arms away from me, which allowed Fleur to move in for her hug. 'Who am I going to drown my sorrows with?' Fleur asked, as I smelled alcohol on her breath. I gave her a muted grin. The taste of our last café meeting, mixed with her wine odour, bothered my nose, as well as my mind, and I didn't like it.

Annie and Fleur moved away to allow others to say their farewells. 'Call me, okay?' Annie asked, as George made his way through the brass players towards me.

'For sure,' I replied, hoping the phone call would be sooner rather than later.

Christopher moved closer to me, stopping George in his tracks.

I looked back and forth between them, not knowing who to speak to first.

Then, Christopher said in a methodical and planned way, 'I'm sorry you're going, Cecelia. And don't worry, I'll keep the section running.'

I stepped away and blinked forcefully at him, feeling sorry for the next person employed in the bassoon section. Their unofficial 'boss' was going to make their life hell, I thought.

As the end neared, orchestra members lined up to hug me and offer commiserations or positive wishes or both. And before I fully comprehended it, my farewell soiree was over. At times, it felt too slow and at other times too fast.

Before Sebastian had finished his second lemonade, we were walking out the front entrance to our car.

As I stepped through the door, I paused to look back and survey the foyer. I had come to know it almost as well as my bassoon. I remembered how excited I was when I first entered the building, starting my new job with the orchestra afresh. The funny thing was, as I looked around, I didn't think about the music I had played there. What I remembered most were the laughs and friendships I had with Annie and Fleur and how they had come to feel like family.

I was leaving the home that I had lived in and loved for over ten years.

CECELIA

48. SILENCE IS TARNISHED GOLD

Sebastian drove me home, and he hardly said a word the whole way. The air inside the car felt palpable, not from tension between us but from shock. Our minds were busy doing the talking, trying to make sense of the finality of what had just happened.

Eventually, Sebastian pulled into our driveway and parked the car. He stopped its engine and sat quietly with me. Instead of opening the car door, I stared silently out the window. It must have been at least ten minutes before either of us said anything. During that time, Sebastian stroked my hair in a vain attempt to comfort me. It made my neck movements worse. 'Sorry,' he apologised, before moving back into his seat.

The rain started pattering on the windscreen, and somehow, that became the impetus for us to talk. Sebastian turned to me again. 'Going away parties are never happy because the going away part is always sad,' he said solemnly.

I turned my body to him. 'It's what they said, except Annie ... no, it's what they didn't say.'

Sebastian laughed to make light of the overly serious situation.

'Christopher deserved a punch. I'd love to have seen Annie's left hook!' he joked.

I smiled a badly needed smile. 'Explaining my condition to Christopher would be a waste of time,' I said. 'But it was Fleur's tone. Her speech was like, 'We made this farewell because we had to. Now you're late, which makes us like you even less.'

Sebastian nodded in agreement. 'So much for friendship,' he added.

I crossed my arms in a huff. 'What about my concertos ... or my good reviews ... how I improved the section and brought a beautiful sound to the orchestra ... how they'll miss me!?'

'But you did achieve all those things.'

'Not enough for them.'

'We can't control what people say or think, darling.'

Sebastian tried to stroke my shoulder instead of my hair. He seemed determined to help, so I let him, even though it felt a little uncomfortable.

'I bet if you were in a wheelchair or had a walking stick, they would have shown more understanding,' he said.

I moved close to Sebastian and gave him a long desperate hug.

'People think I left because I'm messed up!' I declared.

I felt Sebastian's cheek graze against mine as he turned his head from side to side in disagreement.

'That said more about them, not you.'

Tension began to build in my body, and I fought to control my emotions.

I didn't want Sebastian to see me as a blubbering mess, so I abruptly moved back before opening the car door and running to the house in the rain. By the time I reached the front door, I was dripping wet.

Sebastian followed, pleading with me to stop, but I ignored him. Tension rose in me further as I tried to get the key in the front door. It wouldn't fit, despite my many attempts, and when the door finally opened after a big nudge, I noticed a large pile of bills on the hall table. I picked them up and scanned the envelopes: gas, electricity, water and internet. They were all there. Many were unopened due to Sebastian's neglect, as he was responsible for managing the bills. My tension rose to anger. Why did the bills have to come all at once!? They had never done that before. Someone must have done something stupid at one of those large, faceless, heartless utility companies. When did the world become so cruel!?

As I opened each envelope and saw the overdue notices, my anger turned to rage.

Sebastian walked in, leaving puddles of rain on the carpet. I turned to him. 'Did you not see these!?' I shouted.

'Yes, but ...'

I threw the bills on the floor. 'I thought we would be happy!' I yelled.

Sebastian tried to hug me, but I rejected his attempt. The feeling of anything on my skin with my whole body so tense felt uncomfortable and made my neck and body feel worse.

'How are we going to get by?' I snapped.

'We can live in a tent.'

'And after our money runs out?'

Sebastian smiled. 'I'll eat Spam.'

I snorted, and a smile crept up on my face. Sebastian had said that exact sentence to me when we got engaged and were talking about future living arrangements. When he said it to me all those years ago, I realised his sense of priorities, and I loved him more for it at the time.

As we both stood at the front door facing each other, like two wet cats at night, Sebastian's words were what I needed to hear. My body relaxed a little, and my mouth even smiled a little more over his corny joke.

'Will you work?' I asked.

Sebastian nodded. 'I'm trying to.'

Tension welled up inside me again. Our lives had changed now. Sebastian's words weren't good enough this time, and I expressed it bluntly to him, 'It's not fair! I shouldn't have to pay for all this!' I exclaimed.

Sebastian stepped back, and his face dropped. 'Give me a break,' he answered defensively.

I looked at him, turning my head as straight as possible towards his face. Our situation suddenly felt imbalanced. His previous financial contributions to the household coffers didn't seem enough any more.

I asked in a not-so-gentle voice, 'Why don't you find other work?'

'And waste all that study?'

I kicked the bills I had strewn on the floor. 'Money to live isn't a waste!'

Sebastian pulled away further. 'But it's different.'

'Why?' I asked.

'It wasn't your choice to leave.'

At last, something we agreed on, I thought. 'Exactly.' I pointed to him. '*You* have a choice.'

Sebastian shook his head. For a moment, he looked like he was about to go outside again into the rain.

'I'm not going back to work now,' he said in defiance.

I looked at the bills and back to Sebastian. 'But we'll go broke if you don't.'

Suddenly, I realised Sebastian had been holding back his emotions. His face took an about-turn, from compassion to anger.

'We wouldn't be if you didn't pay for that stupid Bowen!' he barked sarcastically.

I stepped back, stunned.

'I thought you came to accept the Bowen therapy, especially when it got me back to playing, at least for a while. Or did you hide your true feelings about it?'

I stepped back again and examined Sebastian, thinking of the support I needed. He didn't look or sound like he was about to give me any.

We stood looking at each other, still wet, in awkward silence.

'Let's not think about it,' he pleaded.

I softened a little. If only *not thinking about it* made our problems disappear, life would be so much easier, I thought.

'Sebastian, we have to work.'

He opened his arms for a hug. 'I know. But not now,' he whispered.

He wrapped his arms around me.

I reluctantly let him.

———

That night, I lay awake in bed, unable to sleep due to another loud rain storm hitting our corrugated iron roof. After our argument, we had quickly and quietly made our way to bed, and mercifully Sebastian was deeply asleep.

Abruptly, the rain stopped, and the room fell into an eerie silence. I lay there, staring upwards, trying to hear a sound, any sound I could use to remind me of music. Random noises sometimes helped me to sleep, and I often turned them into a beat or song. Sometimes I even put words to the beat. But this time, on that night, there was nothing. Normally my mind would be full of music that I was working on and interpreting in many different ways.

I nudged Sebastian, and he stirred slightly. 'Sebastian. I can't hear anything,' I whispered.

Sebastian stirred a bit more. 'Of course not. It's the middle of the night,' he mumbled into his pillow.

I started to panic slightly.

'The music's gone. Now there's nothing.'

'I know. I miss it too.'

'No. I mean in my mind.'

Sebastian rolled sleepily over towards me. 'Go to sleep. It'll be better in the morning.'

I lay awake for the rest of the night, unable to adjust to the new stillness.

CECELIA

49. I'M NOT JUST ANOTHER CUSTOMER
NUMBER

By dawn the following day, even with the drone of distant traffic and the chirping of birds, the world outside my room still seemed quiet. In the early hours, I tried to make sense of my future. Not knowing or being able to control what might happen made me feel anxious, and the churning in my stomach, as a result, kept me awake even more. Eventually, I took solace from the opening sentence in *The Forest of Being*, my favourite book. The author, Agnieska Wlellna, warned her readers, *'The greatest challenge is the challenge of living'*. I realised at some point I would just have to accept those wise words to go on. I just didn't know if I could.

For the first few days after leaving the orchestra permanently, my subconscious hadn't processed that I wasn't actually working, and I had more time to focus on myself. In addition, my neck felt a little better without the pressure of playing, and I was capable of doing a few more things like lifting small objects and jogging slowly. Our finances seemed to be temporarily okay too. The payout I had just received from the orchestra kept us going for a little while, and the possibility of money running out looked like a slightly distant toothless monster.

However, my new-found freedom didn't last long. Having more time for myself didn't translate to more time with my friends. I missed Annie, whom I hadn't seen since my farewell bash. The only contact we had was via a few texts. She said she would make contact when time allowed, as she was in 'overdrive' settling into her new position with the interstate orchestra. I tried to understand and be happy for her latest success but, instead, each message from her made me feel lonelier and lonelier.

Other orchestra members in my wider friendship group initially contacted me to offer commiserations, but they slowly drifted away. When I reached out to them, our conversations were usually short, and not one of them had the time or opportunity to share a coffee with me and have a good old-fashioned chinwag. It wasn't long before it dawned on me that I no longer had friends other than Sebastian. Annie and Fleur were going from my life, so the Terrific Three were no more. Life ahead was looking empty.

Sebastian and I needed to be progressively thrifty as time went on. With less money to spend, we had to forgo or severely limit fun activities, like going out to restaurants and cinemas, which were the mainstay of our dates. As each week passed, it became more challenging and complicated. I realised increasingly that Sebastian and I were on struggle street, financially and otherwise. Making it easier was the knowledge that we weren't the only ones doing it tough and I felt an extra sense of compassion for other people. At least we had enough money to put food on the table. We were the lucky ones in that respect.

Talk about money became increasingly frequent between us. Conversely, relationship talks diminished. By the fourth month, we were too preoccupied to do anything except exist.

We felt like an unemployment statistic when listening to the news. I wanted to work and be around people. But my world was shrinking inwards, knowing I lacked the skills to do anything other than play music. I was confronted by how severely dystonia limited my options. I applied for work in schools teaching music, but they told me I needed to be an active musician who could, on various instruments, demonstrate how to play. I couldn't even play scales on a beginner instrument such as a recorder, so teaching quickly became a non-option. I also applied for jobs in areas outside music to see what would happen. George gave me an excellent reference, but when potential employers read it, they said I was 'too specialised' or 'over qualified'.

My self-confidence, already shaky, took a hit with each job rejection, and the familiar knot in my stomach churned, thinking I would never work again. One of the things that kept me going was routine, and every morning I made sure I got up early, ate breakfast, listened to the news, and learned what was going on in the world.

One morning, nearly five months after leaving the orchestra, I saw an advertisement in the newspaper for a new job agency specialising in long-term unemployed. My previous contacts with agencies had proven humiliating. They weren't willing to help for various reasons. Some were quite offensive too, saying things such as, 'Sorry, we're not set up to deal with people like you.' I was left feeling like a damaged doormat.

In the end, I wasn't sure how long someone had to be unemployed to be classified *long-term*. Still, I knew it was my destiny if I didn't try, so I gave the agency a call and organised an interview.

With persuasion from the agency, a large data processing firm agreed to take me on, under contract and probation, mainly to fill their requirement with the government to employ diverse workers. It felt good to know someone was willing to help me, and finally, after six months in the doldrums, I was about to start work again. However, there was little excitement about my imminent job other than it being an avenue to pay the bills and put food on the table. The position was to be clerical, and it filled me with scepticism. I wondered how I could get through each day in a repetitive and unfulfilling job. Unlike playing in the orchestra that inspired me, administrative work didn't present much of a challenge. There was little spontaneity and room for independent thought or creativity. In the orchestra, my days were full of imagination and inventiveness, where I could add my individual interpretation to the music within the bounds of the composer's vision.

After a restless night's sleep, at eight-fifteen in the morning, I found myself standing outside the big office building where I was going to start work. It felt unusual to dress for work at such an early hour. In the orchestra, my work day started in the evenings or after-noons for rehearsals. As I stood there, thousands of people bustled and hustled around me on a busy city street, and it was easy to be mistaken for an ant in all the hullaballoo.

I walked in and introduced myself to the receptionist. There, I met my new supervisor, Loren. She took me up to my desk in a walk that seemed a mile. Along the way, we hardly spoke. I simply wasn't sure of what to say. Instead, I let myself observe her. She wore a black suit, not unlike the required dress in the orchestra, but her eyes were glazed over and darkened as if she had spent years in a small shadowy room. Loren's clothes made her look like someone I knew in the orchestra, but her face told a different story. I wondered how Loren's wrinkles were formed. Was it the stress and unfulfillment in her job, or was it simply age? She looked older than she probably was, maybe around fifty, and I hoped my new job wouldn't have the same effect on me.

She smiled at me in the elevator, and I tucked my chin a little into my chest in an attempt to hide my dystonia. She was aware of my condition but politely and respectfully hadn't mentioned it, which I appreciated. In comparison, everyone in the orchestra knew and gossiped about my neck, and the result hadn't been good. I worried that if my new colleagues in the office found out, the consequences might be the same. The prospect of hiding dystonia throughout my working life seemed ominous, and my mind raced a little about when and how to 'come out'. It was a question amongst many others, and it remained unanswered as I nervously strode into my new, unfamiliar world.

We arrived on the tenth floor to an ample open space full of what looked like a hundred desks. Loren showed me to one desk in a corner, stacked with files.

'So, this is where you'll be working,' she said.

My eyes scanned the small space. There was virtually nothing: no window, no view, not even a pot plant—just a picture of flowers hanging on a distant wall. Bland is the word that came to my mind as I sat down and adjusted my body awkwardly to look at the computer screen.

'Do you know spreadsheets?' Loren asked.

My tax return was the last time my fingers graced a keyboard, I remembered, and although spreadsheets weren't a big part of my life, I felt confident enough about using them.

'Umm ... yes,' I answered.

Loren smiled again. 'Great.' She opened a paper file, placed it next to my computer, and pointed to numbers on a sheet of paper inside. 'What you'll be doing is entering data from these files into the corresponding fields in the spreadsheet. If you've got any questions, just ask Jenny.'

A middle-aged woman sitting at an adjoining desk put down her paperwork and mutely grinned at me. I smiled back, noting she could pass for a Loren clone.

'Is that all I have to do?' I asked.

Loren nodded. 'Yep! Just for starters.'

I forced a smile, but Loren didn't seem to notice. 'So, head down, bum up, and get to it. Good luck!' she beamed.

I watched her leave, thinking of the enormous yet straightforward task ahead of me. I closed my eyes in desperation and whispered silently to myself, 'I can do this; I can do this,' as my fingers started typing.

The fingers that once graced my bassoon now floated over a keyboard.

Jenny turned to me, sensing my sadness. 'I've been here ten years,' she said happily, trying to cheer me up. I looked back at her, without smiling, and studied her. I quickly realised there was something other than her being a Loren clone that made me feel uneasy. It was her perfume. The smell of it threw me back to another time and place when Sebastian had shown me the *Discoveries in Brain Science* magazine, which had also smelt of the same perfume. I wondered if I could like Jenny, but was wary as a result of the strange reminder.

Thrown by the smell, as I typed, I made many mistakes and hurriedly corrected them. The numbers on my computer screen flooded before my eyes:

CUSTOMER NUMBER: 4765310
CUSTOMER NUMBER:
CUSTOMER NUMBER: 4755310
CUSTOMER NUMBER:
CUSTOMER NUMBER: 4763310
CUSTOMER NUMBER:
CUSTOMER NUMBER: 4764310

My fingers stopped typing with my head in a spin, and I began to think of my bassoon. I struggled to comprehend that what I was doing was so different to my times on stage. Panic started to well throughout my body, just like it had in the orchestra when I couldn't play.

I took a few deep, slow breaths and focussed on a shadowy shape on the floor, imagining what animal it might look like, which was just enough to shake off my nerves and enable me to continue.

SEBASTIAN

50. THE SLOWPOKE

Sometimes doing what you love is a bad thing. Take writing, for example. It's like sport. Even if you're good at it, you'll look like a bumbling fool if you don't play and practise. But that's the thing: *practice*. It's hard to do because life gets in the way.

That being said, writers, including me, Sebastian 'slowpoke' Cavendish, innately find themselves in a catch-22 situation. They need to focus deeply on what they're writing, but that intensity takes their attention away from living. On the other hand, they need life experiences to write something worthwhile. Add to all that writer's block. It's no wonder writers find themselves staring at and sweating over a blank piece of paper before deciding to eat chocolate and play video games instead.

The greatest fear for a writer is failure. They spend years on a beloved novel or script, working their brain cells so hard they bleed. Then, if they are lucky, their work is published and sold in a two-dollar bin before it's used to line the bottom of a parrot cage. For a writer, even that's a victory worthy of an Oscar.

All that dysfunction spills over into real life. That is, the qualities someone needs to be a writer are consistent with those of a living, breathing yet flawed human. Writing requires effort, concentration and persistence, and an acceptance to have a pie thrown in one's face once their work becomes public. That amount of effort is exhausting and addictive. Being a writer, and living with a writer, is like living with a drug addict. For a writer, the constant need for a hit is all that matters. God knows, I know about all this. There have been enough films made about a writer's lot.

———

With Cecelia at work, a part of me guiltily looked forward to the opportunity to do some writing again. I enjoyed being with her when she was at home, and we spent a lot of quality time with one another in close proximity. Often, during that time, my emotions wavered between excitement and disappointment with her, as there were things we could and couldn't do due to her dystonia. But after a while, the biggest let-down became my writing. Each time my attention focussed on Cecelia as her carer, I journeyed further away from my scripts, emotionally and physically. It began to take a toll. I needed to write, and that's all there was to it. Internally, I battled resentment and dumb bad luck that had forced its medical hand on Cecelia and our household.

The day finally came when I was alone, and I felt inspired and motivated enough to enjoy a full day working on my script. My head had been swimming with ideas, and I spent breakfast writing notes and outlines instead of reading the newspaper or watching television. It felt luxurious to have so much free time when usually the best I could do between household tasks was steal ten minutes here or there to write.

I sat down at my computer and started to type a few words, but something strange happened. My motivation suddenly dropped. I just didn't feel like writing. That had rarely happened before, especially in times when I knew with clarity what to write. The compulsion to put words on a page just wasn't there. I drew my fingers away from the keyboard, lay back in my chair, and let my mind rummage for ways to get my mojo back. Eventually, I did what any self-respecting writer would do: I searched the internet. That didn't help either, still nothing.

So I grabbed my car keys and left the house. Whilst trudging along the driveway, I thought a drive in my trusty Jaguar would clear my head. The problem was, the car wouldn't start. Not immediately anyway. It must have taken about five attempts before the engine came to life. When it did, the radio played loud, heavy metal music. I immediately switched the radio station to something quieter and more soothing. A radio announcer introduced the next piece: 'Now, coming up for your listening pleasure, Mozart's Bassoon Concerto in B-flat major.'

Abruptly, I switched off the radio. With the click of the off switch, my car began jerking and stalling to a halt. I shouted, 'For crying out loud!' in exasperation.

Five more attempts and the car still wouldn't start. I banged my hands on the steering wheel angrily. 'For fuck's sake!' I shouted again.

The car door started to slam shut as I got out, and I gave it a hard kick which stopped it from closing. I opened the hood and found nothing wrong.

'Stupid car! Stupid, bloody car!'

I traipsed back indoors and ended up falling asleep on the couch.

So much for my productive day.

CECELIA

51. BITS AND BYTES

I survived! My first day at a new job! Cecelia is working again!

The day panned out slowly and, to be honest, better than expected. Other than lunch and tea breaks, I spent my time at my computer typing into a spreadsheet. That was definitely boring, and I felt a beloved part of my brain shutting down and turning to mush with each keystroke. However, as the day progressed, I became proud of myself for improving my knowledge and skill in using computers and their software. Who would have thought there could be something exciting about learning a whole new language on computers? My fingers were sore by the end of the day, much like they were sometimes after a concert. Interestingly, that was something both careers had in common.

During lunch, Jenny filled me in on essential company details such as policies, pay and human resources. I met a few other employees and was pleasantly surprised by their down-to-earth nature and good humour. Jokes became a way to get through the day and make it more interesting, and I found myself laughing and smiling on more than one occasion. Before midday, for example, I asked Jenny what she was having for lunch, as my tummy was growling and wanting food. She said, as she was eating a banana, 'Gorilla cheese sandwiches.' I giggled at her 'cheesy' joke and began to like her, after initially feeling wary. It made my whole body and neck feel better. Just as importantly, no one seemed to notice my dystonia, perhaps because some other employees had disabilities too.

Still, doing eight hours of work in one day meant I didn't have much energy left afterwards. When I got home, merely walking to the front door seemed like a mountainous challenge with my twisting body. Sebastian's Jaguar didn't help either, as it lay dormant in the driveway behind my car that still had a dented door from the accident. I was surprised to see that the Jaguar's doors were left wide open for all to see.

When I entered the house, Sebastian was lazily typing on his computer and scrolling through puppy pictures. They were cute but annoying images. It didn't seem fair that he got to play around with fun things while I worked my arse off bringing in the money.

'What's wrong with the Jag?' I asked sternly.

Sebastian fell back in his chair, still smiling over a photo of a golden retriever splashing in a pool. He flicked back to his film script. 'It's kaput. Send the damn thing to the junkyard,' he said.

I peered over to see what he was typing and noticed a grammar mistake. 'There's a rogue comma,' I said, pointing to the screen.

Sebastian got up and rolled back his chair for me. 'Feel free to proofread, smartypants.'

I smiled wryly and began to sit down, but I banged my knee on the chair leg in the process. It set off my dystonia in a horrible way, to the point where just getting my bum on the seat became a major logistical exercise.

Sebastian stepped back and his expression softened, looking understanding and caring at my struggle. As I landed on the seat, I groaned, which made Sebastian's appearance change. He watched me, shocked and concerned.

Because of its non-ergonomic set-up, focusing on a computer screen at home seemed more difficult than at work. I shifted my body sideways to compensate, so my face lined up with what I was trying to see.

'Do you know how much your head is at an angle?' Sebastian asked.

'Acutely,' I replied.

Sebastian pulled up another chair.

'Let me show you how bad it is.' He started imitating me, typing on the keyboard but making a lot of mistakes. He stopped abruptly and rubbed his neck. 'Just me twisting like this even for a few seconds hurts my eyes. Everything's blurry,' he exclaimed.

'Try doing that all day, every day,' I said, as I corrected some typos. When I fixed the misspelt word, *broken*, it reminded me of Sebastian's car again. 'Maybe we should sell the Jag?' I asked.

Sebastian scoffed, and the sound of it immediately reminded me of our previous Bowen arguments. Hairs raised on the back of my neck once more.

Sebastian rolled his eyes condescendingly. 'And castrate me in the process.'

I stopped proofreading and stood up curtly, which made my neck tighten. 'We can't afford the repairs,' I said.

'Yeah, right.'

My body immediately tensed as it recognised the possibility of another verbal stoush. I stepped back slightly to take a few deep breaths. 'Have you even tried finding work today?' I said softly, hoping the low tone in my voice would have a soothing effect like it often did.

'Of course,' he said.

'Sebastian, I don't want a fight,' I pleaded.

'Okay. Okay.'

'But I need to know. Did you even try to find work today?'

'Of course.'

'Today?'

'I was writing.'

'All day?'

Sebastian widened his arms as if he had just caught a giant fish and wanted to show me its size.

'It's a big script,' he said exaltedly.

I couldn't believe it. There was something in the tone of Sebastian's voice and his body language that just didn't make his words sound believable. My blood started to boil, and I was getting too tired to turn down the heat. 'You should be looking harder!' I exclaimed.

Sebastian looked at me with disdain. 'Do you even know what it's like to get rejections?' he asked, as if he already knew the answer.

I shook my head, as best I could with a crappy neck, and walked to the door.

'You have no idea,' I whispered to myself.

But Sebastian heard me. 'Fair go, Cecelia. I don't want to argue either.'

'Fair go!' I barked.

'Yeah, fair go.'

That was it. My anger had reached the tipping point. I yelled, 'Fair go! I'm the one with the disability! Fair go! I'm the one who works! Fair go! It should be the other way around!'

I stormed out, leaving Sebastian kicking the chair. Every part of me was so angry, I didn't even care if the chair smashed the computer in the process. 'It's not my fault,' I heard him scream, as I slammed the front door.

I turned back and yelled loudly enough to make the neighbourhood dogs bark. 'It's not my fault, either!'

Still fuming, I got into the Jag. The fact that it blocked Ronnie, my beloved Renault in the driveway, didn't help my mood. I tried to start the car. At first, it wouldn't go, but the engine kicked over and came to life on the third attempt. I ground the gearshift into reverse and tried to turn my head backwards to see where I was going. It was then that excruciating pain shot through my neck. 'Ow!' I yelled.

I quickly realised my body simply couldn't turn enough to look behind me. Attempting to compensate with my legs and torso did nothing. I punched the steering wheel with my tight-fisted hand.

'Ow!' I yelled again. There was nothing I could do. Without the ability to look around me, driving was out of the question.

I got out of the car and picked up a sprinkler from the lawn before throwing it hard through the Jag's windscreen. The reverse force made me fall to the ground.

Smashed glass found its way throughout the car and all over its surfaces, including its interior and the driveway. I lay there panting like a wounded animal, admiring my handiwork, as the shards glistened in the late afternoon sun.

As the steam from my breath filled the air around my face, I took comfort in knowing one critical component of my new self: dystonia stole my freedom, but anger gave me strength.

CECELIA

52. DIVERSITY

The next few days were tense. Life at home became increasingly awkward and stressful. Sebastian and I still talked, and we did our best to be calm and respectful, but underneath, we knew we had problems to resolve. Neither of us seemed ready to take the first step, though. Besides, I was too busy and tired with work, and Sebastian had his mind on his writing like never before.

We mentioned Bowen therapy and Sebastian not working a few times. The conversations became a little heated, but we understood it to be okay to leave things be for the time being. We made some progress and agreed we needed time to adjust to our new lifestyles. The important thing was that I felt we were both willing to compromise, or at least come up with a plan at a later date to live with our differences.

But it wasn't easy to defer communication, which sometimes resulted in us losing patience over the simplest of things. One night, for example, Sebastian accidentally dropped a fork on the floor. That's something we have all been guilty of, including me, but picking it up for him, as a thoughtful favour, became overly upsetting. It was hard for me to bend down where it landed, and he felt it unfair that the cutlery gods made it happen in the first place. It resulted in Sebastian saying several swear words that I hadn't heard in a long time.

Work became a kind of solace where I could rest my mind and not think too hard, a vastly different lifestyle from my previous workplace. My colleagues accepted me into their group, and we got along well. Loren was happy with my work, and I received training on other types of computer software. As the software was new to me, I found it surprisingly interesting.

After a few weeks in the workplace, I realised my neck could more or less handle the tasks required, but hiding my dystonia became too difficult. Rather than holding my head and tucking my chin into my chest for most of the day, which made me sore and look weird at best, I plucked up the courage to come out about it. I was worried it might affect any promotional chances and make me a social pariah. Still, to my surprise, my colleagues took it well. They asked questions such as, 'How long have you had dystonia?' and 'What's it like?' to understand me better.

At first, I confided in Jenny as she was my closest colleague. Knowing her the longest, I felt I could trust her the most, despite the previous strange memories her perfume had awakened in me. She initiated the exchange in the staff kitchen while I struggled to make a cup of tea.

She asked, 'Are you okay?'

I reasoned that sooner or later, my colleagues would realise something was up, so it was better to confess before it caused any embarrassment or conflict.

Coming out about my dystonia certainly gave me a little understanding of what other people from diverse community groups must go through every day.

———

Home life was a stark contrast to work life. What soothed things between Sebastian and me, however, was that eventually, he did find a job. Like me, he was to work in an office, and I felt excited for him. He seemed excited too, if for nothing but the money. He would have enough money to fix his Jaguar. We were going to live on two incomes, and with that came some financial freedom at last. For me, I hoped Sebastian would understand a little more about the nature of my new work, because he would be doing it too.

SEBASTIAN

53. LIFE IN THE DUNGEON

Suits. That's what surrounded me. Various shades of grey suits. White shirts. Black or blue ties. For the ladies, black dresses or slacks. And worse, I wore grey too. I thought to myself, I'm a writer and film-maker! I refuse to do this! Gone were my favourite film-set jeans and cool T-shirts. Just grey office clothes. What an awful, dull, lifeless colour.

Not only that, my grey trousers were tight and uncomfortable. Vinh, my new boss, showed me to my new desk, and it was difficult to walk as my pants were riding up my crotch. But I didn't care. As we traversed through a sea of desks, the only thing on my mind was that Vinh's suit at least had pin stripes. What a rebel, what a neo-James Dean, I thought.

I sat down as my eyes scanned my new domain, thinking: better to be out on the streets and rubbish-filled alleys than here. At least there'd be something interesting to see. Rats, winos, anything as long as it wasn't a grey or white wall. What a hellhole.

Vinh smiled at me. His face looked lined and washed out. God, he looked seventy. Probably not a day over forty. Please, God, don't let me turn into him. Shite. I don't believe in God. Who the bloody hell is going to help me here in this place?

'Welcome to your new home, Sebastian!' beamed Vinh, as he looked sheepishly at me. Maybe he does know how bad it is? I thought to myself.

Before me lay a huge pile of files packed high. If they were joined together, they'd make a long roll of bog paper.

'Grab a file, and I'll show you what to do,' ordered Vinh. In my mind I answered, I take orders from no one! Except maybe James Dean.

I grabbed the top file and opened it.

'Now. Enter the details as listed on the database,' Vinh asked.

'Got it,' I replied overenthusiastically.

'Great! Any problems, just ask Jack.'

Jack, a twenty-something hipster in another grey suit, saluted me. He looked like a Hawaiian politician at a press conference with his long hair and beard. He seemed a little cooler than the other robots around me, so I nodded back to him.

Vinh left, and I started typing on the computer:

THE QUICK BROWN FOX JUMPED OVER THE LAZY DOG

When I finished, a scrunched-up piece of paper hit me on the forehead. I looked up. Jack was looking at me, pleased he had hit his target.

'Welcome to the dungeon,' he said, as he rolled up another piece of paper. I laughed, and we ended up playing paper-ball tennis for a few minutes. Maybe this wasn't going to be as bad as I thought?

Still, I whispered under my breath, 'Welcome to my nightmare.'

CECELIA

54. YES, BUT . . .

It was Saturday night, and Sebastian and I felt beaten after several busy weeks at work. We talked about going out to dinner but decided to stay in, eat pizza, and watch a movie on television instead. We readily agreed that cooking was out of the question, and the night was to be lazy and recuperative. The only things to worry about were not falling asleep before the end credits and whether the pizza had enough mozzarella.

Sebastian handed me a cup of tea before the movie started.

'Milk?' I asked.

'Oops. Sorry. I forgot.'

I sipped it anyway.

Sebastian put the DVD on and relaxed next to me.

'Here we go,' he said expectantly. He was excited. It was one of his favourite films from the 1950s, *Joseph's Gallery*, starring Hunter Michaelwoods and Jennifer Jeremy. I enjoyed it too. It had a lovely romantic, ethereal quality, and I looked forward to seeing it again.

The title credits began, and I let out a big yawn as the star, Hunter Michaelwoods, began his opening monologue:

... there is dystopia far worse than any mortal can bequeath. It is akin to
a death of the creative, where
the world is no longer lived in. In all, I felt I could not continue.

Suddenly, Sebastian got up and abruptly turned off the movie. He startled me. 'Wait. It was just getting started,' I complained, hoping he would start the film again.

Sebastian frowned. 'And now it's finished,' he said.

I shrugged my shoulders, unsure of what Sebastian was thinking. Clearly, he didn't want to watch the film.

It wasn't that important to me in the greater scheme of things, other than a way to relax, so I gave in. 'I guess I didn't feel like watching it, anyway,' I conceded.

Sebastian's head dropped, and his eyes started to tear up. 'Are you okay?' I asked.

'What Hunter Michaelwoods said. It's too close to the bone.'

'The bit about dystopia or the death of the creative?'

'Both.'

He turned to me. 'Why don't you ever cry, Cecelia?' he asked. His face looked stern in a way that pressured me for an immediate answer.

I resented his tone, and I thought the question was disrespectful, but I tried to remain calm. 'What good will that do?' I asked, wanting to know more about how his mind was working.

'Crying is a healthy way of releasing emotion,' he said.

'Yes, but other ways do that too, like listening to music.'

'Yes, but I've never seen you cry.'

I rolled my eyes. 'Yes. But. Can you say, *"Yes, and"* instead? It's a much more healthy and productive way of talking.'

'Yes, and I've never seen you cry.'

I grabbed a cushion and put it between us. Goosebumps appeared on my arms from Sebastian's attitude, and I checked myself, realising a new feeling was building up inside me. Then, almost without thought, I said, 'You don't need to tell me how to feel or what to do, Sebastian.'

Taken aback, Sebastian stood up and paced around the room. I watched him in silence.

'Cecelia. Office work is sucking our souls!' he exclaimed.

'Tell me, what's the alternative?' I asked.

Sebastian shrugged his shoulders. 'I don't know. I don't know. All I know is that I don't want this.'

I sat up straight. 'Sebastian, this is our life. If you don't like your work, you can always find something else.'

'Why don't you feel the same?' he responded.

I stood up. I didn't like the way Sebastian was above me when he spoke. 'I don't like the situation any more than you do,' I retorted.

'I know. Neither do I.'

Sebastian dropped his shoulders in defeat. He whispered, 'I just don't have your strength.'

I stepped forward. 'Sebastian, you know I can't support you not working.'

'I work,' he bit back. 'I do housework. I do gardening. I do lots of stuff because you can't.'

My voice softened. 'Of course,' I said. 'And I appreciate it.'

Sebastian backed away and headed for the front door. As he turned to me, he said softly, 'I just don't have the energy anymore.'

'Wait! What do you mean?' I asked.

'I can't help you. Not as much as you need help anyway.'

The front door slammed shut just as I shouted, 'You sound like a shrink!'

CECELIA

55. EVERYONE NEEDS A LIZZY IN THEIR LIVES

When I woke up the following day, I didn't know where Sebastian had spent the night, yet again. My thoughts and feelings were torn between not caring too much when I was angry, and desperately wanting him in bed when I felt lonely.

I felt annoyed at Sebastian but also somehow thankful to him. His words were valid and hard to hear, but they also gave me the impetus to do something more. So, during the dark alone hours of the early morning, I decided to do some research. I realised there were still unanswered questions, and if Sebastian couldn't help me, I'd just have to help myself.

With my laptop's screen shedding a dull light around my bedroom and Wills' coat shedding fur over my blanket, I typed 'dystonia' into the search engine. Hundreds of results came up, and I started scrolling. My eyes darted across the screen, reading its contents. A link soon appeared:

AUSTRALIAN DYSTONIA SUPPORT GROUP

My body relaxed as I exhaled deeply. As I read more, I smiled a bittersweet smile and clicked on the group's contact button. I began to type:

Hi, my name is Cecelia, and I am reaching out. I feel so tired and so alone. I have cervical dystonia, and it is destroying me. It's ruined my job, my greatest love, and my relationships, and now my enjoyment of life itself. Is it just me, or is life with dystonia really hard? I've tried everything, and nothing has helped. Not in the way I want it to anyway.

Later that day, as the afternoon was settling in, I found myself unexpectedly sitting in a quiet café, sipping tea. My eyes and mind were in a kind of trance as they stared at a young couple nearby who were obviously in love.

My spell was broken by a lady wearing a bright yellow coat. She was about my age and walking towards me. Her attention was on the young couple, too, not in the direction of where she walked. I feared she would bump into my table, and that's precisely what she did.

'Oops,' she said, as she stretched out her hand towards me. 'Hi. You must be Cecelia. I'm Lizzy.'

'Oh. Hi,' I said, shaking her hand lightly. 'Please ... sit down.'

Lizzy removed her coat and proceeded to sit down as directed but she bumped the table once more. I watched her struggle to look at me squarely. It's then it hit me. Lizzy was just like me. She had dystonia too. My mind searched for something to say, but all that happened was my cheeks reddened.

Lizzy moved her seat to a forty-five degree angle, so we looked at each other face-to-face. 'Hey. It's okay. You get used to it,' she laughed.

I smiled quietly and took another sip of my tea. My eyes were in a trance again. They couldn't stop watching Lizzy's head turn uncontrollably.

Other café patrons stared at us, and it made my cheeks redden some more. Lizzy noticed. She gently and reassuringly held my hand and said, 'I was the same when I first saw someone else with dystonia.'

'Oh. Sorry,' I apologised.

'As I say, it's okay. Welcome to the family!' Lizzy punched her fist in the air in a kind of salute. 'Solidarity, right!?'

Her words and gentle nature sent a wave of relaxation through my body, and I was still a little awe-struck about what was going on. 'Oh ... right,' I smiled.

A young waitress walked past, and Lizzy grabbed her attention with such presence and ease, she could easily be a prime minister. 'What are you having?' she asked.

'Another tea ... please.'

Lizzy turned her attention back to the waitress. 'Can I have tea, please? Chamomile.'

'Me too,' I rushed to answer.

The waitress nodded and headed off to get our orders. Lizzy turned back to me and grinned. I noticed she had perfect teeth and wondered how she kept them that way. Since my dystonia, brushing mine became a massive task, and I worried that I had a mouth full of cavities. She took some brochures out of her handbag and gave them to me. I scanned them. They were all about living with dystonia and what services the dystonia support group offered. I couldn't help but smile again. I said with surprising ease since Lizzy was still a stranger, 'Not so long ago, I didn't even know what dystonia was ... and now there's a group for it.'

Lizzy squeezed my hand again. 'It's like a comforting backup I carry with me every day. No one else understands. In hard times, I just think of the group and feel supported.'

I nodded as best I could, which seemed to attract the attention of prying café patrons again. My cheeks didn't burn like before, though. I simply shrugged them off. 'Sometimes, I wish they could experience it for just one day,' I said. 'Then they would know the pain.'

'Even then, I'm sure some still wouldn't understand.'

'You're probably correct,' I said, as the waitress returned with our chamomile teas. I took a sip which soon turned into a gulp. 'This is yummy.'

Lizzy agreed. 'I find it relaxing. Sometimes herbal tea helps my dystonia a little too.'

We sat there in silence for a few seconds, happily sipping and enjoying our teas. My mind wandered towards my new work colleagues, which made me realise I hadn't asked Lizzy what she did for a living yet. It interested me as I read that many people living with dystonia have to reduce their career choices, and I still felt alone in my experiences. 'So, how do you get by? I mean ... do you work?' I asked.

'Oh! I haven't done that for years,' she said. 'I used to be a teacher if that's what you mean.'

'What happened?' I asked, conscious that my questions may come across as an interrogation. Lizzy seemed to take it in her stride.

'Other than dystonia? People who thought they knew better made decisions about me.'

'That sucks!' I said a little too loudly.

We laughed and continued chatting until long past dinner time. It felt terrific and, later, as I left, I wondered if Lizzy was my long-lost twin sister.

———

My time with Lizzy couldn't have been in more contrast to my home life. As I came home and walked to the front door, I noticed that both our cars sitting in the driveway were in a state of disrepair that, in some ways, resembled our relationship. The good thing is that cars and relationships can be fixed and, with the confidence and high borne of my time with Lizzy, I resolved to have a good heart-to-heart with Sebastian.

When I entered the house, Wills and Sebastian had already made their way to bed, and both were half asleep. I exhaled with the knowledge that Sebastian had made it safely home again. As I tip toed into the bedroom, they both mumbled, 'Grrrff', upon hearing me put my pyjamas on and slip into bed. It made me giggle.

I stroked Wills gently behind his left ear and turned to Sebastian to whisper, 'Good night,' into his right ear.

Sebastian awoke slightly and said abruptly, 'Really?'

I moved closer to him. 'Never go to sleep angry,' I whispered, hoping it would start a conversation.

Sebastian pulled the sheet over his shoulder. 'Cecelia, I'm tired.'

'Sebastian, talk to me, please,' I pleaded.

He turned around to face me. 'Okay, I'll talk to you. I'm exhausted.'

I softened in understanding. After all, I felt exhausted too. 'I can see that, but there is a solution.'

Sebastian's body tensed, and it quickly became apparent sleep was out of the question for both of us. 'What!?' he snapped.

'Perhaps you can find other work? Something more challenging.'

Suddenly, Sebastian jumped out of bed. The force from the blankets pushed Wills to the floor, and he ran out with his tail between his legs as if it was all his fault. Sebastian moved to stop him but banged his foot on a side table. 'Shit!' he screamed.

'Are you all right?' I asked.

'Of course not! he retorted.

Sebastian stepped further away from me and grabbed Wills. Before he left, he turned back to me and said angrily, waving his arms around, 'Cecelia, this is … this is shite! I'm in a dead-end job! I'm too tired to look for another one! My soul is dead, and having money won't fix it! And your Bowen … and … and … dystonia. It's all … all … shit!'

'Well, thanks for your choice of words.'

Sebastian scanned his foot. 'Shit! I've broken a nail!' he snarled.

I ignored his foot, my mind still squarely on his rant. 'What are you saying?' I asked. 'You know I had no say in getting dystonia.'

Sebastian stepped back apologetically. 'Look. I'm sorry to say this, Cecelia … but … I need space … I think we should separate.'

CECELIA

56. VOWS

What is the best thing to do when someone's partner says they want to separate? That's the question I asked myself as I heard Sebastian and Wills leave and shut the front door that day. Night after night afterwards, I lay in bed for hours, searching, not sure if I found the answer to that question.

At first, I was angry at Sebastian for what he said, especially as he said it with a few choice four-letter words. His profanity was a side of him I didn't particularly like. I could see he had a lot of pent-up anger, but there was no need for him to express it the way he did, even though he had something huge to say. I hoped that was the last time I would ever hear him speak in such a manner, and with that, I wondered if I would ever speak to him again at all.

As for my anger, it didn't last for long. My world cooled living alone, and I spent a lot of that time thinking of our wedding vows, *for better or for worse*. For me, vows were forever. My dystonia certainly made life worse, and Sebastian had every right to be angry about it. So was I. But no one could be blamed for my medical condition or our feelings because of it. A new awareness was growing in me that some people develop chronic conditions even if they have lived healthy and happy lives. They live on, and many still do great things. I was starting to learn that opportunities, despite my disability, or disabilities anyone had for that matter, still awaited to be grabbed and enjoyed. And opportunities, like they had been since Sebastian and I first met, were one of the many driving forces in our relationship.

But without any close friends, I desperately wanted to talk to someone, anyone, so I drove to my mum's house to break the bad news to her. She took it supportively, but my positive resolve started to fall apart as I spilled the beans and told her the sordid details.

I sat in the kitchen, trying in vain to look at a photo of Sebastian that Mum kept on the counter. 'It's gone! It's over!' I shrieked, as Mum handed me a cup of tea.

I took a sip, but as I put the cup down, my neck jerked sideways. It made the tea spill all over the benchtop and floor.

'Jesus!' I screamed, as I frantically attempted to clean up the mess.

Mum grabbed a paper towel. 'Now calm down. Let's think about it,' she said, as she began to wipe the spillage.

I covered my face in my hands and tutted between my fingers, 'I've lost everything!'

Mum started to sound annoyingly motherly. 'We all have our crosses to bear,' she said.

Her words didn't help. I took a deep breath and lowered my voice a little, and it felt and sounded husky. 'So much for following our dreams,' I croaked. 'All we had was next to nothing. I've failed at everything!'

Mum spoke in a tone I hadn't heard since I was a teenager.

'Don't be silly!' she said. 'Why can't you see how strong you are and all you've achieved?'

I slapped my fist on the table. It hurt. 'I've achieved nothing!'

Mum stayed silent and let me vent while she continued to clean up the spilt tea.

'That's what I love about Sebastian. He's not giving up on his dreams. But my stupid neck has stopped him!'

Mum interrupted. 'He's been a carer. That's hard for anyone.'

I uncovered my face and softened. 'Was I too hard on Sebastian, Mum?'

She threw the dirty paper towel in the rubbish bin dismissively with a that's-the-end-of-that brashness. 'No,' she said. 'Your neck was too hard on Sebastian.'

I saw my reflection on the clean benchtop, and it wasn't a pretty sight. I smiled a little anyway.

Trust Mum, I thought. She always had the right attitude.

––––––

The next day, I arrived at work bleary-eyed and tired. As I sat at my desk to begin, the day ahead seemed long. A lot of work had piled up, and there wasn't enough time to finish it before 5.00 pm.

I opened a file and stretched my body. Before my fingers touched my keyboard, Loren walked up to me and interrupted. 'Good morning, Cecelia. I thought you might like to know this. I've received some great feedback on your work.'

She took me by surprise, and my cheeks reddened. 'Really?'

'Yes. And there's a new position available. It's a promotion. Are you interested?' Loren asked.

In the corner of my eye, I saw Jenny looking on jealously.

'Yes, I am,' I answered, embarrassed.

She patted me on my back gently. 'Good work. I'll talk to you more about the position later. So go out and celebrate tonight. Just not too much!'

I nodded slowly, not wanting to hurt my neck. 'I'll do my best,' I said.

For a moment, I felt pleased, but then, all of a sudden, thoughts of my home life entered my mind. They overwhelmed me, and sadness gripped my body.

Luckily, Loren had already walked away and didn't see me.

SEBASTIAN – EARLY YEARS
57. A BOY AND HIS DOG

A young boy once learnt a rewarding method for dealing with change when he spent a night alone in the wilderness with his dog, a corgi crossbreed named Sophie.

His family had moved to a new suburb the week before, and he missed his old friends. He didn't like having to start a new school and find new friends either. For a shy little boy, that sounded way too hard.

Realising his fear, one day his mother drove past some kids playing cricket. She stopped the car, and said, 'Sebastian, go make friends.' Sebastian argued with her, but as mothers often do, she won, and he ended up having to obey her. So, the boy nervously approached the kids and asked if he could join in. They laughed at and mocked him instead.

That night, to cheer himself up, he cuddled Sophie while he planned a big adventure: returning to what he saw as his rightful home.

Early the following day, Sebastian packed his lunch and set off with Sophie. They got onto a bus Sebastian thought would go straight to his old suburb. Instead, it took them to a nature park where they alighted and began to explore. As they walked around, the park soon turned into a wilderness, but they didn't care. Sebastian and his dog were having too much fun seeing the wild animals. Sophie enjoyed chasing them. Night arrived quickly, and they set up camp under a tree, much like they had camped in their backyard during summer. They watched the stars and munched over his remaining sandwiches and biscuits. By good luck, police found them early next morning and took them home. For the boy, that was all part of his big adventure.

Naturally, his parents were angry when they arrived home. The young boy argued with his mother again before she grounded him in his room, where he spent hours recapping his journey, playing with toys and writing short stories, Sophie by his side.

They were escaping the pressures of their new life.

SEBASTIAN

58. RUNNING WILD

As I sat in a crowded café tapping on my laptop, writing my script, the words came easily for me that day. I had just left Cecelia behind, and despite everything, being away from home freed my mind, and I felt in the zone. It had become a rare state of being for me of late, and I savoured every minute. I wished I had more.

Several hours passed, and I sat back, admiring my work. Just then, a familiar blonde woman slinked past. She still looked as much like Marilyn Monroe as when we first met. I smiled in recognition and was glad to see her.

'Well, kiss my thirsty lips!' she said in a perfect Californian accent. 'Working on your next Oscar winner, eh?'

I laughed. 'We live in hope.'

Before I could do anything about it, she flung her arms out and wrapped them around me. It felt nice, even nicer when her large chest squeezed against mine, and I found myself returning her affection with almost as much enthusiasm.

She pushed my plate aside and sat opposite me. 'So, how's your protagonist getting along?' she asked.

I sat there, wondering what to do or say. Reading aloud didn't seem a good option in such a crowded place, so I invited her to read what I had typed, even though I felt reserved about it. 'Go ahead. Check the ending for yourself,' I said.

'Sure!' she beamed.

I turned my laptop screen towards her. We sat in silence while she read my work. Occasionally, she looked up at me to smile again. I smiled back, self-conscious and a little embarrassed about the fact that she was reading my work ... and that I was admiring her rose perfume and glistening golden hair.

'Hmmm,' she nodded. 'Not bad.'

She slid her hand across the table to touch my hand. At first, mine pulled away. Then I let her, and we continued talking.

After all, I could do what I wanted. I was free.

CECELIA

59. TORRENT

I walked to the train station with Loren's unexpected news buzzing in my head, trying to control a raging sadness growing inside me. As I stumbled along, something caught my eye in a café window, and I looked inside.

I couldn't believe what I saw. I froze as my body filled with shock.

Inside, Sebastian was holding hands and talking with an attractive blonde woman I didn't know. They looked way too affectionate together.

They didn't see me, but I ran to the train station as fast as I could.

When I got home, in my music room, I stared at my bassoon for hours. The torrent of sadness inside me had grown to the size of Niagara Falls.

As I stared at my beloved old friend in the dull light, two things hit me at once.

I was alone.

And I was crying.

SEBASTIAN

60. RUNNING WITH THE HORSES

My name is Sebastian, and I am now a free man!
Freedom! Woooooooo hooooooooo!

CECELIA

61. AULD LANG SYNE

Eventually, my tears dried and Annie entered my thoughts. I desperately wanted to share my struggles with her and get everything off my chest. I picked up the phone and dialled slowly, but when her phone started ringing, I grappled to keep the phone to my ear due to my twisting head and neck. It dampened my upbeat mood a little too quickly and made me feel solemn.

When Annie picked up her phone to answer, it was clear she was in a backstage room. All I could hear were musicians practising vigorously on their instruments. I talked loudly to compensate and blocked one ear with my finger so I could listen.

'Annie?' I shouted.

'Cecelia. Is that you?'

'Yes! It's been so long!'

Just as Annie was about to speak, a loud trumpet sound interrupted her. 'I'm sorry, Cecelia. We've got Wagner tonight.'

'Nothing can stop the ride of the Valkyries, right?' I giggled.

Annie's loudness softened slightly. 'I'd love to talk. You know that, but ...'

'I'm wondering when you can come back to see me?'

For a moment, there was silence before Annie spoke again. 'It's a crazy schedule here,' she said.

I tried to sound upbeat. 'It always is.'

'It's not the same as the Weistar Symphony, though.'

'There's no Christopher?'

Annie laughed. 'God doesn't exist here, Cecelia.'

A smirk, and then more silence.

'We'll always be the Dynamic Duo,' I said.

'Maybe at Christmas, eh?'

I smiled gently, hoping that would be the time we reunited, but I knew we probably wouldn't. 'I'd like that,' I replied.

Suddenly, our conversation was interrupted by the auditorium bell. I knew Annie had to leave.

Annie blew me a kiss over the phone. 'I gotta go. Sorry, Cecelia. Love you!' Her voice faded.

'Annie?' I asked again loudly.

'What was that, Cecelia?'

I took a second before answering. 'I just wanted to say ... goodbye ... Annie.'

'Oh! Bye!'

The auditorium bell rang once more, and I heard Annie move her phone away from her ear.

It sounded like she whimpered and I could picture tears in her eyes as she hung up.

Left in silence, I remained motionless and deep in thought, wondering if I really would see Annie again. Our lives had suddenly taken such a steep and different trajectory; it seemed unlikely and destined. Coming to that conclusion made my tears well up once more. However, I was determined not to break down in a bawling mess again, as tears had soaked away nearly all my energy, so I rubbed my neck and dried my eyes.

SEBASTIAN

62. PROWLING

I could get used to this. Okay, I'm in a crappy job and a dingy motel room right now, but hopefully not for long. That's the plan. Maybe I can get my own place? You know, a bachelor pad. Nothing fancy. A one-bedroom apartment will do—king-size bed, of course—Sebastian's lair.

I can get up when I want and come home when I please. Bring home whoever I like. Eat pizza. Watch movies. Write when my creative brain tells me to.

No pressure. No demands from anyone. Do what I desire and not put up with someone with so many problems.

And maybe someday, be free of Cecelia.

And be with someone else.

CECELIA

63. ANTIGRAMS

The prospect of losing Annie made me think of Fleur as well. My mind hurried with thoughts and memories of all the good times with her. Fleur and I didn't have a lot in common I conceded, but somehow, we gelled, and our times in and out of the orchestra were happy memories for both of us.

Time has a way of letting us reconsider things differently. With Fleur, she hadn't been at her best in times of trouble, but I felt compelled to know urgently if she still was my always friend or just a fair-weather one. With a heavy heart and a strong sense of scepticism, I phoned her.

'Hi, Fleur,' I said, not quite knowing what to say next.

'Cecelia!' she shouted, making me jump. She sounded out of breath as I heard her rustle around and compose herself.

'How are you?' I asked.

It also sounded like she had someone with her, of the deep breathing kind. I concluded she must have a new conquest again and rolled my eyes.

'It's been ages. Simply *eons*!' Fleur joked.

'I was hoping you could come over for a cup of tea?' I asked.

'I'm sorry, darling. I'm kind of busy right now.'

I sat in silence for a few seconds, not knowing what to say again, before suddenly blurting it all out senselessly. 'Sebastian and I have separated. I really could do with a friend.'

'Aw, darling. You two are so lovey-dovey. I'm sure you'll work it out.'

'It's a little more serious, Fleur.'

'Cecelia,' she said. 'I'd give anything to have a relationship like you and Sebastian. Why do you think I read all those self-help books and date all these men?'

It's then I heard a playful slapping sound and Fleur blowing her conquest a kiss. 'Men and women are made for disagreements,' she laughed. The male laughed in the background too. I was correct; she did have a new man, and my mood hardened.

'We used to be good friends when I was in the orchestra, Fleur. What's happened?'

'Well, you're not in the orchestra anymore.'

Taken aback by that comment, I felt anger rise inside me, although it quickly dissipated. Interestingly, I noticed it was a lower level of rage than when dystonia was new to me. I concluded that people just didn't seem to push my buttons as much anymore.

Nevertheless, Fleur was the focus of my feelings, and she proved disappointing once again. 'So, you're only friends with musicians now?' I asked.

'No, it's not that.' I heard the man try to kiss her. 'Can we talk later?' she replied.

She giggled again. 'I'm sorry, darling. I'll take a rain check on that tea.' It sounded like the man had progressed to nibbling her ear.

A tear ran down my cheek. Losing two friends in one day wasn't a good day, and it was becoming clear Fleur, just like Annie, wasn't going to be a big part of my life anymore.

I didn't feel like hearing Fleur wrestle with her man again, so I slowly pushed the phone away from me. I heard Fleur say, 'Cecelia. Cecelia!' before the man grunted, and I hung up.

The last words I ever heard her say were, 'I'm not in the mood anymore.'

Perhaps she was right. As far as orchestra politics and all of its problems were concerned, I was starting to feel the same way.

SEBASTIAN

64. I'M RIDIN' THE MUSTANG, BABY!

For a movie fan and scriptwriter, it felt like a perfect night in.

- Couch.
- Movie: *Bullitt* starring Steve McQueen (is there anyone cooler than Steve McQueen in *Bullitt*?)
- Me on said couch pining for a green 1968 Ford Mustang GT, just like the one McQueen drives in the movie.
- Popcorn.
- Eating popcorn.
- Corgi on lap eating popcorn.
- Corgi on floor, vacuuming spilt popcorn.
- And no one to bother me.

CECELIA

65. SECOND HOME

Thank God for taxis. They're a miracle for those of us who can't drive. I sat in the back seat of one, staring out the window, while the driver and I waited for a large crowd in front of us to disperse.

The surroundings were very familiar to me. We were outside the concert hall I had played in many hundreds of times.

Lost in my thoughts, I stared at the great hall. Sure, it was sad that I wasn't playing there anymore. Still, time and space since my concert days added a sense of romanticism to my memories. My lips even managed a small smile. A car beeped its horn, though, and it took me back to the present.

The way became clear, and the taxi driver steered the car into the concert hall car park. He turned to me and said, 'You know, I never really cared for that type of music.'

I smirked and paid him his fare. If only he knew, I thought.

'It's a matter of perspective, I suppose,' I laughed.

'Maybe.' The taxi driver shrugged his shoulders.

I got out and smiled at him. 'Thanks for the ride,' I said, as I made my way through the crowd and inside the hall.

Once inside the auditorium, I took my seat in the back row. The

Weistar Symphony Orchestra readied on stage. The piece began, and it was played with such intense enthusiasm, I worried I'd lose my hearing. I sat and listened, transfixed the whole time.

In the first bassoon position sat Christopher, looking like he was playing his little heart out. It wasn't to a very high standard. The poor souls playing second and third bassoon, who I didn't recognise, struggled to keep up with him, and I felt for them.

When the first movement ended, I had heard enough, so I got up and left.

SEBASTIAN

66. DOGS AND CATS

After watching *Bullitt*, with a belly full of popcorn and a satisfied mind, I sat back and relaxed on the couch some more. Wills had fallen asleep on my lap, his slumber no doubt brought on by a tummy full of popcorn too. I stroked him softly and slowly, thinking of my new life.

I mulled over what it would be like to have a life without Cecelia. Could I do it? Did I really want to leave her? Yes, it would be a new lifestyle being single, and it would be lonely at times, but I would just have to adjust. I had been there before, living several years on my own before I met Cecelia. So I'd need to stick the difficult period out for now, and the rewards would come later.

As I started to list those rewards in my mind, the idea of being a footloose bachelor definitely sounded more and more attractive.

Suddenly, the phone rang. I went to pick it up, thinking it would be Cecelia. Remembering what we had gone through, I braced myself for a difficult conversation.

But it wasn't Cecelia. It was the blonde.

'Hi, can I speak to that famous scriptwriter, please?' she asked.

Taken aback and nearly dropping the phone, I didn't know what to say. 'Umm,' was all I could manage.

'How about that famous director?' she continued.

Realising who it was on the line, I sat up and relaxed.

'Well, they're both here. One and the same person actually,' I said.

'That's fabulous!' she exclaimed excitedly.

I put my feet up on the couch to relax further. 'How are you?' I asked.

The blonde's voice perked up, and she sounded brighter. 'I'm fabulous! I've been doing some writing,' she said confidently.

'Hey, that's great! What's it about?' I asked.

'Well, my mind's been going wild,' she said raunchily, sounding like Marilyn Monroe again. I thought of Marilyn singing 'Running Wild' in the film *Some Like it Hot* and happily concluded that the blonde was not quite in the same league.

'Hello-ohhh,' the blonde sang.

I woke from my thoughts. 'Oh yes! Minds can do that to you,' I replied.

'You're going to laugh,' she said, sounding more serious. 'You're not going to judge me too harshly, are you? It's my first proper attempt at writing a novel.'

I smiled slightly to myself, flattered that she wanted to share her work with me. 'Of course I won't,' I said supportively. 'Us writers have to stick together, you know.'

'Okay ... It's about these golden retrievers, you know, with superpowers.'

'What sort of superpowers?' I asked, puzzled.

'Well...ninjas, X-ray vision, lasers, that sort of thing.'

'Ah, yes. I saw one yesterday. The dog tried to pee. That took out a fire hydrant and a city building before anyone knew what happened.'

She giggled. 'Anyway, they fight this planet of mutant Abyssinian cats.'

'Why are they mutant?' I asked, trying not to laugh.

'Radiation.'

I slapped my forehead with my palm. 'Of course,' I said. 'Silly me.'

I scratched my nose. 'Tell me, dear writer ... what's the target market for your fine piece of literature?' I asked.

'Young adult,' she said thoughtfully.

I slapped my forehead again. 'Of course. Who else?'

'So ... I was wondering,' the blonde asked, a little tentatively. 'Do you want to meet up on Saturday at the café ... and read what I've written?'

'Sure, I'd love to,' I answered. 'As I said, us writers have to stick together.'

'Fabulous!' she beamed.

I smiled, and we continued talking.

And just like when I first met her, all I could think about throughout the whole conversation was, is she for real?

CECELIA

67. TAKING FLIGHT

It was raining heavily outside as I sat on the couch one particular night, absentmindedly twirling my curls with my fingers. The gushing water against the windows brought back memories of long-gone dreams of the wild sea and soaring ospreys. I soon realised those dreams had stopped, and they now felt like a very old part of me that had moved on.

SEBASTIAN

68. WILLS AND THE BLONDE

Still thinking of my meeting with the blonde in a couple of days and uninspired by my writing, I decided to take Wills for a walk.

As I trudged along the footpath, my thoughts jumped between Cecelia and the blonde. I questioned how much I really felt single. After all, it hadn't been that long since my break-up with Cecelia.

I thought about what a relationship would be like with the blonde. She definitely had a way of moving and talking that most men would drool over. Her attractiveness had a lot to do with her hips and swagger, as well as her slightly lower beguiling voice. Despite initial perceptions, she was actually quite intelligent and thoughtful, putting aside her lapses into ditziness.

Having come to those conclusions, I still chastised myself, feeling guilty and pretty low for seeing another woman so soon. Still, the blonde was intriguing, and I had promised to read her work. Maybe I would just stick to that for now, I resolved—writer to writer, like two writers in a writers' room at a big TV or film production house.

After passing several shops that sold products I didn't care to buy, I soon found myself stopping outside a bookstore window. Wills whined, seemingly disappointed that his walk had ended, so I bent down to hug him.

It was then that I noticed, reflected in the window, the blonde.

She was a fair distance away, and she appeared to have a man with her grasping a walking stick. He was older than her, perhaps in his fifties, and he looked rather dashing. They were holding hands as she helped him into a car. Once the man was seated, she turned towards me, seemingly not looking for anything in particular. Then, suddenly, her face turned red. She had seen me.

She whispered to the man, kissed his lips quickly, and ran towards me. For a few seconds, we stood face to face in silence.

'Hi,' she whispered.

'G'day.'

Her faced dropped in guilt, and she looked at Wills, who, thankfully for her, was the perfect distraction.

'Oh! He's adorable,' she said, as she gave him a huge embrace. To her joy, Wills responded appropriately by licking the end of her nose.

The blonde stood up and turned towards the man, who looked impatient and a little angry at us. Then she turned back to me with a sweet smile. 'I'm sorry ... I didn't ... it's just that ...' she said.

I interrupted and nodded. 'It's all good. I understand.'

In the corner of my eye, I saw the man signal to the blonde.

'You'd better go. Your man needs you,' I said.

She smiled admiringly at me for a few seconds and kissed me momentarily on the cheek.

'It was nice we shared something in common,' she said softly.

'Yes, it was.'

With a tear in her eye, she turned away and ran back to the man.

That was the last I ever saw of her.

CECELIA

69. BENEATH THE SOUTHERN CROSS

It's one night-time walk, in particular, that I remember. Virtually the whole time, my mind was purely and simply focussed on Sebastian and my ex-career as a musician.

Along the way, when my mind wandered onto other things, and I took in my surroundings, I was comforted by what was above me. I gazed up into the stars and found the Southern Cross constellation shining brightly. I smiled, knowing that those four simple stars gave me a feeling of home, just as they had given other Australians before me a sense of identity and pride. In those moments when I looked upwards towards the constellation, I felt a sense of place, and the place I belonged was right there, in that suburban street in my neighbour-hood, on my way home.

It also felt comforting to realise that the Southern Cross had guided me there, just like it had guided many lost souls before me. I was part of a journey, not only as myself but for all of us—a small piece of something much more profound and extensive on this planet and in this universe.

SEBASTIAN

70. HOLLOW

What the clusterfuck hell was I thinking!?

I was seeing another woman while still married to someone else! And for fuck's sake, someone else who's in another relationship! Oh my fucking non-existent God, will I have some explaining to do!

All the best things I believed in had been thrown away by the person I had become. Monogamy, altruism, self-enhancement, all gone, replaced by a selfish, inconsiderate shite of an idiot! I walked back to the motel, swearing several more expletives to myself. I replayed over and over in my mind, 'For fuck's sake, Sebastian, get your shit in order!'

Then, once back in my room, I splashed water over my face. I looked in the bathroom mirror. All I could see was a ragged, tired, sad man who didn't look like me.

I made my way to the bed, and Wills lay next to me, panting and staring at me the whole time. Finally, he demanded attention, and eventually, I gave in and signalled for him to join me on my lap. He happily obliged. It earned him a long pat and scratch behind his ears while I stretched back, deep in thought.

The thing was, I realised that loving and living with someone for many years just *couldn't* be forgotten. Not in a day anyway. Perhaps not even in a lifetime. I tried to reconcile that, but the more I told my mind *not* to think of Cecelia, the more I thought of her.

It was too late. I grabbed my computer and typed into the search engine:

WHY DO MEN LIKE BLONDES?
GUILT!

As soon as I typed those words, I threw the computer across the bed and looked at Wills. He stared back, seemingly trying to tell me something.

I laughed at him and scratched his ear while saying, 'Yeah, right, coming from a dog who steals chicken from the table.'

I grabbed my computer again and typed:

DYSTONIA SUPPORT FOR PARTNERS

Scores of results came up, and, transfixed, I scrolled through them. One stood out:

CARERS SUPPORT

My eyes scanned the screen taking in the information. Leaning forward, I clicked on a tab that revealed:

Carers are often forgotten when their loved one is
diagnosed with dystonia, but they need support too …

Tears welled up in my eyes as I read on intently.

That night, neither Wills nor I slept well. The noise of sirens and shouting from some God-forsaken ruckus outside kept us awake. Lying in bed with my eyes wide open, habitually staring at the clock, I wished slumber would take me away from my abyss. But, instead, what occupied my mind in the dark hours was Cecelia. I felt compelled to know more about her suffering, and I wished more than anything that it would miraculously go away.

The following day, I got up and looked at myself in the mirror. What I saw was still a dishevelled and spent man. Or someone who once was a man. He needed help for Cecelia's sake and his own. So I decided to see a doctor, hoping some light could be shed on my malaise.

———

I sat in a squeaky chair in a room smelling strongly of antiseptic, trying to get comfortable as I dried my eyes.

'I'm just trying to understand, doc?' I asked, as he studied me from the other side of his desk.

'I can give you something. Diazepam, a Valium derivative ...'

I interrupted and dropped my head in thought before lifting my eyes. 'But that's not what I need here now.'

The doctor leaned forward to press his point. 'Yes, but it would help. We could try Cognitive Behaviour Therapy as well. I've had a lot of success using that on my patients.'

My cheeks reddened. Anger began to surge in me. 'It must be easy for you,' I said forcefully.

'What?'

'I mean, it's so easy for you to dish out the drugs and therapies.'

The doc leaned back defensively. 'I'm just trying to help.'

Even though I had only been there a couple of minutes, it felt enough, and I got up to leave.

'You're not the one on the other side of the table,' I said, as my knee bumped my chair. 'Shit! That hurt!'

The doctor scanned my knee and then looked back into my eyes. 'Mr Cavendish, Sebastian, are you okay?' he asked.

'You're not the one losing everything!' I said, as I rubbed my leg to ease the pain.

Realising my temper may get out of control, I hid my face in my hands to compose myself.

'We can only do so much,' the doctor pleaded.

I turned around and left. My legs couldn't take me out of there fast enough. 'This isn't what I need right now,' I barked, as I slammed the door.

The doctor's other patients in the waiting room looked at me, stunned. So much for composure.

I felt in the wilderness again, but not of the kind I had enjoyed when I was a young boy.

CECELIA

71. BUDS

I had been doing a lot of thinking lately. But, of course, being on your own lends itself to it, and truth be told, I was starting to enjoy my new solo lifestyle, even though Sebastian was often on my mind.

Without him, I was reconnecting with the single Cecelia of years ago. I was finding my way and finding a new way to live. For example, I started to enjoy cooking thanks to gadgets that made the tasks more manageable, such as an automatic bottle and can opener given to me by Lizzy. I ate healthy meals, nothing fancy, just simple one-pot wonders that were very tasty. I was thrilled to realise then that day-to-day activities that were difficult when I was first diagnosed with dystonia became more manageable with a few modifications.

Cooking and walking were 'me' times when I could ponder over new challenges and map ways to navigate and complete them. Walking soon became a new passion, and it didn't take me long to realise I could still do it, albeit with a bit of a side step like a crab. With my head at an angle and my eyes not looking straight ahead, walking around left-hand corners was interestingly more straightforward than walking in a straight line. Sometimes, when out treading paths and streets, I found that a little amusing. It felt good to be able to laugh at myself.

The big question was, what was the new me going to be like? I pondered further some of the philosophical discussions Sebastian and I had about being the best we could be and our best selves. Then I asked myself, was the new Cecelia going to be an existentialist or universalist? Would she focus on herself as an individual, or would she absorb herself with truths that we are all equal without question? As an amateur philosopher, that was the big question I had asked myself in my late teens. But now I was alone, it became a significant consideration again. In the end, I decided that I was to be a blend of both, a blend of many things, but as I had the room to do it, I could be a little more attentive to myself as an individual. The new Cecelia was to be better than she had ever been before.

But what of Sebastian? Since my diagnosis, part of me knew he was unhappy, but I was too lost in my own struggles to appreciate it fully. I hadn't realised he had thoughts of separation. The signs were there, I suppose, but I just hadn't seen them. When I realised that, I found myself wanting to understand him more. His unhappiness borne from his rocky career was clear to me, but was it something more? Was it a mid-life crisis? Was it boredom?

Often, before I fell asleep, I'd gather up inside me an optimistic attitude. Sometimes, I thought there were still signs of success between us. We had still communicated, and I believed we always loved each other. If love had gone, perhaps we could even learn to love again? I always thought we were right for each other emotionally, intellectually, spiritually, physically and more.

But I was starting to enjoy the new independent Cecelia.

In all of that, I couldn't decide what to do. In the end, it came down to one question I asked myself.

Was Cecelia's new world going to have Sebastian in it? That question especially couldn't be answered.

I had seen him with another woman.

SEBASTIAN
72. WE GO TOGETHER LIKE . . .

I sat in the motel room in a trance, reflecting on my past and future while lazily stroking Wills. I came to realise that, for several months, I hadn't known what I was thinking. However I reasoned myself out of my relationship with Cecelia, my gut feeling, my common sense, said I should be in it. In the end, it was a no brainer. Cecelia was the one. I couldn't imagine being with anyone else or that anyone else was better or better suited to me.

She was intertwined forever with my happiness, my centredness and who I was as a person. The person I wanted to be was the person who had Cecelia in their life. Life was unfulfilled without her and definitely wasn't better without her. I more than just loved her, she was my best friend, and friends are always there for each other through thick and thin.

CECELIA

73. THE MOST ROMANTIC CITY ON EARTH

Gazing at a photo of Sebastian and me, my mind wandered to distant lands and what felt like long-gone times. It was a gorgeous photo of us in Venice at the Doge's Palace and Bridge of Sighs. Sebastian had always wanted to go there and recreate a scene from one of his favourite movies, *A Little Romance*. In the film, the two lovestruck young stars find a gondola and ride it under the famous bridge at sunset, while the bells of St Mark's Campanile chime. Local legend said that any couple lucky enough to kiss in these circumstances would enjoy everlasting love. And that's what the two stars did in the movie, and Sebastian and I did, on one of the most romantic and memorable days of my life. We did it in front of many hundreds of onlookers and we kissed twice, on the way there and back, for good measure.

My mind came to conclude what I steadfastly believed to be one simple everlasting fact: any man who loves a woman that much just cannot stop loving her.

I needed to talk to him, so I made my way to the front door. Along the way, I noticed Wills' dog leash hanging on a hook. I ran my fingers over it nostalgically, picked it up, and left.

SEBASTIAN

74. MYOPIC

A few days after the doctor offered me Valium, I found myself in the front row of seats at the Festival Theatre, listening to the Weistar Symphony Orchestra play a loud piece of music with gusto. The music drowned out the noise of the rain outside.

Everyone else seemed to be enjoying the concert. But for me, it didn't sound the same as when Cecelia was in the orchestra.

My heart just wasn't in it like it used to be, and my mind was busy looking back to another time.

I thought about how much I enjoyed listening to Cecelia practise at home. I thought about how beautiful she looked when she walked on stage. I thought about how overjoyed I was when Pavarotti gave her flowers. I thought about what it felt like when Cecelia was playing on stage, seemingly just for me. I thought about how much I loved her, no matter what.

Tears welled up in my eyes, and I left.

When I arrived back at my motel, as I opened the door, Wills greeted me in his usual overly excited way. I gave him a big hug, and we went to a nearby park to play a game where I lay on the ground, and he tried to lick my nose. He won several times, and I gave him scratches behind his ears each time as a reward.

Just as we settled down to go back inside, a car beeped its horn. We both turned around to look. At that moment, Wills pricked his ears up at a woman who looked like Cecelia but wasn't, walking on the other side of the road. He immediately barked with excitement and bolted towards her.

I bolted after him, shouting, 'Wills, stop!' as he ran in front of several cars, ignoring the danger.

Focussing heavily only on Wills and with myopic vision, I did the same thing.

And a couple of seconds after leaving the curb, I was hit by a car.

CECELIA

75. I ONCE KNEW A MAN

I made my way to an old motel we used to frequent, hoping Sebastian would be there. I hadn't seen him in several weeks.

The receptionist confirmed there was a Sebastian at the motel.

My heart skipped a beat as I neared his door. It was in a dingier part of the motel, and I stood there for a few minutes, not sure of what to say, even though I had rehearsed it in my mind several times. Eventually, I laughed at myself. It wasn't a stranger I was about to see. It was someone who had shared my life for many years. Talking with him had always been the most comfortable thing, so really, there was nothing to stop me.

I knocked on the door and waited, looking around in hope just in case he was hiding behind the plants or something. Nope. I knocked again. No answer.

A little disappointed, I slowly placed Wills' leash on the doorstep, along with a note that simply read: *Call me.*

When I arrived home, I saw Wills at the front door. He was looking around anxiously and panting nervously.

I ran to him and cuddled him. 'What's up, Wills? Where's your master?' I said worriedly.

I tried to open the front door, but it was locked. 'Sebastian, are you here?' I shouted.

No answer.

'Sebastian?'

Still no answer.

Just at that moment, a police car pulled up, and an officer got out. My face dropped.

'Are you Cecelia Cavendish?' he asked, as he walked towards me.

'Yes. What's wrong?'

'Do you know Sebastian Cavendish?'

'Yes.'

'I'm afraid I have some bad news for you.'

'What. What is it?'

'Sebastian. He's in hospital. I can take you there now if you like.'

My face dropped again, and my body stiffened. My neck went crazy too.

'Is he okay?' I asked.

The policeman ignored my question, simply saying, 'Let's go.'

I quickly put Wills inside and got in the police car as fast as I could.

———

When I walked into the hospital room and saw Sebastian unconscious, tears immediately gushed from my eyes. They were already moist, as I had just spoken to his doctor, who told me that he was concussed and under observation. Sebastian also had a broken shoulder blade and leg. He had cuts and bruises on the visible parts of his body that weren't under blankets or bandages. His prognosis was unclear.

The room seemed to spin. First, it was my bassoon and music career, and now I was facing the complete loss of Sebastian too. Life was throwing everything at me again, and like before, it all seemed so unfair. Grief, anxiety and fear gripped my body. I reflected on how

Sebastian had been central in me coping with dystonia, helping with cleaning, cooking and, except for our arguments, being a shoulder to lean on. He had been there with me, and as such, my grief would always be a part of him too. Without him, I realised I would have to deal with it totally alone. I wished we hadn't said and done some things, especially argue and separate, and all for what? To see Sebastian in a hospital?

I sat on the bed and scanned Sebastian's body. I wasn't sure what to think. Was he lucky that things could have been worse? I took some comfort in knowing that our hearts were still beating and we were still breathing. I held his hand, squeezing it gently, the whole time wishing and wishing he would awaken, and worrying that the other woman might show up in his room. Occasionally, his eyes seemed to flutter, but he remained asleep.

I thought of how the dystonia journey had been for him. He had put aside his dreams to take care of me. That must have hurt the essence of who he was as a person with plans to do great things. At that moment, I felt incredibly thankful and loving towards him. Despite our arguments, I could see that he was still a kind and selfless man.

I cried for him, and I cried for me. A litre of liquid must have flowed from my eyes as I emptied two tissue boxes. I cried the tears of someone whose soul and being had been hurt, maimed and destroyed more than anything imaginable.

I cried not just for losing the job that best suited me in this crazy world, or for losing the love of my life, or my friends. I cried for my future, the life that I would never live, and all the most profound things my heart was so set on to accomplish and continue. I cried for my lost plans to be creative and my dreams of becoming a well-known soloist and creating recordings for the enjoyment of listeners and students. My plans to travel the world and play music, which I loved so much, were all gone too. I cried for the lost beauty and the lost chance to reach the transcendence music had given me and the opportunity to bring that to others. I cried for all the hard work and lost years of preparation to be a musician and perform with superstars like Pavarotti.

Most of all, I cried for the lost *me* and for my contorted body I could no longer control. I cried for children I wasn't sure I could have. Even though I didn't have them, it didn't matter. It felt like dystonia had cruelly and unjustly taken that choice away from me. I cried for my inability to get lost in kissing Sebastian and for all the small things like tying shoelaces or easily making a cup of tea. I cried because never again would I live as a dynamic person. It all sucked so badly. It should never happen to anyone, but it happened to me.

The fact that it was a Saturday night added to my tears. Saturday was the main night in the orchestra when I played my bassoon to entertain others. That felt so bohemian, and I still missed it a lot. Being anywhere else other than a concert hall on weekends was a state of being I hadn't fully grasped yet, and it felt so unfamiliar.

When I finally composed myself, my eyes stung, and my face burned. Conversely, though, I felt soothed and relaxed. My whole body had been so angry and sad for months, if not years. Crying seemed to purge many of the horrible feelings that had dwelled deep inside me.

I thought of my favourite composers and how their music connected to what I was going through. My whole teary experience felt as cathartic as playing *Scheherazade* by Rimsky-Korsakov or a Rachmaninoff piano concerto.

But when the tears were gone, Sebastian was still before me, lying in the hospital bed, still unconscious, and his future still uncertain.

I sat there for hours watching him, hoping, willing him to wake up. And when I couldn't wait any longer, I decided, very reluctantly, to go home, get some sleep, and come back early the next day.

Maybe he would improve by morning.

CECELIA

76. ALIVE

Just as I was about to leave, I turned back to take one last look of the day at Sebastian.

But then, suddenly, he opened his eyes.

I jumped in the air, startled.

After a few seconds of silence, he smiled at me. 'Hello,' he said softly.

'Hello,' I said back, equally as soft.

He looked around for a couple of minutes, then seemed to wake up a little more.

'I have a gnawing sense we're not at home right now,' he whispered, as he smiled at me again.

'That's a quote from one of your scripts!' I replied, giggling and crying at the same time.

'I'm glad you read them.'

Sebastian looked around once more, and I could see he was taking in his surroundings with increasing awareness.

'Where's Wills?' he asked, as I made my way back to my seat.

'He's at home, safe.'

Sebastian exhaled in relief.

'You know, for someone with little legs, he's quite a runner.'

I laughed again in joy. 'Perhaps we should have named him Logan. *Logan's Run.*'

'That's two film references in less than a minute. One of them mine,' Sebastian said with a grin.

'We must be doing well then,' I replied.

Sebastian sat up a little. 'Do you think I can have a cup of tea?' he asked.

'Tea? Now?' I said, feeling somewhat puzzled.

'Tea.'

'Okay. I'll ask the nurse.'

'That's tea, with milk,' Sebastian clarified.

'Okay.'

Sebastian's face brightened. 'Like so many other things, tea is part of my life, part of living,' he said softly.

I looked at him deeply, my mind ticking over.

'Yes,' I replied, pausing, my heart still pumping. 'But we can't just accept that this life is all we've got.'

Sebastian gazed at me as if he wanted me to create world peace or something. 'What about my writing?' he asked.

His face yearned for an answer, but I wasn't sure if I had the right one. 'I know that means a lot to you,' I said.

'As much as music means to you?'

I smiled. 'As much as you mean to me.'

Sebastian smiled back and laughed to himself. 'Coming from a lady who seeks the meaning of life.'

'We choose whatever meaning we want,' I replied.

Hearing myself say those words made me stand a little taller.

Sebastian softened even further and had an expression of love in his eyes I hadn't seen for a long time. 'And we get to choose who we spend it with,' he said.

We looked at each other in silence, our faces plastered with huge grins. No words seemed necessary, until Sebastian suddenly looked bewildered.

'I just don't ... I just don't understand why you didn't try everything ...'

He looked downwards before lifting his eyes back to me. I smiled back, which seemed to give him strength, '... to get back to playing. Perhaps there was something more. I don't know. I thought we'd never give up on our dreams.'

'Some things just can't be beaten,' I said softly. My heart skipped a beat, and I held back a tear.

'Want some tea, too?' he asked. 'It would be selfish of me not to offer.'

I dropped my eyes.

'You can trust me. It's good,' he said.

I looked up, and my eyes widened. There was an understanding look in Sebastian's eyes that reassured me and made my heart glow.

We were going to be all right.

'Yes,' I smiled.

CECELIA

77. PAVANE FOR A DEAD PRINCESS

Suffice to say, when I arrived home knowing that Sebastian would recover well, I felt incredibly overjoyed, relieved and happy.

I thought about how much of a turn-around it had been from the time I cried alone to the time I saw Sebastian in hospital. In a newfound way, I realised that crying gave me empathy for myself, Sebastian and so many other things. Feelings needed to be acknowledged, and through my tears, my frame of mind felt more extraordinary than ever before. The benefits of my crying were felt instantly afterwards and flowed through me like a warm wave.

Putting the keys in the front door of my house proved challenging, just like it had been since my dystonia started. I spent several minutes trying to fit them into the slot, but my dystonic head and neck movements prevented me from even focussing on the keyhole. After what seemed like the tenth attempt, I dropped the keys and tutted in frustration.

Instead of picking them up, however, I turned my body to survey the driveway. Sebastian's Jaguar still sat there, as damaged as it had been since Sprinklergate. I exhaled in determination and walked over to remove the sprinkler. It was sitting in a pool of glass on the back seat.

I then tried to connect the sprinkler to the garden tap. Just like the front door keys, I found it difficult, but the click of the sprinkler's connection to the tap brought a defiant smile to my face. Proud of my minor, yet significant, success, I grabbed the keys.

On my next attempt, the front door key fitted perfectly into the lock.

Inside, I looked around the room. Everything looked different, even though the walls, floor, windows and furniture around me were the same. Objects everywhere shone brighter, and the feel of the place seemed to hold much more meaning. I didn't understand specifically why, other than I felt at home, but I did punch my fist into the air with a kind of suppressed joy.

I walked around the lounge room, deep in thought. My mind turned to the orchestra again, and I felt inspired to try to remember some significant highlights of my career. There were many, but I was sad to realise details were beginning to fade. Much time had passed, and so much had happened since my fateful farewell shindig. Of all the concerts, what music did I play, and where and when? Who was with me? Who was the conductor? Did I play well? What were the notes in that piece? What did the reviews say? I couldn't recollect everything, whereas before I could. My mind, once a steel-tight filing cabinet, had turned somewhat into a foggy mess.

On a side table I saw an old scrapbook and opened it with curiosity. Within its worn pages, a headline from a 1990's newspaper article read:

CECELIA CAVENDISH WINS
ABC TV YOUNG PERFORMER OF THE YEAR
INSTRUMENTAL SECTION

There was a photo of me taken from TV wearing a bright, blue shiny dress. I shut the book softly, feeling proud of the achievements I could recall, happy that I had the chance to complete them. Not everyone got that chance, and I was the lucky one who won the opportunity.

Memories of dancing to the music as I played, and dancing while listening to music, came into my mind. I became aware of how much I missed that feeling since my dystonia symptoms had reared their ugly head. I could still listen to my favourite compositions and songs, so I grabbed a compact disk and put it on to play. Hearing the music still filled me with the urge to dance, especially in my joyful state, but when I stood up to try, my neck and unbalanced body almost made me fall over. I tried several times, each time unsuccessfully.

Eventually, I turned off the music and sat down, staring at the compact disk player as if it were a gladiator needing to be conquered.

Taking a determined breath, I rose to my feet and turned the music back on.

This time I used the back of a chair to balance, and found myself swaying gently instead of dancing.

Lost in my own world again, a smile slowly came across my face.

———

As Sebastian slept beside me in bed, finally returned from his hospital stay, I reminisced over a passage from my book, *The Forest of Being:*

God is within, in the form of our human spirit.

I looked gently at Sebastian, and got up to go to the bathroom. I turned on the radio, although softly so as not to wake my lover. Then I smiled. Ravel's *Pavane for a Dead Princess* played, one of my all-time most loved pieces.

I gazed into the large bathroom mirror, where I could see a whole twisted body struggling to stay straight. My eyes and fingers ran inquisitively over it.

I struggled to run my fingers over my lips.

Yet, what I saw in the reflection were long graceful fingers running over full lips.

I struggled to run my fingers over the curves of my body.

Yet, what I saw in the reflection were fingers effortlessly sliding over lingerie.

I ran my fingers down my sides. It almost made me fall.

Yet, what I saw in my reflection was a woman standing firm, with her fingers illuminating her beautiful outline.

I smiled a little.

The music reached its climax.

My body and neck twisted again.

But this time, the mirror reflected my body as it actually was.

As I stared at the new Cecelia, I thought, what of beauty? When I was a teenager, my self-image intertwined with my self-worth. It took a few years of growing to become satisfied with my physical attractiveness. With my physical beauty now altered, I missed that happy young woman, taken so unforgivingly and surreptitiously because of dystonia.

In my twenties, I liked to think that it was more than looks that had given me my success. I hoped that my positivity, openness, honesty, confidence and a healthy, joyful outlook all contributed. Dystonia made me doubt those qualities of my younger self, and for a while, it took them away. And it took all my bravery and strength for them to return and subsequently shine. Now I felt that they were back, and I felt me again.

I smiled with satisfaction.

A wave of happiness washed through my mind and body, and for the first time in a long time, I felt comfort and peace.

Acceptance cleared the way for the next chapter in my life.

CECELIA – TWO YEARS LATER
78. SPOTLIGHT

Peggy, a young employee, had just started work, and it was my responsibility to ensure she knew what to do. We sat in front of a computer with its screen facing us.

My neck still twisted, but I felt comfortable, thanks to the specially designed chair and desk set-up Loren organised soon after I started with the company. Around me, dozens of employees tapped away on their keyboards.

Peggy tried, unsuccessfully, to type a particularly tricky piece of jargon and she turned to me for help.

'It's okay,' I said. 'You can use the keyboard command control-Z to undo, and then do it all again how you want it.'

'Thanks,' Peggy laughed. 'If only life was like that.'

I couldn't help but laugh with her. If only that were true, I thought.

Another employee shouted for my attention. 'Hey, boss! I'm stuck here.'

I looked at my watch. 'Loren will be here soon. She'll help, okay?' I answered.

Perfectly timed, Loren rushed in. 'Cecelia, have you got time to discuss your disability support group for our upcoming all-staff meeting?'

I looked at my watch again. I was running late. 'Sorry, Loren. I'd better go. Talk about it tomorrow, though. Bye, everyone!'

Just as I walked out, Loren grabbed my attention. 'Thanks for the CDs,' she said. 'You sounded great.'

'Thanks.'

Loren looked me in the eyes.

'I don't think you have been thanked enough, Cecelia.'

I smiled at her and walked out brightly.

———

In a crowded room, I was relieved to have my two new friends with me, Lydia and Charlotte. Lydia had dystonia that affected her face, while Charlotte had dystonia in her legs and hands. We stood out, wearing our bright orange T-shirts from Dystonia Europe and T-shirts with the words: *Dystonia – 'Muscles Behaving Badly'* from the Dystonia Network of Australia Inc. My two friends hovered around a table displaying promotional flyers for the Australian Dystonia Support Group.

Charlotte hugged me tightly, and Lydia soon joined in for good measure. 'The Three Dysmusketeers!' we shouted in unison.

Lydia beamed. 'This is amazing!' she said, through teeth clenched with dystonia.

Charlotte nodded in agreement. 'Thank you, Cecelia.'

'No, thank you,' I said.

Sebastian cut in. He looked cute in his bright orange dystonia T-shirt, and I couldn't help but laugh. He added to his cuteness by doing a funny robot dance, tripping over himself intentionally.

'Now's your time to shine, darling,' he said like a cyborg, as he recovered his balance.

I made my way to a podium, giving my old friend Lizzy a hug as we passed.

I scanned the audience before me. Doctors were there, as well as Parkinson's disease and dystonia patients, many also wearing bright orange dystonia T-shirts. It looked like a citrus orchard.

Sebastian took his spot and focussed his camera on me. His film crew shone spotlights on me as well. Behind me hung a banner:

PARKINSON'S DISEASE AND DYSTONIA CONFERENCE
PARKINSON'S AUSTRALIA – DYSTONIA NETWORK OF
AUSTRALIA INC.

In the crowd, Dr Hayworth and Indira smiled proudly.

Everyone applauded as I stepped onto the podium.

'Organising this conference has been a great joy for me,' I began. 'When doctors first diagnosed me, I tried everything to hang onto the life I wanted to live. Dystonia made me feel like I lost my creativity, my passion, my achievements ... as I'm sure it has for many of you too.'

I took a deep breath and glanced at Sebastian before continuing, 'Now I've learnt to embrace a new life *with* dystonia. There is so much to learn, and so much to enjoy.'

I could see Sebastian wink at me from the corner of my eye.

'But most of all, I've learnt to appreciate something other than my musical life.'

The audience gave me a standing ovation.

A moment in time came to mind, a younger me, bowing on stage, as I held my bassoon aloft.

CECELIA

79. THE NEVER WOLF

Sebastian had just spent months writing and making a film titled *Dystonia*. It was a joyous grand gesture, a beautiful film, and one of the most loving things he had done for me. At first, when he wanted to make it, he asked me lots of questions about my journey, and I felt a sense of uneasy trepidation. I wondered if putting all the difficult things I had been through into a script would make my body and mind react as they did when I was at my worst. However, to my surprise, the process turned out to be cathartic, although sometimes bittersweet. In addition, I had many cheerleaders in the form of Sebastian, friends and fellow sisters and brothers with dystonia to support me.

Just as importantly, as I watched on during the film's production process, something clicked inside me, a new creative urge. I thought to myself, I can do this. I could write a film myself. So I raided Sebastian's film books and sat down to complete the task, my head swimming with ideas and prose. At the time, little did I realise it would take me down a wonderful, eye-opening path.

Previously, I had never seen myself as Cecelia the scriptwriter, but putting words on paper seemed easy and fun, especially as my first subject was Wills and his contribution to our lives. He was enter-taining and full of character, and with his cute features and personal-ity, he almost *demanded* to be put on film. I titled it, *A Canine Connection*.

So, there I was, watching Sebastian prepare to shoot a big scene in my film. He had spent many weeks training Wills, and he had his crew ready and waiting to finish the opening shot. They all seemed keen and happy about the film, except Wills, who lay down and panted nervously.

Sebastian made his way around the back of the film camera.

'Okay, Wills, ready to be a star?' he asked.

Wills pricked his ears up and looked excitedly towards his master. His enthusiasm didn't garner much of a response from Sebastian, though. And there was a good reason, too. It was take seventeen, and everyone was getting fed up and tired. Still, the shot had to be done while the light was good, so we all carried on.

Unfortunately, Sebastian's weeks of training Wills were to little avail, and Wills' actions on set surprised everyone. Before the film, Wills knew all his commands and knew what to do when asked. We had high hopes for him, confident he would be the next Rin Tin Tin or Lassie. The problem was the film set itself. As soon as Wills saw the lights, camera and sound gear, he ran for cover, usually behind the lavender bushes in the garden corner. He was pretty happy for his picture to be taken with a photo camera on holiday, but a moving shot with a film camera—nope. He acted like a real diva. In previous takes, Sebastian had tried everything, including a group Wills and film crew hug, food, and even stroking Wills with the sound boom pole. Nothing seemed to work.

Sebastian was at the end of his rope and dispensed with the on-set protocol.

'Let's get straight into it,' he pleaded.

The second assistant cameraperson nodded. 'Shot four, take seventeen ... marker!'

The clapper guy clapped his thingamajig.

Sebastian looked around the set. Everyone seemed ready, even the star. 'Steady ... and action!' he shouted.

Wills' human co-star bent down and patted his hands on his thighs to call Wills. 'Come on, Wills!' he shouted excitedly.

Wills ran towards him, but again, as soon as he saw the film set, he fled for cover behind the lavender bush.

'CUT!'

We all looked at each other, totally spent and overly disappointed. The first assistant director rolled his eyes for the umpteenth time. 'Sebastian, it'll be take one thousand before we get this in the can,' he cried.

Sebastian tutted at Wills, who proceeded to wag his tail cutely.

I burst out laughing. It was impossible to be mad at either of them.

'Wills, Wills, Wills! That's a wrap ... Thanks, guys. We'll try something new tomorrow,' offered Sebastian.

The film crew wasted no time in packing up. Before anyone could say, 'Wills is a very naughty boy,' they left, and I was still giggling to myself as I waved them off. When I turned to go back inside, I chuckled again, seeing Wills' wet tongue happily licking Sebastian's face. Sebastian didn't take kindly to being laughed at by me, so he proceeded to wipe the dog drool off his face and trace it on my chest in the shape of a heart. I screamed like a teenager.

As I planned a playful way to get back at Sebastian for giving me a slobber shower, the situation quickly became uncontrollable. I ran inside and half-filled a bucket of water, ran back outside, and with one fell swoop—KERSPLASH!

Oh well, I thought. Filming will just have to wait for another day. And we did wait.

But not for long. Despite Wills' mishaps and many, many retakes and subsequent laughs, we finally completed the film a few days later.

It was my first film script, one of many to come.

CECELIA

80. ROXANNE

I was in the music room, carefully cleaning the wood and chrome of my bassoon, until it all looked as beautiful as the first time I laid my eyes on it. I then checked all the keys were working correctly and placed it gently back on its stand before taking a step back to admire my handiwork. It looked as good as new.

Suddenly, the doorbell rang.

Sebastian hurriedly finished typing a sentence in his film script and shouted, 'That'll be Roxanne! Ready?'

I walked to the door. 'As I'll ever be,' I replied.

When I opened it, a young, trendy, wide-eyed, enthusiastic girl smiled at me. She instantly reminded me of myself, albeit twenty years younger, and I smiled back. However, instead of the customary, 'Hello', she greeted me with her hands shielding her eyes. My Renault and Sebastian's brand-new, historic Jaguar were parked right next to her, and the sun was reflecting off their shiny, new paint jobs straight into her eyes.

'Oh, sorry about that!' I apologised.

The girl giggled and held out her hand nervously. 'I'm Roxanne. We spoke on the phone about your bassoon.'

'Hi. Come in!' I said, holding my head to keep it still as I spoke.

As we made our way along the corridor, I couldn't help but glance at Roxanne. Her naturalness and friendly smile made me feel instantly comfortable, and I started to feel more relaxed than I thought I'd be.

'So, what's your next orchestra gig?' I asked.

'Mozart's Bassoon Concerto.'

She immediately took me back to another time and place.

'One of my favourites. I did it with the Weistar Symphony many years ago.'

'Yes. I was there. I was ten years old.'

I shivered, feeling a sense of uncanniness in her words.

We entered the music room, and I saw Roxanne's eyes widen as she noticed my bassoon. It sat peacefully on its stand, silver keys glistening in the light and beckoning Roxanne to pick it up.

All of a sudden, I realised the reality of the situation, and my eyes welled up.

'May I?' she asked.

'Yes. Be careful.'

Roxanne picked up the bassoon and ran her fingers admiringly over its polished wood and shiny keys. Her lips engulfed the reed, and she began to play scales and passages of music, including Mozart's Bassoon Concerto.

She stopped, and a huge smile beamed across her innocent face. 'It's lovely,' she said.

'I know.'

Sebastian walked in. In a solemn tone, he murmured, 'That music sounds familiar.'

Roxanne turned to him. 'Sounds perfect,' she said.

She played some more while Sebastian and I listened intently.

The music stopped, and we all stood in silence for a few seconds. Roxanne was eager to speak and blurted out, 'It certainly sounds as good as a Heckel bassoon ought to.'

'There's nothing like it,' I said.

She surveyed the instrument lovingly again. 'Cecelia. My mind was pretty much made up before I got here. It's a yes from me,' she said happily.

Sebastian looked adoringly at me. He put his arms around my shoulder as I teared up some more.

'Darling?' he asked.

Both of them looked expectantly at me.

'And it's a yes from me,' I said quietly.

'Thank you, Cecelia.'

I looked at Roxanne a little seriously. 'You take the best care of it.'

'Rest assured, it's going to a good home.'

I nodded as best I could. 'I know.'

Sebastian smiled and hugged me closer.

'I'll help you pack it up,' I said.

Together, Roxanne and I packed the bassoon back into its case. Not a word was spoken. As I handled each piece, I held back a tear.

We walked to the door slowly, where Roxanne handed me a cheque. She looked so at ease with my beloved instrument in her hands.

'So, this is it,' I said.

'This is it.'

I forced a slight smile.

Roxanne turned to me, gazing with affection.

'You know, Cecelia, if I hadn't seen you play Mozart when I was ten, I'd probably be doing something else now. Thank you. Really. Thank you.'

I whispered to myself, 'It was my pleasure ... it was my pleasure.'

Roxanne smiled and walked into the bright, outdoor light towards her car.

At the front door, I closed my eyes briefly. I held Sebastian's hand, squeezing it tightly over and over, as we watched Roxanne drive away.

I looked back fondly into the music room to see the sun illuminating the bassoon stand, now empty. Thoughts of my music career entered my mind and, as I stood there, those many years of music felt like another time and another place. Now I was in a new, joyful place making a different kind of music within myself and with Sebastian. I was as happy as I had ever been.

THE END

ABOUT MONTY RAYMOND

Monty Raymond was born in Hampshire, England, in 1965. After completing a post-graduate Creative Arts degree at Flinders University of South Australia in 2002, he wrote scripts for children's television programs in Australia and wrote several short and feature film scripts.

Monty also directed and produced short films, including *Dystonia* in 2018: https://www.youtube.com/watch?v=dCapqLSkb60.

Monty lives in South Australia with his wife. He spends his days writing, walking on the beach, patting dogs and eating tiramisu.

Life and Music is also a feature film script, and further information is available at *Corgipawfilms and Books* on Facebook.

https://www.facebook.com/Corgipawfilms-and-Books-562284584156297

Use this QR code to go directly to the Facebook page.

ACKNOWLEDGEMENTS

When I first sat down to write the feature film script, *Life and Music*, in 2015, little did I know at the time it would take me on an incredible journey. That journey has taken me to the UK and California, and enabled me to meet so many inspirational and wonderful people.

In making the short film *Dystonia*, and writing the feature film script that led to writing this book, I wanted to tell my wife's story and help raise awareness of dystonia. Unexpectedly and in return, I received more support from the dystonia community, and film cast and crew, than I ever imagined. The financial support from the dystonia community was overwhelming and invaluable. Thank you, thank you, thank you! I will always be grateful for the support you have given me, and the care and love you have shown for my wife.

I'd also like to especially thank the Australian Dystonia Support Group (ADSG), the Dystonia Network of Australia Inc. (DNA), Brain Foundation and Writers South Australia (Writers SA). You've all been amazing and encouraging and kept me going with this project.

To the many thousands of people who have watched *Dystonia* on YouTube, thank you too! Keep watching and keep spreading the word about dystonia!

And of course, my darling wife. Our lives changed forever when you were diagnosed with dystonia in 2000, yet our love and creativity never stopped. It only grew, and here we are, happy as rabbits. Every day, I am inspired by your strength and compassion and so many other qualities that you have in spades.

LIFE AND MUSIC ON FILM

Dystonia, a short film based on this novel, is a proof of concept for the feature film script, *Life and Music*. Use the QR code or link to watch:

https://www.youtube.com/watch?v=dCapqLSkb60

https://www.youtube.com/watch?v=QYMBSwxiXrM
(subtitled version)

The *Life and Music* film script is 101 pages and is a biographical drama and romance.

HELPFUL DYSTONIA LINKS

AUSTRALIA:
https://www.dystonia.org.au
https://australiandystoniasupportgroup.wordpress.com
https://brainfoundation.org.au/disorders/dystonia

USA:
https://dystonia-foundation.org

UK:
https://www.dystonia.org.uk

EUROPE:
https://dystonia-europe.org

NEW ZEALAND:
https://www.dystonia.org.nz

Ingram Content Group UK Ltd.
Milton Keynes UK
UKHW020749030523
421098UK00016B/17